THE

KILL

FLOOR

JOHN DESJARLAIS

THE
KILL
FLOOR

JOHN DESJARLAIS

Torchflame Books

Durham, NC

The Kill Floor
John Desjarlais
www.johndesjarlais.com
johndesjarlais12@gmail.com

Published 2022, by Torchflame Books
an Imprint of Light Messages Publishing
www.lightmessages.com
Durham, NC 27713 USA
SAN: 920-9298

Paperback ISBN: 978-1-61153-470-2
E-book ISBN: 978-1-61153-471-9
Library of Congress Control Number: 2022914374

For Pop

Once a farmer, always a farmer.

Woe to those who add house to house
And join field to field
Until everywhere belongs to them
And they are the sole owners of the land.
The Just One has sworn in my hearing:
'Such a house shall be brought to ruin.'
Isaiah 5:8-9

CHAPTER 1

"Bravo-12, do you copy?" crackled the radio.

"Bravo-12, copy that," Gordon said. He flicked on the cruiser's windshield wipers *shoo-fly, shoo-fly*. The retreating storm spat a few more drops of rain. "10-76. Almost there."

It wasn't the first time Officer Francis Gordon dealt with a domestic violence call at the Prairie View Trailer Park. With large families packed into sweaty single-wide mobile homes as tightly as the swine in the slaughterhouse where the men worked—men who killed all day and drank all night— fights happened. Trouble was, this was during the police department's second shift, late afternoon into night, not the usual 2:00 or 3:00 a.m. after the bars closed.

Dispatcher: "9-1-1 is reporting calls about a 10-32 on the scene; use caution."

That's just great, Gordon harrumphed. *Man with gun. Always a gun.*

"Can I get backup?" he barked.

"Bravo-15, I'm on it," interrupted Paul Pembroke, a fellow town officer on patrol—where the devil *was* he?

"What's your 20, Paul?" Gordon called.

"Sinnissippi Forest Preserve. Just helped some tourist with a flat. I'll *spaat*." The static of a prowling storm cut him off.

A good thirty minutes away even if he high-tailed it with the siren keening and the bar flashing—if he wasn't blocked by a tractor or a combine or some loose cows on the way.

"Any troopers nearby for assist? Or county?" Gordon asked the dispatcher. Almost pleaded.

"Checking—deputies—county route—" the radio sizzled like fatty meat on a grill. "Stand by."

Well, I can't stand by, Gordon complained silently. He gunned the Impala. He cranked the AC; there was no way he'd have the windows down in this August heat, at this blazing speed, and with farmers spraying the fields with liquefied manure. He figured that the swine lagoons must be close to flooding with all the rain. They needed emptying, even if onto saturated ground. He zoomed past acres of low fields where the stunted corn was drowning. The stench, like a backed-up sewer, had clearly put people in a foul mood.

Through a gauzy haze that veiled the green sea of corn on either side of Illinois Route 40, watery mirages flickered ahead. The mobile home park sat ahead like shoe boxes in a circle. Gordon wheeled in with a fishtail stop. Wet gravel sprayed behind his blue-and-white cruiser. A knot of women and a few children were clustered behind a pockmarked pickup. Seeing him, they babbled nervously, waved at him, and stabbed their fingers over the truck toward the aqua trailer two spots away. *Okay, so it's gotta be that one.* He drew a deep breath that pressed his belly against the bullet-resistant vest beneath his fire-retardant shirt. His stubborn bulge pinched between the rigid vest bottom and the top of his utility belt. Why couldn't he lose that last inch? Why did he have to wear a clay vest on such a blistering day? *It's gonna be stinkin' hot.* He passed his fingers over his brush cut and stepped out.

The rush of heat roasted his cheeks, and the sickly smell of airborne fertilizer stung his nose and throat. He repressed an urge to clamp a handkerchief over his mouth and nose. He secured the car with the key remote; no need to have a suspect escape in his vehicle. The radio crackled inside and on his shoulder mic. Garbled. Probably his backup. Or not. He couldn't wait.

A couple of hand-wringing women made a stuttering motion to approach him, but after glancing wide-eyed at the trailer, they hesitated and retreated hastily behind the pick-up.

"Hey, Rosie, Maritza—just stay back, okay?" Gordon ordered, raising a hand. From experience—previous domestic violence and visits with the library bookmobile—he knew they spoke English. The Spanish-only workers were usually bunked in barracks close to the plant or in renovated farmhouses by their employers. "Stand right there, okay?"

His eyes darted this way and that behind the polarized Aviator sunglasses, assessing the familiar area. Laundry lines. Bent awnings. Rusty BBQ grills. Children's toys and bikes. Trash cans, lids askew. Rattling window air conditioners. Beater cars without hubcaps. A red Ford pickup with a gun rack. Empty.

"He has a gun," one woman squealed, tearing at her red-dyed hair. "In there." Again, the rapid pointing.

Gordon rested his palm on his sidearm. "Who is 'he'? Who are we talkin' about?"

"It's Richie—Richard. We call him Richie. Richie Valera."

A shouting tirade erupted through the screened windows.

"I DON'T CARE, YOU STUPID BITCH! HE'S MY KID, MY KID, AND YOU CAN'T STOP ME!"

The woman hollered back. A baby wailed.

"MAKE HIM SHUT UP!"

Oh, great. Richie again. Drug charges, assault, DUI. A bar fight. Now this: a custody dispute. Domestic battery, reckless endangerment of a child, possible violation of an order of protection—

And the guy sounds wired.

The shouting continued.

"What kind of gun?" Gordon asked over the clamor.

"A big one," a woman said.

"A shotgun," said a teen girl. "A fat one. Two barrels."

"Has he fired it yet?"

"No," the girl said. "He went in first, and we all argued, and then he left, but only to his truck to get his gun, and he went back in. We called 9-1-1 again to tell—"

Twelve-gauge, two shots, Gordon told himself. *With extra ammo, maybe.* His heart pumped faster. *I'm probably interrupting a kidnapping. Gonna be a possible hostage situation as soon as he realizes I'm here.*

Gordon jerked his thumb at the trailer. "Anyone else in the house?"

"No, just the three. When he left that first time, we came outside, too."

"What's his beef?"

The women looked confused by the question.

"His problem, what's his problem?"

"It's his baby," the redhead answered, "and she is the mother. It's my sister, Krystyl. They are not married. He wants it, and she will not let him."

"That's cuz he is always pissed," added the teen. "You know, I mean, like, high on crank."

Meth. It was a big problem with slaughterhouse workers like this. Kept them awake and strong for the brutal work and the long hours. Easy to make in farm country with all the anhydrous ammonia around for fertilizers. "Is he high now? Could you tell when he came here?"

The teen rolled her eyes. "He is, like, *always* high."

If it was meth, it would take four officers to wrestle him into cuffs. These guys had superhuman energy and couldn't even feel the pain of a taser c2. They ripped out the darts and laughed.

A Sinnissippi County Sheriff's Deputy Ford Interceptor crunched its way into the stony circle drive. No lights, no siren, thankfully. Two brownshirts emerged. They coughed and held their noses.

"OOO-eee, smell my dairy-air," said Otis Anderson, the paunchy partner, waving sausagey fingers in front of his face. "Whew."

"That there is the smell of money," the younger, Tim Creasy, agreed, his mirrored aviators gleaming. "What do we got, Flash?"

"10-16 Domestic. Custody fight. In there. And a 10-32. It's Richie Valera—"

"Oh, crap. Him again?" Anderson grumped.

"—with a double-barreled shotgun. No shots fired. There's one woman and an infant in the place with him. No one else. He hasn't seen me yet."

The blast of the shotgun deafened him and threw him to the ground by instinct. An aluminum screen frame arced into the sky and bits of pink insulation spewed into the parking circle.

The woman inside screamed. The baby screeched.

"SHUT UP! SHUT UP! THE NEXT ONE IS FOR YOU IF YOU DON'T GIVE ME MY BABY, NOW! NOW, I SAID, YOU WHORE, OR I KILL YOU BOTH!"

"I gotta go in," Gordon said.

"Flash, for God's sake, get behind the car," Anderson urged. "We'll call the tactical team right now to contain this guy. They'll set up a perimeter and—"

"No way," Gordon fired back. "There's no time. He's gonna kill her and the kid."

"He'll kill you, first. We should get a Crisis Unit negotiator down here right now."

"It'll take him an hour to get here from Rockford, or Moline, whichever office you call. He won't—"

"I'M GONNA COUNT TO THREE! THAT'S ALL YOU GET! DO YOU HEAR ME? DO YOU? ONE."

"That does it." Gordon scrambled up.

"Francis, what the fat?" Anderson rebuked him. "Get down!"

"I'M NOT KIDDING! TWO!"

Gordon dashed to the rickety wood stoop, stretched out his fist, and hammered twice on the flimsy door.

"Richie! Richie, Police! Let's talk!"

Gordon twisted aside, dropped, and pressed his chest and cheek to the dirt.

The second shotgun blast exploded through the door, splintering it.

Gordon brushed bits of debris from his scalp. *Think you're smart, dontcha?* Gordon launched himself up, drew his Glock, anchored his left foot, and snap-kicked the splintered doorjamb into pieces. He shouldered inside, the gun double-fisted and raised.

The stringy Richie glared at him through glowing eyes that looked like coals, hot and hard. Under a white t-shirt with the sleeves rolled up, colorful tattoos writhed as if alive. He held the emptied shotgun firmly in two boney hands, and Gordon expected him to swing it like a club now that he was cornered.

Gordon's skin goose-bumped. The trailer was cold as a meat locker.

"Drop the gun, Richie," Gordon commanded, aiming at his heaving chest. "It's not loaded anyway. It's of no use to you now."

"Back off, Gordon! This ain't none o' your business!"

Richie's breath steamed in the frigid air.

"It is when there's a gun involved. Drop it, Richie."

Richie swore twice and tossed the weapon behind him. It landed with a dull thump on the yellowed linoleum of the kitchen nook where the woman, Krystyl, pressed her back against a cabinet. She clutched a diapered child to her damp blouse. Krystyl had a split lip and a bruised eye. Cut-up pork loin sizzled in a skillet on a hot plate. A half-diced onion sat next to it with a butcher knife stuck in it.

"There! No more gun. Now get out." Richie's rapid breathing rose and fell to the rhythm of a country ballad on a tinny radio. *When the lights go down, and it's near the last round, all the girls get pretty.* His nostrils flared and his hands curled and uncurled into fists. He was totally amped all right, with soaked armpits and hair matted from sweat.,

Gordon kept the gun trained on Richie's chest. "Keep your hands where I can see them, Richie, okay? Now listen to me, Richie. Are you listening? Listen real good, huh? We can all walk out of here and figure things out, huh? No one is hurt. Look at me, okay? You're not looking at me. Look at me, Richie. Richie?"

"Pig," Richie spat. Then he laughed. The teeth—the ones that were left—were urine-yellow and cracked. "Ain't that what they call yous? Pigs?"

At least he wasn't shouting at the top of his lungs. Gordon tilted his head toward the busted-out window. "There's two more pigs in the yard, Richie, and more pigs comin'. Lots of 'em. Can I be honest with you? Huh? They're not as nice as me. They're tactical. Do you know what that means? Huh?"

"Tell me, Pig," Richie rasped.

Hyperventilating. Flushed. Dehydrated, no doubt. With luck, he'd just pass out.

"It's cop talk for Special Weapons and Tactics," Gordon said evenly. "You know, SWAT. That's what they do, huh? They *swat* guys like they were bugs. They're snipers, and they'll shoot first and *not* ask questions later. They're gonna be real mad, comin' out on such a hot day wearing helmets and all that heavy body armor, huh? So they're gonna want business to be over fast."

"Lemme tell you about *pigs*," Richie said, his sweat-speckled chest heaving. "At the Diedrich plant, I kill 'em. That's my job. I stick 'em with a knife in the throat even if the stunner screws up and they ain't knocked out when they're hung up on the line. I kill near three hunnert hogs a day, *one every three minutes, all day, every day,* and ya know what, pig?"

Keep him talking. De-escalate. "You tell me, Richie. It's dirty work, huh?"

Richie sneered. "It's a *riot*. It's *hilarious*. I think it's *funny* how they scream. How they dangle by one hoof, and kick and spin, and their blood sprays everywhere. There's no time to stun 'em again. So I just kill 'em. I don't care about killing. I kinda *like* it. I'm pretty *good* at it."

"No one needs to get killed here today, Richie."

"I DON'T CARE ABOUT BEING KILLED EITHER, PIG! So let your pig friends come! Let 'em come! Get that, *Pig*? Huh? Huh?"

Richie laughed at his mocking imitation of Gordon's nervous tic. It was more of a wheeze coming out of Richie.

Gordon tightened his grip on the Glock. *Don't lose it,* he scolded himself. *Buy some time.*

"You don't want that, Richie, okay? This didn't start out as suicide by cop. You're smarter than that. You just wanted what was yours, and you feel cheated of it, huh? You just came to claim your rights—"

"Damn straight," Richie gruffed.

"So, I wanna hear your side of the story, okay? To do that, we're gonna let the girl and the baby leave so we can talk, the two of us, man to man, okay? Just you and me."

"NO WAY! NO WAY! THE BABY STAYS WITH ME!" He thumped his sunken chest, ape-like. Then he bared his fangs.

"Maybe you're just jealous because you an' yer missus can't have one, HUH?"

Gordon's jaw tightened. How could he know that? Was he trying to make this personal? *Don't let him.*

"Francis?" the sheriff's deputy, Anderson, called from outside. "Hey, Francis! You all right?"

"Those the other pigs?" Richie snapped.

"Just a couple," Gordon said. *Always tell the truth.* "But I'm telling ya, the bad boys are on the way. A lot of 'em. Military-grade. But there's still time to do the right thing, okay, Richie? We're gonna let the girl and kid out now, okay? So, we can talk, is all. Those guys will keep them here. They won't take them away." He wasn't sure about that.

Gordon treaded backward a few careful steps to give the girl and baby some room to get by. "Krystyl, you and the baby get up and walk by me, on this side." The girl struggled up while cradling the baby and moved closer to the kitchenette countertop. Gordon fixed his gaze forward. You don't turn away from a trapped criminal jacked on drugs who finds killing fun. Gordon leaned slightly toward the open doorframe and called, "The girl's coming out."

"What?" Anderson called.

Gordon turned his chin a little and shouted out the side of his mouth, "The girl! She's coming out with the baby! Tell the tacticals to *hold the line* and don't—"

Richie drew a Microtech Flick Knife from his pocket. He thumbed open the blade.

Krystyl froze behind him.

Gordon braced into a firing stance. Adrenaline electrified his arms. If he reached for the pepper spray, Richie might lunge at him. "Put that thing down, Richie. Right now. It's not gonna help you, okay? We can still fix this."

"I'm gonna show you how to stick a pig," Richie growled, bear-like, low in the throat. He wagged the blade.

"Don't do it, Richie. Put it down."

"It just takes two slices."

"Put it down! Right now!"

"It's fast, Pig."

"Drop it now, Richie. It's the *crank* talking. I know that. Let Krystyl pass by you. You can still walk out outa here, too." *Unless I shoot your kneecap out, but I might hit the girl or the kid—*

"On the neck artery. Right here." He tilted his chin and tapped his own carotid with the tip of the blade.

Krystyl snatched the onion knife. Plunged it deep into that very spot on his neck.

Yanked it free.

Rammed it in the other side to the hilt. Let it go, fell back.

Saucer-eyed, Richie clapped his palm over the first cut. Blood spurted from between his fingers. It bloomed like a flower unfolding on the other side. He looked at his hand, then to Gordon, puzzled. With each heartbeat, a red stream jetted from his neck.

He grimaced, all fury. Reached to his clavicle and tried to pull out the knife. Couldn't get a grip. With a wet gagging, he swung his blade once behind him, but Krystyl had stumbled out of his reach.

Gordon raised the Glock.

Richie collapsed to his knees. He dropped his MicroTech and slapped at his twin wounds like they were demons perched on his shoulders. With a horrid gargling noise, he crumpled, shuddered, and lay still.

The deputies stooped inside, guns drawn. Anderson cursed. Creasy ran out and threw up.

"Call tactics and tell them to stand down," Gordon said over the din of the woman's sobs and the baby's wails. "Get an ambulance here." He secured his weapon, choked back stomach bile, and controlled his rubbery legs to kneel beside Richie.

An ambulance would not arrive out here in the boonies in time. Gordon might put a compress on the artery wound, but the windpipe was probably sliced clean through. That second stab had been at more of an angle than he realized. Krystyl, whimpering, sat on her haunches with the baby wriggling in her lap.

Gordon stepped over Richie, still twitching and foaming at the throat, and took a knee beside Krystyl, whose cheek was turning deep purple. "It's all right, now," he lied, heart still bucking in his chest. "But you're hurt. We're gonna get you to a doctor."

Then these brownshirts will probably arrest you and charge you with voluntary manslaughter, he thought.

"We got this, Flash. It's our scene, now," Anderson declared.

"What? This was my call," Gordon protested. "It's within city limits."

"Once you call in county tactical, it's county jurisdiction," said the sheriff's deputy. "You know that. Coroner's office and county crime scene unit are on the way. We'll get your report later."

Gordon swallowed a lump of pride. "Sure. Okay. Yeah. All yours. As soon as your partner is done talking to Earl and selling Buicks outside, call an ambulance for *her*. It's too late for our friend Richie here." He jerked a thumb at the now-still Richie and the widening pool of bubbly blood staining the orange shag carpeting. "And good luck cleaning that up when they're done."

He addressed the girl seated on the floor. "You have relatives here, don't you, Krystyl, to look after the baby?" He pulled out a handkerchief from his back pants pocket. "That red-haired girl outside?"

"My—my sister," she said with a wince. "Lu—Lucy."

"Fine. I'll tell her you're okay, but you need to go to the ER." He swallowed hard. *And probably the county jail after that.* "Can I leave the baby with her?"

Krystyl whispered, "Okay." She struggled to stand up.

"No, no," Gordon said, palm up. You'll need to stay here." *Flight risk*, he thought. "I'll take the little one to Lucy. What's his name?"

"C—Cody."

"Cody. Hey, Cody. C'mere. Come on. I gotcha."

Krystyl hesitated and then handed over the baby. Gordon gathered the boy into his arms, levered up, and stepped outside with the child against his chest, his kerchief over the kid's face. No need to remember Daddy looking that way. The diaper was leaking on his hand and shirt. "Lucy" ran up to him and took the squirming boy. Gordon told her that Richie was dead.

"But how? There was no gun shot and—"

"Never mind that," Gordon deflected. "Take care of Cody, huh? Stick around because someone will be asking you for a statement."

"Not you?"

"Not me. I gotta go." *I've got more important things to get to: traffic stops for seat belt violations, barking dog complaints, he-said-she-saids, underage smokers. Ya know, threats to civil order.*

Lucy ran to the gathering crowd, getting peppered with questions. Gordon's damp hands trembled. He wiped them with the handkerchief. Acid churned in his gut. He dug in his shirt pocket and pulled out two Rolaids. Cop candy. He tried to take a deep breath of fresh air, but it stank like he was face down in an outhouse. He lifted his square chin as a throaty grumble rippled across the roiling clouds.

More rain coming. At least a good shower might clear the air of that God-awful smell. And cool things down. Oddly, the heat was comforting. *Man, it was cold inside there.* He studied the trailer to see what kind of tiny window AC unit could turn it into a butcher's freezer. There wasn't one. *Must be in the back.*

Creasy sidled up to him, sunglasses in one hand, the other hand wiping his reddened eyes with a kerchief.

"You all right now?" Gordon asked.

Creasy shook his head. "Not really. 1 got bad news, Francis. The smell isn't from farmers spraying the fields. Well, not *just* from that. Dispatcher says the main manure lagoon at Diedrich's Swine Op breached 'cuz of all the rain. There's gotta be near two million gallons of pig waste filling every creek that feeds into the Sinnissippi River. The smell is gonna get a lot worse."

"1 thought you said it was the smell of money."

"1 mean it's gonna rot trees and kill fish," Creasy clarified.

"That *will* be worse," Gordon agreed.

"That's not the worst of it," Creasy said.

"It's not?"

"There's a body in the muck."

Gordon made a face. "That's gross. Do we know who it is?"

"I'll give you one guess."

Gordon didn't have to guess. Given the raucous town hall meeting last night, he knew.

CHAPTER 2

WHEN JACOB DIEDRICH, the CEO of Diedrich Delights AgriProducts and all of its CAFOs, or Concentrated Animal Feeding Operations, had strutted into the high school gym for the town hall meeting last night, two hundred protestors sprang up from their folding chairs and erupted:

"N! O! No CAFO! N! O! No CAFO!"

Out had come the blood-red stop-sign shaped placards, reading NO CAFO, bobbing to the chant. Other signs, held by those standing along the back wall, read CAFOs STINK and SAVE OUR SOIL with the SOS in bold letters.

"Save! Our! Soil! Save! Our! —"

Diedrich had ignored them while shaking rain from his umbrella. Ahead of him, a train of state officials; his adult daughter, Chelsea; and the mayor, Ami Pratt, had shrugged out of wet ponchos and dropped their dripping umbrellas in a crate before climbing up to the dais. Pratt had motioned the officials to their seats and seized a wooden gavel, banging on the folding table three times. "Please! Order! Please sit down! We won't get a thing done, folks, if we don't listen to each other!"

"N! O! No CAFO! N! O! Save! Our! Soil! Save! Our! N! O!—"

They were having none of it. Gordon stood at parade rest by the entrance, thumbs looped into his belt by his hips, scanning the boisterous crowd. Other town cops and a few sheriff's deputies stood at the ready too, shifting their weight nervously left, right, left. An ambulance and a police van were running in the rear parking lot.

The officials moved uneasily in their assigned seats: someone from the state Department of Natural Resources, a biology professor from Sinnissippi Community College, a public health inspector from the state Department of Agriculture. Diedrich enthroned himself beside his prim daughter, Chelsea, who was the acting CFO in charge of negotiating a joint ownership partnering contract with the Chinese. In the front row, stone-faced, sat State Senator Ronald Michelson and State Representative Jeb Harmon, with County Commissioner Terence B. Sellers, who owned a swine operation with Harmon, between them.

Mayor Pratt tapped the microphone and spoke too close to it. "Let's get started." It screeched with feedback. Palms flew to ears. People slid into seats restlessly. Pratt backed off from the mic. "Okay, is this better? We're good? Okay? Look, everyone, let's get started. The zoning board has already granted the required agricultural use district permits, and we're not here to dispute that. In that meeting, everyone had to be quiet while the lawyers made their cases, but we wanted this to be more open. We want to assure everyone that this farm operation will be safe, even with the record rainfall left over from Hurricane Gertrude this week that has moved up here from Texas. You may have heard of problems downstate with these kinds of farms, but the technology has changed and—"

"Hog farms like that, with 3,000 head in crowded pens where they can't even turn around, aren't farms at all!" a woman called out. "They're factories!"

The room broke into applause.

"That was you, right, Autumn?" the mayor said, her hand shading her brow until she spotted the Humane Society shelter director. "Well, you may be right, but remember, we got other factories in town: the metal finishers, Landis Fasteners, First Choice Tool and Die, and we don't mind them, not to mention the Perkins Ranch with—how many heads, now, Travis? Where are you sitting?"

Travis Perkins half-stood up and tipped his Stetson. "Near 500, Your Honor, but we don't pen up the cattle or smell like a hog farm do."

The crowd applauded.

"I can't sit on my patio anymore!" someone complained.

"I can't hang out the clothes to dry! They get brown!"

"My kids can't play outside!"

"My yard smells like a sewer!"

"That lagoon is gonna flood with all this rain! What about my well?"

"All right, all right," the mayor conceded, "when the wind shifts it can be an annoyance. Dr. Charles, do you want to address the rain issue?"

A *ba-boom* of thunder rattled windows, and rain hammered at the metal roof.

Owen Charles, the public health inspector from the state Department of Agriculture, had run an industrial poultry farm before his appointment. "Well, there's two things," he began, loudly enough to be heard over the clatter of the rainfall. "First, like all you farmers out there do, the compost gets jet-sprayed on the fields for fertilizer. That's a good thing. That there is the smell of money."

Common farm humor. No one laughed but Charles.

"So, uh, the second thing is, the lagoons are built better than before when they were just lined with clay and breaches caused by rain were a problem. They got these high-tech membrane linings now, and levels are inspected every week, and sensors channel off any excess in a safe way."

Malcolm Brandt, the thirty-something academic whose

shock of dark hair no comb could tame, craned toward the mic. "I'm sorry, I need to jump in here. There's no 'safe way.' The Spoon River and its tributaries experienced excessive levels of nitrites last year, soon after Mr. Diedrich's plants opened in Tazewell County and West Peoria, that resulted in massive fish kills and the widespread loss of trees and crops."

Many nodding heads, whispers of "See, I told you."

Diedrich folded his arms and shook his head, *No.*

"But, professor," Charles rebutted, "there's no telling where those nutrients came from, isn't that true?" He sounded snide. "Our studies say most of the nutrients didn't come from the Diedrich operation but from municipal sewage and lawn fertilizers from upstream."

The professor shook his head. "I wouldn't call it *nutrients.* The Pfiesteria, E. Coli, and Enterococcus bacteria levels from fecal matter clearly boosted algae growth that clogged every stream, depleted oxygen levels, and killed four million fish—"

"Let me ask you, *Professor,*" the official sneered, "do *you* use lawn fertilizer?"

"That is not the point—"

"Everyone in this here auditorium does, I'll bet. I mean, who doesn't?"

"It's not nitrogen and phosphorous from lawn fertilizers, it's fecal bacteria—"

"I'm a scientist, too," the public health inspector broke in, "and the bugs you grow in your lab aren't the same as what's in the rivers. It's likely a disease brought in by the Asian Carp, an invasive species."

The gym filled with boos. Some laughs. "Of course it's pig shite!" someone shouted. "Cain't you smell it?"

"It's more complicated," the inspector claimed. "It's a combination of fungal invasion, wastewater, pesticides, and other chemicals. Besides, the bacteria are beneficial, like the ones in your own septic systems, and the levels are below the threshold for harm to human health. Not for certain kinds of fish, obviously, but for humans, safe."

Gordon wondered how much Diedrich was paying him.

"Then why do so many people get sick?" A stately older gentleman in a sport coat and bow tie levered up to address the panel. "I lived in Peoria a long time, and I was never sick until these hog farms opened a mile from my house. I got asthma-like spells from the ammonia smell, so I moved up here to be away from the hog farms down South, and now you're here in the North, too."

"Not for long!" the audience yelled. "N! O! No CAFO! N! O! No—"

"Save! Our! Soil! Save! Our! Soil! Save!—"

"That's enough! SQUEEEAHEE," the mayor shouted into the mic. Again, the piercing feedback squeal. The crowd sat uneasily. "Tommy Samuelson, is that your hand I see up? Go ahead."

"Hey there, Ami, I just got one question. See, I petitioned the county health department for a 500-gallon septic system for my cabin, but they said I'm too close to the Sinnissippi River. So how come these people, whose hogs are gonna produce up to twenty million gallons of poo, can have a manure pond that ain't filtered near the same river?"

Scattered applause and catcalls sounded throughout the room.

The mayor looked down the row of panelists. No one looked up.

"I just need to know," Samuelson repeated, "why they can build an open cesspool the size of a football field, and I can't put in a tank?"

A cheer from the crowd.

The mayor pointed down the row. "Mr. Diedrich, do you have an explanation?"

Jacob Diedrich stood up, a barrel of a man, his dark hair brilliantined and brushed straight back from a high forehead. He thumbed his suit coat lapels and the diamond in his tie clip glittered. The crowd booed. Diedrich smiled and nodded in recognition as though he were being awarded a prize.

"I'll answer your question, sir, if we can be calm but for a moment. I'll wait—that's better. For one thing," he boomed, "hog waste does not contain communicable human diseases."

Samuelson flushed red. "Are you suggesting, sir, that I have some kind of dis—"

The crowd jeered and hissed. Some stood, shaking fists; placards were raised.

"How dare you!" called a thirty-something woman in a headband and ponytail. She stepped into the center aisle and approached the stage. "We've all been insulted enough!" She was steaming. "We all know what's really going on here. All our elected officials, including you, Commissioner, and you, Senator, and you, Mr. Representative, are either in the pork business or received campaign donations from hog bosses and then passed laws to deregulate hog farms and maximize their profits while polluting the land and oppressing workers—"

Diedrich raised a wide palm. "Little lady, let me stop you right there and tell you that your town's tax base is about to increase by an assessment of twenty million dollars which will build a library, a rec center, a new firehouse, and employ hundreds."

"That's a lie," the woman shot back, her honeyed ponytail bobbing. She marched toward the stage, pointing her finger like a pistol. "The money is going to lobby politicians like these—these swine—who happen to be major shareholders who are now planning legislation to prevent anyone from suing pig operations—"

"Someone get this—this *extremist* to sit down," Diedrich ordered.

"—and these so-called jobs have gone to people you brought in from the *outside*, poor immigrants, not to *us*—"

"Officer, over there, yes, you, could you please restrain this person," Diedrich bellowed with an urgent beckon to Gordon.

"And in fact, we'll *lose* jobs," the woman shuddered, "because family farms like *my* family's farm will go out of business and your factory will employ *fewer* workers who will get no protections because they are undocumented—"

"Officer, now, if you please."

Standing at the dais' edge, the woman stabbed a finger at Diedrich. "You should be stuck and bled out like one of your hogs!"

"Officer, do your duty!" Diedrich commanded.

Gordon froze.

How could he arrest his own wife?

CHAPTER 3

GORDON LEFT THE COUNTY DEPUTIES to their grim task, notified the dispatcher, requested Officer Pembroke for backup, and headed for the Diedrich hog lots. The sprawling CAFO—Concentrated Animal Feeding Operation, or as his wife, Stephanie, and her fellow activists called it, a Confined Animal Feeding Operation—lay within the jurisdiction of The River Falls Police Department. Since he was the only officer ranked detective sergeant, chances were he'd be the lead investigator unless the chief deferred to the state police or the county sheriff's office bullied their way into heading it. There was an election for sheriff coming this Fall, after all, and getting a solve on a high-profile case would be good PR.

He kept the windows shut and the AC blowing. Even so, the sweet-sick smell seeped through the vents. Lord knows it was bad enough on breezy days when the noxious clouds from manure spraying made kids puke, old people faint, and townsfolk grumble about the gummy brown film that coated their cars. But now, even a few miles away, the raunchy odor began to turn his stomach.

The radio scanner chattered non-stop. The Fire Protection District set up a command post in the fire station. The Illinois Environmental Protection Agency was called. Illinois Emergency Management. Department of Natural Resources. State Police to close any flooded roads. The mayor. Aldermen. State rep. County supervisor. *Hope he isn't drinking yet.* Township managers downstream. Lou Willis, the county coroner, of course, who was on his way to the trailer park. That would delay his arrival at the Diedrich operation. Gordon knew he needed to secure the crime scene before a throng of guys in suits—whether hazmat suits or Brooks Brothers—showed up and contaminated things. Funny thought, that—*contaminating* an area ankle-deep in a noxious brew of swiney sewage.

The windshield splattered, and he switched on the wipers. The spots smeared. Not raindrops. Flies, suddenly clouds of them, coming for the feast. Gordon scowled and pressed the washer button. The smears arced across the glass, and he hoped for a sudden downpour. He rocketed over a bridge that crossed Leaf Creek, a tributary of the Sinnissippi River. Already, a frothy pink film ribboned through the waters, foul effluent eddying in pools on the way to the river. Just as the locals had feared and Creasy had noted, the algae, and ammonia, and God-knows-what fecal bacteria would kill catfish and walleye by the thousands, and their stinking carcasses would bring quarreling swarms of turkey vultures.

So, the very waste lagoon breach that the whole town feared had now occurred. And the dead body found in the sludge? Could be a worker trying to fix a problem and overcome by the fumes. But Gordon's gut said it was Diedrich.

Officer Paul Pembroke met him at the razor-wired gate and guardhouse of the Diedrich complex. The company security men, in forest-green uniforms that looked borrowed from a Balkan state, lingered behind the chain-link fencing, standing near black Dodge pick-ups, clasping walkie-talkies at their mouths that were covered by green and yellow company-logo bandanas. *Stagecoach bandits.*

Gordon rolled down his car window and skewed his nose at the stench.

"You're gonna need one of these," Pembroke said,

coughing once before handing over a single-use filter mask. He put on his own. "I just got here. We'll need the fire boots, too."

Gordon affixed the half-face mask and popped the trunk. He stepped out and retrieved the rubber bunker boots. "I saw the creeks filling up already on the way," he said.

"The whole county is gonna turn into a toilet."

"We'll get numb to it in a few minutes." Or so he wished. Seated on the bumper, Gordon loosened and slipped off his nylon athletic Oxfords and tugged on the high boots by the straps. "Won't need the hip boots, I hope." He grabbed some blue nitrile gloves from a box and pulled them on with a snap.

"Lou is on the way," Pembroke said. "Busy day for the coroner's office."

"I'm not waiting," Gordon said, retrieving his digital SLR camera and slamming the trunk shut. "Let's have a look at the stiff."

Pembroke waved at the guards, who activated the gate. It yawned open. Gordon swatted away some flies and strode past the garish WARNING: NO TRESSPASSING sign. VIOLATORS SUBJECT TO ARREST. PASS AT OWN RISK. SURVEILLANCE CAMERAS IN USE. ABSOLUTELY NO PHOTOGRAPHY.

Double standard, Gordon thought. He hoisted his Nikon to his shoulder to clearly display it in defiance and glanced up. Sure enough, a security camera mounted on the guardhouse eyed him. There were cameras everywhere, no doubt; someone would have to check the video archives for activity around the plant and lagoon as soon as the coroner gave a reasonable time-of-death. Had to be an accident, and if not, an inside job, Gordon surmised. That or someone took a big risk and somehow got past these mercenaries and all these cameras.

A trim young man in khakis and a corn-colored company polo shirt emerged from one of the pick-up trucks. A respirator covered his lower face, making him look like an enormous insect. His black hair glistened with mousse into a hundred mini antennas. He extended a hand.

"Gordon, right?" he said. "Remember me? Dennis Quayle? Communications Office?"

The fancy-pants Diedrich company PR man. He was the guy with a piano-key smile two octaves wide who had commanded the open house when the facility was near the end of construction. For the highly publicized event, he had supervised chaperones in white coveralls. He had sported a pleated chef's hat while handing out free BBQ pork sandwiches to vetted visitors and friendly reporters. The guests toured gleaming empty pens, shining corrugated aluminum ceilings, and pristine farrowing crates lined up in neat rows. Nearby had sat samples of composted manure—no smell.

"Quayle. Sure. This here's my partner, Paul Pembroke." They all shook hands. Good thing they had spare gloves in their pockets.

"This is awful," Quayle lamented. "I mean, it's just so, how could it, I mean, how could such a thing happen?"

"That's what we're here to find out," Gordon said. "Has anybody touched or moved the body?"

Quayle snapped his fingers. "No, no, no. Two of our workers, because of the heavy rains, were inspecting the lagoon for a freeboard measurement—"

"Freeboard?"

"How much room remained around the rim above the liquid content. In Illinois, a legal two feet is required. We were worried that the storm surge overnight might result in overflow that even the safe channels couldn't manage."

"And one of them passed out from the fumes and fell in?"

"No, oh, my heavens, no. The workers found a breach by the main drainpipe, where the seal is weakest. The resultant lower water level revealed—well, they saw—I can't believe it. Mr. Diedrich."

Just as he suspected. "Had he been on the premises earlier?"

"Two days ago. But yesterday? No. Not to my knowledge. And I would know if he was, so I was astonished that he was here. Stuck in the breach point. He slowed the leakage."

A company man to the end. Not exactly like putting your finger in the dike.

Quayle shrugged. "Don't we need to wait for the crime scene technicians? Command center truck, cameras, crime scene tape, all that?"

The kid watched too much TV. "They're at another call. They'll come later. For now, *I'm* the crime scene technician. It's a small town."

"Oh. Very well. This way." Quayle pivoted and led the men past a row of trailers and around the first hog barn of eight. The hangar-sized structures, two stories high with gleaming ribbed metal roofs, were punctuated regularly along the walls by humming exhaust fans. Feeder silos, looking like lunar landers, squatted beside them. Clearly, Quayle did not want to pass through the barns but wanted to go around them. No need to see five thousand animals crammed into steel pens too small to turn around in, some injured from the bites of stressed-out neighbors, lying in whatever filth did not drop through the gridwork beneath them. As Gordon recalled from an animal rights circular his wife had written, the daily waste equaled the raw flushings of 20,000 people. And all within a mile or so from homes.

As soon as the coroner calculated a reliable time of death, everyone else on duty around those hours would be interviewed by the canvas team. Hopefully, they wouldn't have much time to discuss the matter among themselves and conflate their stories to match whatever Quayle wanted them to say—and not say. Even so, every good cop knew that eyewitnesses often made up stuff that they imagined *should* have happened for the sake of a good story. Everyone lied to cops, each for his own reason. To exaggerate one's own importance or connection to the excitement. To distance oneself from it. To cast blame on an enemy. To protect a loved one. Even to flirt.

And a professional liar like Quayle would feed *The Sinnissippi Observer* a positive press release that they'd gladly print as is, being too busy covering 4-H shows, high school sports, and church soup suppers to do their own reporting. The weekly paper was a promotion piece for the county as it was, appealing to Chicago-area tourists who came here for vacations. They wouldn't come if they heard the place smelled worse than a gas station urinal. If *The Rockford Register Star* or *The Pantagraph* or *The Dixon Telegraph* or Rock Island's *Dispatch Argus* or other news outlets showed up, he'd give them the same pretty press release, PR photos, and a canned speech to con the public into believing that *everything is under control*. By protocol, the chief would do the same in his press conference. You couldn't say more. Why tip off the bad guys? The politicians and the suits from Natural Resources and Emergency Management? Yup, the same. *We're on it*. The public was already angry and anxious enough.

Gordon plucked a spiral notebook and a pen from his chest pocket to record his narrative details: day, time, weather and temperature, names of those present, what doors were open and closed in nearby buildings, and, in a moment, the location and condition of the body. He began to sketch the layout of the barns and the location of the lagoon, made a plus sign for compass points, and then decided he should get a better map from the County Planning Board office later on. He put away the notebook. Rounding the last barn, he studied the waste lagoon, a three-acre artificial lake unseen beyond a raised earthen berm planted with sod and intermittent pines for soil stability, perhaps, and privacy, for sure. Some bristly oxtongue, stink grass, and bedstraw had taken hold in spots, but the herbicides used in the adjacent cornfield to control broadleaves had mostly worked on weeds around the perimeter too. A series of pipes fed the lake, with gauges and valve wheels at the elbow joints.

A fetid brown muck, foaming pink at the edges, lapped at the gravelly access road where it sloped into a soggy cornfield. The ground was submerged in Pepto-Bismol ooze, and the relentlessly marching rows of cornstalks, sharp leaves upraised from their stalks, all looked to be calling desperately for rescue. Crops in deeply pooled areas were stunted and crisped. Gordon's eyes itched, and he blinked away more buzzing flies.

He followed Quayle up the embankment to the lagoon's rim; there were no steps or railings to brush for fingerprints. The rains would have washed them away anyway. At the top, he tried not to retch as he considered a reconstruction theory. Did Diedrich drown in this foul stuff? Stephie once told him that workers who have entered these "manure lagoons" to perform maintenance tasks like clearing blockage from a pump were instantaneously asphyxiated by the release of hydrogen sulfide gas. Thank goodness his mask was working. Once unconscious, workers quickly drowned in the liquid manure. Often, these deadly incidents involved multiple coworkers attempting to rescue one another. At first, he figured that's what had happened. But Diedrich would certainly not be doing a menial task or assisting in a rescue. And Quayle would have mentioned it. He was killed, here or elsewhere, and then dumped. It was a good place to hide a body unless security cameras got a good image. No one would smell the submerged corpse decomposing, that's for sure. And it might decompose faster. Who would think of searching here, anyway, in the heat of August when the smell was worst? If a gun was involved, would he need to dredge the lagoon for the weapon? *Ick.*

The men followed the grassy rim to the far corner where it seemed the earthen wall fell away, as though it had been a sandcastle wall dissolved by a wave.

"There," Quayle said with a nervous gulp, pointing.

The limp body, coated in sludge, draped over the drainpipe face down, almost as though clutching it to avoid being washed out. The corpse had probably been carried along by the outflow when the heavy rains broke through then got stuck. If so, then it was dumped closer to the other end, near the barns. Made sense. Why drag it all the way out here? The body was clothed in trousers but no shirt. Because of the hot weather? Wouldn't he just unbutton it and roll up the sleeves? Was it stripped by his attacker?

Gordon stepped up to the spot, rebuking his nausea, and tested the saturated grounding with a heel. The plastic lining, stretched out over what looked like clay, would probably hold him. He snapped a few shots with the camera—wide-angle, close-ups—and then asked Pembroke to grab his forearm to anchor him in case of a slip or a plunge so he could get closer. After this was over, he thought, he might ask to be hosed down in the barn where workers probably sprayed the concrete floors. A long shower at home with lemon soap and a disinfectant shampoo would be in order too.

Thus locked in Pembroke's grip, Gordon stepped forward and strained closer. It was Jacob Diedrich, all right. His face, smeared by a ghoulish mudpack, hadn't yet bloated. Neither had his neck puffed up much; the exposed portly belly didn't look inflated by gases. He didn't see the yellowish froth around the mouth and nose common in a drowning. The arms and legs were untied, unbound. No gag, though it was possible it'd been removed. An autopsy would show it. No rings or wristwatch or ear stud or other jewelry that he could see. No neck chain, which could be used for strangling. No visible wounds. Again, the autopsy would confirm. He took a few more one-handed snapshots.

"Help me back up," Gordon called through a tight throat. "I've seen enough."

His partner yanked him to the solid walkway. "So, what do you think?"

Gordon pinched the nose of his mask. "I think it stinks," he said wryly. "It's Diedrich, all right. I can tell even with all the junk caked on the face. I'll get the evidence kit from the car." He called to the PR man, keeping his distance. "Mr. Quayle, you'll have to come with me and stay away while we process the scene. Have you notified anyone yet of the incident?"

"No, I thought I should wait for the police."

"Good. Sometimes news gets leaked out and the next-of-kin learn from a phone call or the media."

"But something like this—I mean, it's all over the plant already."

Gordon grumped. "Well, let me be the one to notify next of kin. It needs to be timely, accurate, and in person. Say, is the lagoon under video surveillance?"

"Everything is."

"Okay. We'll need to see the footage from 9:00 p.m. last night to when the body was found today." Nine o'clock was when the town hall meeting let out.

"I'll tell the security office."

Big corporations like Diedrich must have the latest equipment, Gordon surmised. Digital image storage for a month, remote access, motion-activated cameras. Should make the job for the state police's forensic lab easy.

"And I'll need a list of everyone on duty for that shift and the logs of all visitors— livestock drivers, delivery people, salespeople, I mean, like, whoever came and went."

"Human Resources again, reception, shipping and receiving," Quayle recited, escorting him back to the squad car. Gordon ignored his pestering questions on the walk—*How'd he die? How'd he get in there? Is the company in trouble?*—replying with the standard *I can't tell you in an ongoing investigation,* and *We won't know until after the autopsy and pathologist's report,* and the generic *That's not for me to say.*

"When can I begin making phone calls about it?"

"Wait until I call you after I visit with family," Gordon replied as he popped open the trunk to methodically gather paper and plastic evidence bags with pre-printed ID tags, eyedroppers, tweezers, and vials.

"I thought you had to notify the family."

"One thing at a time, Mr. Quayle," Gordon said. "I need to keep the scene secure until the Crime Scene Unit shows up."

Once Quayle dismissed himself, the radio snapped and popped; the dispatcher notified Gordon that the coroner was on the way, but the Crime Scene Unit would be delayed. No surprise there.

The big surprise was two killings in one day. Homicides were few and far between in corn-and-soybean country. Some drug-related gang violence found its way here from Chicago last spring and about a year ago, another domestic dispute, this time with a .380 ACP semi-auto pistol—favored by concealed carriers—involved. Sheesh, come to think of it, nearly everyone had a gun out in the country, mainly rifles for hunting deer and pheasant, for self-protection in such isolated places where a cop might be half an hour away, or for shooting the coyotes that preyed on livestock. But Bobby Ray Thornton, in that domestic call, swore he didn't know the gun was loaded. Bobby Ray was loaded, that's for sure, with malt liquor, and he got off with a lesser charge for shooting his third live-in girlfriend, LauraLynn Sheer. 'Course he knew it was loaded; he was a licensed concealed-carrier and knew guns. Gordon had shot skeet with him as teenagers at the Sinnissippi Rod and Gun Club, and he often bragged about shooting and skinning squirrels. Gordon didn't buy his story when he arrested him. *It just went off, Flash, I swear. What went off, Bobby? The gun—or you?* And so Bobby Ray became another one of Gordon's old high school classmates he'd arrested at one time or another, mostly for traffic violations, public drunkenness, disturbing the peace, disorderly conduct, battery. Maybe he'd be arresting one for murder.

The coroner rolled up in his van and parked behind the cruiser.

"This one's gonna be messy, eh, Francis?" Willis said, stepping out of the cab with a respirator in his grip.

"Just the usual, Lou," Gordon said.

"Sure," Willis said sardonically, "Boss Hogg found in his own pig manure lagoon. Happens every day." As the third-generation director of the town's funeral home, twice-elected coroner, and licensed pathologist, he'd seen plenty of messes. Car crashes. Hunting mishaps. Farm accidents. They were the worst. You always knew the families.

"It's just gonna take a while," Gordon replied resignedly. "Everything's wet and smells like a full diaper."

Willis fussed with his face mask ear loops. "Sure you don't want to wait for the techs, Francis? This will be gritty work."

Gordon checked the frowning steel wool sky. "We'd better start before it pours again," he said. He had a few hours left to his shift, anyway, time to bag any evidence easily found such as shell casings or cigarette butts, a weapon if he was lucky, and maybe begin to process the body: put each soaked shoe in a separate bag, each dripping sock, any effects: a wallet, a pen, a phone. He'd leave it to the techs to try getting anything else: fingerprints, fibers, soil samples, and such, all mixed with the fetid feces-and-urine glop. But it wasn't likely they'd find anything.

"Your call," Willis agreed. "I'll get the EMTs to help me move Mr. Diedrich out to the van when we're finished."

"Can you still do a preliminary exam and get me an estimated TOD?" Gordon asked. "I could use more information for the notification."

"I'll try. I can get to the autopsy pretty fast."

"I can't wait. Small town news travels faster."

"Got it. Anyway, it looks like we got a two-for-the-price-of-one sale today. That hasn't happened for a long time. That'll slow things down a little."

A livestock trailer truck rumbled by with a load of fattened swine on the way to the nearby Diedrich processing facility, where Richie had worked.

Gordon slammed the trunk shut. *The killing never stops here.*

CHAPTER 4

"EIGHT HOURS," Willis announced. "Not as specific as you wanted, Francis, sorry. The full body rigidity, those milky corneas, and the lividity in the back where the purple blotches didn't blanche when I pressed with a thumb say so, but they can't tell me it was 10:15 p.m. or whatever. Body temp doesn't tell me much either, being in this heat and sewage."

The techies arrived, sheathed in white full-body suits despite the humidity, hoods up and snug, facemasks affixed, high boots at parade rest, and their blue nitrile gloves lugging an assortment of silver cases and plastic sacks. Someone hauled an air-compressed pressure washer unit up the berm slope.

"All yours, gentlemen," Gordon invited with an exaggerated sweep of his hand. He briefed them on what he'd done, handed over the bags he'd collected and labeled, and promised to email the photos. They'd be taking their own, of course. It might take a couple of days to process all the data, including his tediously written report, which would take the rest of his shift to write up. But the first forty-eight hours were critical in an investigation like this. Witnesses who had not stepped forward would probably not appear, or if they did, they wouldn't remember details well. New clues were unlikely to emerge. Interviews would need to begin immediately.

He might have begun to question employees in the barns,

but someone from PD's First Shift, the same shift as the workers present at the time, would have to do the canvassing. He urgently needed to notify the family before the town grapevine did. Telephone, telegraph, tell a neighbor.

He decided to transfer what notes he had to the laptop later, at the end of his shift, while sitting in the squad car in a vacant lot near the edge of town where the weekly farmers' market was held, so he could be seen by anyone needing help. It might be different in the city; sitting in a squad car made you an easy target, but in the country you were a shield. First, he needed a shower and a fresh uniform before visiting family members with the news, accompanied by the chaplain. "See ya, Lou," he said to the coroner with a wave.

Willis was already unfolding a blue polyethylene body bag. "Sure, later. After I bag him and tag him, I'll be in touch," Willis called after him. "And Francis, rub a lemon on your skin for that smell."

CHAPTER 5

IT WAS THE WORST, truly the worst, part of his job. Not gruesome car crashes. Not autopsies.

Notification of kin.

Like the time a just-retired sixty-six-year-old hiker was struck and killed in a crosswalk in Sinnissippi State Park late on a Sunday afternoon by another vacationing RV-er.

Or when that suicide driver accelerated across the double yellow line and smashed head-on into an eighteen-wheeler just before dawn one Saturday on a remote part of Route 251 by the Benson Farms.

Or poor Jimmy Blankenship, the college-bound high school basketball player who was stabbed to death outside Pop's Pizza after a Friday night game by a jealous and drunken rival.

"You or me?"

Police Chaplain Christina Balfour, in the cruiser's passenger seat, asked every time.

"Gotta be me," Gordon said. "It's the uniform. It makes it real to them." It was his answer—every time.

She might have a Police Department Chaplain shoulder patch and a gold cop badge with a prominent cross on it pinned to her chest, but in that singular moment of shock, on the worst day of their lives, survivors would only see the man in blue. He had showered and changed into the fresh uni at the station. Funny, ironing the shirt was one of the last things Stephie had done before leaving.

At the guard house for Alton Heights Golf Club and Estates, Gordon flashed the tin at the attendant. After the gate lifted, he followed the GPS directions. It wasn't a community he visited much.

"In 800 feet, turn left onto Driver Lane," the GPS chirped.

"There's no telling who will answer the door," Gordon said. "Like I said, the two adult kids live with him—which is weird—but they might be away. I don't know if he had housekeepers or gardeners."

"How about the divorced wife? Do you have to visit her?"

"Lives in Arizona," Gordon said. "Not our jurisdiction. I called the sheriff's department there. They'll send somebody. They won't be able to say much. Not before the autopsy."

"The destination is on your left. Arrived."

An Audi convertible was parked at the crest of the long brick drive. Someone was home in the stately antebellum mansion with a broad porch and high windows. They ascended the veranda steps between white colonnades. Wicker furniture overlooked a manicured fairway where a golf cart hummed. It was a long way from the Prairie View Trailer Park. Gordon noted the security camera, took a deep breath, and rapped the bronze knocker.

He considered pressing the doorbell button when the lock *ker-chicked* and the heavy paneled door swung open. A willowy blonde woman, late twenties, in a tennis outfit and a red headband, looked him over.

"Chelsea Diedrich?" Gordon asked, even though he recognized her. "I'm Detective Sergeant Francis Gordon and this is Officer Chris Balfour—"

"Is he dead?" she asked evenly.

The words *May we please come inside* and *I'm very sorry to inform you* stuck in his throat. "Excuse me?"

"My brother Logan. He's been using again?"

"No, I mean, I don't know, I mean—"

Chaplain Chris cut in. "We're so sorry to tell you that your father is dead."

Sometimes they fainted. One time a woman ran outside screaming. Another time Gordon got punched. Usually they stood there, silent, quizzical, as if they'd lost their hearing or suddenly no longer understood English.

Like Chelsea.

Gordon let it be. Why say anything to make it worse?

Chelsea cocked her head and pursed her lips as if considering an oddity. *Who knew that "natural" red food coloring is actually derived from crushed cochineal insects? It takes forty thousand dead bugs to make a pound. How about that?*

"Won't you come in?" she finally said.

A broad staircase greeted them. He might have been walking onto the plantation home set of *Gone with The Wind*. The crystal chandelier cast arcs of rainbows on the gilded paintings. The chairs looked like they should have velvet ropes on them so no one would sit on them.

"Please," she said with a wave of her lean hand, "have a seat."

"We won't be long," Gordon promised. "So sorry for your loss." Routine.

"How did it happen?" Chelsea asked.

"We're not exactly sure. Your father was found behind the farrowing plant, in the pond." He had rehearsed this. "We don't know the circumstances yet. The coroner is conducting an examination."

She didn't pale or pink. She didn't cry or sigh. She looked past Gordon and Balfour to the upper wall as though checking a stock ticker. "So, you suspect foul play?"

"We're trying to find out," Gordon said. It was incomplete

but not a lie. "The coroner is running some tests. If you'd care to see the remains—"

"You're here, aren't you?" she said curtly. "You don't need me to identify the body."

"Truth to tell, miss, we do need a positive ID in person. It's the law. And we need for you and your brother to sign some papers to authorize release of the body to a funeral director for final arrangements that conform to the stipulations of a will, if there is one."

"Oh, there is one," she said. A smile tempted the corner of her lips. "I'll need to call Winston. The family lawyer, I mean."

"I'm sure there are many other calls you'll need to make."

"I'm not calling my brother. That's on you. He'll ID the body for you."

"He's not here?"

"Dad kicked him out a couple days ago. Weed. Pills. Again. I'll give you an address where he's probably at."

"Appreciate it."

She drilled into his eyes. "Do you have suspects?"

Someone angry, revengeful, or who could benefit from his death. Like you. Maybe that's why you're asking. To see if we're on to you.

"We're looking into it," Gordon replied dryly. "The coroner needs to rule it accidental or otherwise. Until he does that tomorrow, I have a few questions for you. We're in a gathering phase, and then we'll be in a sifting phase. I promise you we'll be thorough." He tried not to make it sound like a threat. He pulled out a memo pad and a pencil.

"Will this be long? My tennis partner is due any minute."

Gordon ignored the comment. He ran her through the drill.

"Are there other relatives in the area?" *People to inform.*

"No. Mom's in Arizona, with her sister, my Aunt Betty. I have two uncles, aunts, and some cousins in North Carolina."

More family hog operations, no doubt, Gordon thought. *And that explains a Southern touch to the house. The relations are probably too far away to be suspects. I'll have the locals inform them and check their travel.*

"Did your dad ever mention threatening letters, texts, social media postings, or phone calls?"

"He stopped mentioning them, there were so many."

"We'll check the phone texts and social media. Other than that, is there a record or file of abusive letters or calls?"

"No. He ignored them all. Part of doing business, he said."

"Know of any enemies he had?"

She laughed. "You were at that town hall meeting last night, right? I'd say just about everyone in the room. One lady, some whacko activist, even made a verbal threat."

Stephie, for goodness sakes ...

Chelsea stabbed a finger at Gordon's chest. "I'd start with her."

"Anyone he had an ongoing dispute with, a suit, a quarrel?"

She harrumphed again. "When has he *not* been in a dispute? Picking a fight and threatening a lawsuit was his way of controlling a situation."

"Like with your brother? You said he was kicked out."

"Logan was in rehab, out, in, out again. What parent wants a freeloading addict in the house stealing things?"

"Is that what your dad said?"

"Something like it."

"So, he was stealing things from the house to pay for a drug habit?"

"Dad thought so."

"And how did you two get along?"

"Well enough. I'm handling the Chinese accounts. I'm fluent, you know."

I know Pig Latin, Gordon thought. *Ig-Pay Atin-lay.* "So, import/export terms?"

"We're in acquisition talks. Weng Feng of Shanghai wants to buy our North Carolina operations outright and partner with us here."

"How are the talks going?"

She grinned. "They'll go well."

"Now that your father is gone?" Gordon asked.

Her face clouded. "No, because I'm good at what I do."

"Any disputes or quarrels with anyone else?"

"Are you kidding?" She counted on her fingers. "Some sub-contracted local pork producers don't like their sales terms for the rendering plant. Some farm families quitting the business don't like the prices they got for their land to build the CAFO. Some crazy environmental group wants to file a suit about the manure lagoons. That crazy lady at the meeting is one of their leaders. Animal rights people are on us, like the head of the dog shelter here. She was at the meeting too; maybe you should talk to her. She's used to euthanizing animals. The union at the packing house has filed an 'intent to strike' now that the contract talks have deadlocked. I mean, who *isn't* mad at Dad?"

"Maybe the politicians who were at the town meeting," Gordon said.

"Diedrich Delights is good for the state's economy," she retorted.

And for the politicians' pocketbooks, too. They would not want him dead. *Follow the money.*

Speaking of money, how much do you stand to inherit? he wanted to ask.

"So, the meeting must be the last time you talked to him or saw him."

Her eyes rolled up to the cathedral ceiling, impatient. "After the town meeting last night, yeah. So, like, 9:00 p.m., I guess. We left in separate cars. He had a driver."

"Who is that?"

"Lo Phat."

"Excuse me?"

"Chinese."

"Nickname?"

"That's what Dad called him. Lo Phat."

Like pork? Gordon almost said. *The other white meat?*

"An amenity, of sorts, provided by the Chinese company we're negotiating with. Kinda his bodyguard, too," Chelsea added.

Didn't do the job. Contrarily, did the job he was asked to do: earn the boss's trust, then eliminate the boss for better trade terms with the daughter. "Where can I find him?"

"I think he has a condo in Naperville."

"I'll need his real name."

"Lo Phan. Xi Lo Phan." She spelled it out.

"Thanks. Do you have an address?"

"Ask Human Resources."

"I will. What kind of car and where is it kept?"

"Lincoln Continental. White. After Lo Phat drops him off here, he usually parks at the farrowing plant. Sometimes he drives it home to the condo in Naperville."

He would look for the car in both places. "Did you think it unusual that your dad didn't come home last night?"

"Not really. He could be away for days. Married to his work, like Mom said."

It's what Stephie told me more than once.

"Do you have a recent photo of your dad we could borrow?" Gordon asked. "To show people in the process of the investigation."

"There must be a dozen in his room," Chelsea said. She noted Gordon's quizzical look. "Oh, he printed off selfies with business associates and people in politics. Come on in and pick one."

The broad chest of drawers displayed a veritable rogues' gallery of suspects, a photographic line-up. There was the big business celebrity himself who clearly had told the orthodontist to give him the high beams, posing—imposing— beside the governor, a few mayors, the state agriculture secretary, the U.S. Department of Agriculture secretary, the president of the Illinois Pork Producers Association and his board in a row holding gold shovels for the CAFO ground- breaking, a circle of Asian men in chef hats, state senator Ronald Michelson, state representative Jeb Harmon, and county commissioner Terence B. Sellers, all of whom had attended the town meeting.

No family photos.

"This one will do," Gordon said, choosing the best close- up. "We'll make a copy and return it. An investigations team may visit and ask to photograph the other photos," Gordon said. "If that's all right with you." *And if not, we'll get a warrant.*

Chelsea nodded.

"In the meantime," Gordon added, "please leave everything in the room as it is. Here's my card with my cell number. If something comes up or you recall something, please call."

Chaplain Balfour cut in. "Is there a family priest or pastor you'd like us to call?"

Chelsea made a face, as though she'd bitten into a lemon. "Are you serious?" she said.

CHAPTER 6

"MY MORON BROTHER WON'T PICK UP, as usual," Chelsea complained.

"Geez, Chels, you wanna go over to his place and tell him?" Molly Tiffin asked, her knuckles whitening on the steering wheel.

"And deal with those cops again?" she snorted. She tucked the phone under her thigh. "They're on the way there now. Wait'll they smell it."

"But tennis? Now? After you've been told—"

"After I've been told I'm finally free?" she said with a smirk.

Molly eyed her like she'd grown a horn. "Like, aren't you mad or sad?"

"I can't do anything about it. One call took care of it. Paid pre-arrangements. I signed the cop's release form. The family lawyer will call the board members. The trust falls to me and Logan and there's nothing to sign. Death certificates get mailed. What am I supposed to do? Stop my life?"

It's like beginning a whole new life, she thought.

CHAPTER 7

GORDON FOUND A PARKING SPOT between a rusting Chevy
Cavalier and a Buick Regal missing its hubcaps a few doors
down from Logan Diedrich's Pleasant Vista Apartment unit.
Never park in front. He didn't bother to run the plates on the
adjacent vehicles, not with Christine in the car. He did it
on his patrols, when he regularly passed by these north side
public housing projects, a part of town most residents denied
existed. The only ones to encounter the smell of urine, weed,
garbage, B.O., and matted dog were the cops and, as they
kidded among themselves, *the other trash collectors.*

When he stepped out, his quick scan caught the snap of
Venetian blinds and the rustle of curtains. *It's the fuzz, man;
flush it, flush it; ay, es la policia otra vez; get that thing outta
sight.*

"Number Seventeen," Balfour said, slamming the door.
"Over there? Won't the entry need to be buzzed?

"I got it," Gordon said. After locking the squad car, he
strode smartly to the stoop, hands out to the sides as though
for a quick draw. He pulled a plastic card, credit card sized,
from his vest pocket, slid it into the latch, and yanked the
door.

"Open for business," he said. "After you, Reverend."

Balfour pinched her nose. "Oh, heavens."

"Not the worst I've smelled here," he said.

They passed Unit Thirteen (water running, tink of dishes)

and Unit Fifteen (TV chattering *get cash fast, fast, fast with your title loan from KwikKash*) before reaching Seventeen.

Gordon back-fisted the heavily varnished door, then stepped aside. Habit. "Logan Diedrich? Police. Open up."

The crack under the door was dark; the curtains or blinds were down. The sweet-sick stink of weed crawled out to say hello.

Gordon hammered the door again.

The crack lightened. Shadows played there. A security chain chinked. The door creaked open. A short brunette in a terry robe peered around it. She muttered an expletive and tugged the robe tighter with a fist.

"River Falls Police," Gordon said. "I'm Detective Sergeant Gordon, this is Officer Balfour. We're looking for Logan Diedrich."

"He's, um, he's—" she threw a glimpse over her shoulder.

"Is he here or not?" Gordon pressed.

"Who's that, babe?" called a sleepy male voice.

"It's, um, it's the police."

Gordon listened for a window being opened for escape or a drawer for a weapon.

"What's your name?" Chaplain Balfour calmly asked the girl who appeared to be trying to quickly wake— or sober— up.

"I'm Bunny—I mean, um, Beverly."

"Got a last name, Beverly?"

"Stimpson. Beverly Stimpson."

"May we come in, Beverly?" Balfour said, all sweetness.

"Don't you need a warrant or something?" Beverly said.

"We just have some questions for Logan," Gordon said. "Routine."

Logan came out of a hallway buttoning a shirt that hung loosely over sweatpants. He swung bangs from his squinting eyes. Scratched at his stubble.

"Cops? Really?" he said, indignant. "Did my father send you to check on me? I've been clean, I swear."

Gordon was in his gun-draw stance, firing side foot just behind the support foot. "Mr. Diedrich, I am very sorry to tell you that your father is dead."

The young man stopped dead in his tracks. Paled. Planted his feet in the worn carpet pile. Grabbed his hair over both ears as though to rip it out. If he went into shock, Gordon would have to get him to the ER.

Logan tried to shake the confusion out of his head. "He—what? What happened?"

Beverly rushed to his side. "Babe, I'm so sorry."

"He was found unresponsive on the grounds of the main feeding operation this afternoon," Gordon said. *No need to leak details yet.*

"My sister—"

"We already informed her," Gordon said. "She gave us this address."

"What else did she tell you?"

"Only that your father made you move out. A day or two ago, was it?"

Logan pressed his head as though to keep it from exploding. "Yeah, we fought, but I wouldn't hurt him. You don't think I did this, do you?"

"Did you?"

"No! I mean, he was—he was killed?"

"You seem to think that he was."

"It wasn't an accident or something?"

"The coroner will decide that after his exam in the morning," Gordon said. "Then you can visit his office, sign off on arrangements, and make a positive identification."

"Why? You know it's him already."

Gordon nearly said *It's the law* when he decided to test a reaction. "We need to be sure. There's some disfigurement.

The body was found submerged in a manure lagoon behind the CAFO."

Logan raised a palm up to his nose. Was he recalling the smell?

Beverly squeezed Logan's bicep. "I'll take you, babe," she said. "Okay, officers? I just need the address."

He doesn't have a car? License suspended because of the drug use? He'd check with the DMV. Or is she just offering to drive? She might high-tail it in the opposite direction, Gordon thought. But they wouldn't be hard to find. He scribbled on his pad, ripped out the page, and handed it to her.

"We'll be there," Beverly said. "Just call and give us a time."

"I will. It will probably be tomorrow, late afternoon," Gordon said. *Logan should be sobered up by then and ready to answer questions.* "Meanwhile, if you have a question or something comes up, give me a call." He fished out his card.

Gordon and Balfour left.

Balfour clicked the seat belt. "You think he knows something?"

"We'll find out tomorrow."

—m—

Behind the door, Logan wailed, "They're gonna think it was me! Because he kicked me out! They're gonna think I was getting back at him!"

"Babe, you don't know that. You said you wouldn't hurt him. You thought he sent the cops after you. You thought he was still alive."

"I told him to drop dead when I left! Chelsea heard me! What if she told them that?"

"I dunno. Maybe they'll say you got your wish. He dropped dead." A sudden thought puckered her brow and puffed out her lower lip. "If he *dropped dead*," she emphasized. "But then why would he be in the, you know, the manure pond? No one just drops dead in there. Do they? From the smell? Or someone had to put him there. Is there something you're not telling me, babe?"

—ɯ—

After dropping off Christine at the station and telling dispatch that he was 10-8, back on the street, Gordon returned to town and wheeled the cruiser into a QuikStop gas station for an iced coffee. Weary and parched, he felt like he'd swallowed glue. The heat of the day was finally relenting, but he felt damp and grimy, despite the change in uniform. City detectives could wear cotton street clothes to be a bit cooler and not bother with the polyester blend uniforms and clinging clay vests. Sometimes he did. But a small-town detective sergeant, when working traffic and on patrol, didn't have the luxury.

Before parking, Gordon scoped out the place to make certain he wasn't walking into a robbery in progress. "Stop and Robs", as cops called them, were often held up. This one had been hit up twice in the past six months. The silvery owner, Donny Delmonico, appreciated him checking in now and then.

Gordon carried his cup to the counter, ice cubes rattling, glad to have poured and prepared his own in order to be assured that no one had spit into it. Donny turned away from an afternoon TV talk show, wrinkled his doorknob nose, and peered at him through Coke glasses. "Frankie, is it true? Diedrich?"

News in a small town traveled faster than cold germs in Stephie's preschool.

"What have you heard?"

"The pissed-off workers drowned him in the pig shite pond," Donny said. "What a way to go."

A grapevine always has some sour grapes on it. "We don't

know that for sure," Gordon said. "Lou Willis is doing an exam, and I'm sure the chief will have a press conference or something tomorrow when we have some facts. So don't go spreadin' no rumors, huh?"

Donny crossed his heart. Gordon finished the rest in his mind: *Hope to die, stick a needle in my eye.* But Gordon knew it was too late to put the toothpaste back into the tube. The cat was out of the bag, the horses had run from the barn, and the bus had left that station.

Back in his cruiser a short while later, Gordon turned into the vacant lot by the railroad trellis where honey locust saplings and leafy mulberry trees provided some shade. He kept the engine running, rolled down the window, and sipped his iced coffee. A train hooted in the distance. The cicadas sawed in the trees. A row crop tractor thundered by and a bumper-to-bumper parade of passenger cars with irate drivers followed it. Gordon pulled up the "Death Scene Investigation Report" on his Toughbook laptop and started with the lagoon incident. He moused through the forms, clicking boxes, mostly *unknown, pending, in process,* and *yet to be determined.* He filled in "Jacob Diedrich" for the vic, though this was officially preliminary. The man lived up to his name, all right, Gordon mused: he Died Rich. Hilarious. He added what he knew, referring to his notes for name spellings, and dates of birth, glancing up now and then to check the traffic. He stopped typing *Details Regarding Place of Incident* when a Nissan sedan rolled up near him and the driver stepped out, a fifty-ish man in khaki cargo shorts. White male, 5'9", a hundred and eighty pounds, Hawaiian shirt. Clip-on sunglasses. Wispy mustache. Clogs. Poor taste. Gordon levered out of the cruiser. Always thinking tactically, he never had someone surprise him while sitting down.

"Hey, officer, I'm looking for—"

The man reached into his right cargo pocket.

Gordon tensed.

The man extracted a postcard. Squinted at it. "Tall Pines Park?"

Gordon gladly directed him. He returned to the report. He saved it and proceeded with the trailer park incident. The sheriff's deputies would have their report, too, but he had to fill one out nonetheless. Typing, typing. Mouse down, type some more. There were blanks here, as well, to be filled in once the CS Techs and Willis had finished their work.

But his work was just beginning.

Once he submitted his forms electronically to the Central Reporting desk, he drove back to his apartment. On the way, he observed a Toyota in front of him slowing down, speeding up, weaving across the lane line, braking unpredictably. Gordon followed him for a block to determine if the car was malfunctioning.

Nope, it's the guy.

He hit the siren and lights. The Toyota swerved left, then angled right and jerked to a stop in the gravel. Gordon parked behind him and kept the flash bar strobing. He typed in the plate numbers. It always amazed him how fast the information came through. *Boom*, there it was on the green screen: year, make, model, color, licensee, expiration. Car not stolen. Registered to: Mr. Curtis Putnam of 912 Corncrib Lane, Worth Township, age fifty-five. Out of towner. No warrant. That was probably him bending across the seat—getting his license, registration, and insurance card from the glove compartment? Or a weapon? Not likely but look out.

Approaching the vehicle with trained caution, Gordon patted the trunk to be sure it was closed. Checked the back seat. No bodies, guns, or contraband visible. The driver-side window *whirrrred* down. The stale odor of beer was unmistakable. In the golden slant of sunset, Gordon noted the driver's watery and bloodshot eyes, his papery lips, his twitchy hands clutching his paperwork. "Offisher, whasha matta? I got a, a light out or, or shomthing?"

"Your lights aren't even on, sir," Gordon said. "License and insurance card, please."

Back in the patrol car, he ran a check on the license. Two moving violations and a previous DUI. *Quelle surprise, monsieur.*

Back at the car window. "How much have you had to drink, Mr. Putnam?"

"Couple beers is all. Visiting, visiting family. You know."

"Could you step out of the car, please?"

As a matter of public safety, it wasn't the time for a mere warning, even though his shift ended barely twenty minutes ago and it would take another two hours to deliver the man to detention and to do the paperwork after. And it wasn't right to call in back-up for a routine arrest he should do himself. Following the man's shaky performance on the field sobriety test, Gordon dutifully made the arrest, hauled him back to the station for the breathalyzer test and jail processing, and started typing.

So here he was again, opening his front door nearly four hours later than expected. How many times over the years, depending on the shift, had supper long gone cold, or Stephanie had curled up and dropped off to sleep for the night, or she'd already eaten breakfast and left the house for the day?

Too many times, that's how many. Gordon twisted the key and knob, pressed open the duplex door, and trudged inside. The two-bedroomer was costing almost as much as the monthly mortgage on the house where Stephanie remained. *Please, two weeks, Frankie. That's all I ask. I just need a little space.*

It turned into two-plus months. So far.

He passed through the living room decorated in

Salvation Army Chic and rummaged in the kitchen cabinet for the vinegar jug. He set three bowls of vinegar through the apartment to counter any smells in the air; it had worked once when his cat, Batman, came home with a stink of skunk clinging to him. A vinegar wash of the clothes would work well, too, well enough to bring them to the dry cleaner without Mrs. Pierce asking too many questions. *What's this, Francis, they got you doing the latrines at the station now? You been there how many years? Don't the rookies clean the cans? Or a custodial guy? I thought you got promoted? Did I hear wrong?*

He unclipped his duty belt and laid it within reach *ker-clank* on the toilet tank, peeled off his smelly clothes and sweat-darkened vest and piled them at the vanity, and then stood sighing in the steaming hot shower for a long time. Rivulets ran down his face and torso like tears. Poor Richie. The stabber stabbed. The sticker stuck. Was that justice? He lathered up with lemon soap to wash away the filth and fatigue. When he turned, the jets pounded his neck and shoulders. He thought of the techs power-washing off Mr. Diedrich and zipping him up in the sanitized human remains pouch.

After toweling off, he tugged on athletic pants and, utility belt draped over his shoulder, slogged into the kitchen. He zapped leftover mac-and-cheese for dinner and passed on having a beer with it. Now detective rank, he was on call. He opened the front door to call Batman in. That's when he noticed the half-of-a-chipmunk on the stoop. Guess Batman wasn't going to be hungry, after all. But when he whistled "Shave-and-a-Haircut", the cat streaked inside, straight for the bed. He pawed and clawed at the foot and then curled into a black ball. With the white patch on his face, he looked like a fuzzy 8-ball. And with those tall black ears? Hence the name. *Good idea, Batman. But I can't sleep yet. The gerbil in my brain is running the wheel. Can you kill the gerbil like you killed the chipmunk?* He flipped through cable TV channels, skipping by all the cop and crime shows and the news channels, which were basically cop and crime shows, too. He settled as usual on HGTV where every show benignly moved in a predictable pattern from goal to setback to happy finale. What a comforting fantasy. If only his cases were resolved so easily in an hour. When the screen blurred, he dropped into bed. He closed his eyes but saw Richie's contorted grimace and Diedrich's slimed face before drifting off. In his dream where Batman finished herding all the pigs into a barn, a loudspeaker in the rafters droned to celebrate his achievement, and it buzzed and buzzed and *buzzzzzzz*

Gordon jerked awake. The lime-green clock read 2:12 a.m. His phone screamed like a cicada. He reached for it in a fog. Knocked it to the floor. *Gotta be dispatch with a signal 7. "Good morning, Detective, are you ready to copy?" she'll say. Here we go. Where's my notepad?*

"Gordon here."

"Frankie?"

A woman. Not dispatch.

"Frankie, you there?"

"Stephanie?"

"Frankie, come home." A sniffle. "Now."

CHAPTER 8

WHEN HE WHEELED INTO THE DRIVEWAY and killed the cruiser's headlamps, a waxing gibbous moon was slicing through ragged clouds. Heat lightning flickered through the high honeysuckles. His familiar bedroom window fan *whirrrrred* above the front porch, where Stephanie sat on the top step, elbows on her knees. It was exactly where he'd left her in tears in late May, when the lilacs had begun to brown. It was as though she hadn't moved an inch.

He jack-knifed out of the car, hurried to the first step, and froze there. "Stephie, sweetie, what's wrong? Are you okay?"

She was in shorts with a camisole top; her sandals crisscrossed beside her at her hip. "I'm getting eaten alive out here."

"You could have waited inside."

"Too hot," she said. She slapped at a mosquito. Considered the blood on her hand and made a face. "Just as hot and too buggy here. Maybe you're right."

She stood and pushed through the door into the foyer, barefoot. The dimmed chandelier cast a glow on her strawberry hair, and in the spinning shadow of the ceiling fan, the freckles on her bare shoulders danced. "Get you a beer?" she asked.

"I'm on call."

"Of course. Shoulda been a teacher. You get the summers off."

Her preschool was full of the children they could never have.

"So, you go back to work soon, right?" Gordon ventured, picking up on the clue.

"Next Monday. Honestly, Frankie. You never remember, do you?"

Gordon regretted asking. He stayed in the parlor while she padded into the kitchen, seized a beer from the fridge, and snapped it open. "How about a water instead?" she called. "I got Ice Mountains in here."

Gordon smoothed his palm over his usual spot on the living room sofa. "Sure, sounds good." He dropped into position, but it felt like someone else's house at two-thirty in the morning, dim and damp as it was, the knickknacks a lifeless gray, and the mirror over the credenza blank.

Stephanie handed him the plastic bottle. "Here you go." She took a swig from her can.

This was clearly not the first beer she was having. All those traffic stops told him that. Not as bad as Mr. Perkins but even so. And in the tenebrous light, her eyes looked pinked, from sleeplessness, from a good cry, from exceeding her three-beer limit, or all three.

She plopped into place on the opposite side of the sofa. The light bounce loosened a strap from her shoulder. She took another sip, her jaw tight.

"So, are you going to tell me what's up?' Gordon hazarded.

"Maybe I was just lonely, you know?" she bit back. "It's not the first time you've been away a long time without calling."

"I thought you wanted me away for a while."

"Yeah, but not all the other times."

"Is that what's on your mind? Still?"

"Frankie, you're always on my mind." She sniffled and wiped her nose with the back of her hand. He still adored the splash of freckles across the bridge of her nose, and how they fanned across her high cheeks and spilled to her silky shoulders. "I mean, like, summer brings out the crazies, I know. So, I worry."

"I do too. Sometimes."

"Like today?" she asked.

He tensed. "What about today?"

"I mean, you got a lot going on, right?"

"Enough." The two killings hadn't made the news yet, but the town seemed to be buzzing already. Should he tell her? She hated the Diedrich swine operation as much as anybody else, maybe more, for the way the nauseating smell sickened kids at her school. No wonder she was a leader in the No CAFO Coalition that organized protests and was threatening to sue the company to shut it down and had made a scene at the town hall.

She took a long swallow from the can. A few drops spattered on her chin. Maybe her mouth was already numb. "So, like, how's Batman?"

"You miss him?"

"Nah. I'm a dog person. You know that. So, no. But I know why you got a cat."

Another dig. One needed to be home at regular hours to care for a dog. "He comes when I whistle. Like a dog. And he hasn't smelled like a skunk lately."

"Just as well he was out of the house at the time," she said.

Let's not talk about animals, please, not now, Gordon begged. *We'll just argue as always about the cruelty of CAFO confinement pens and stun pistols and scalding pools and ammonia levels and—*

She drained the beer. Wiggled the can in her hand. "Uh, oh," she grinned mischievously, "someone—someone needs a refill."

Already? She'd had plenty, but he wouldn't start a fight over it. "Lemme get it."

"I'll letcha."

Gordon leaned up. Stephanie stood with him and sidestepped in his way. She seized his face and kissed him hard on the lips. She brushed her hand against his cheek.

"Oooh, someone needs a shave."

"Stephie, I don't think you—"

"Missed you? Heck, yes, I missed you. Not the cat, so much, but you." She wrapped her arms around his neck. Kissed him again, lingering.

"I missed you, too," he said.

"I shouldn't do this," she said, looking him in the eye. The gold flecks in her hazel eyes glittered.

"You shouldn't," he whispered.

She grasped the hem of his T-shirt and yanked it up over his head. Stephanie tilted back her dimpled chin and accepted the kisses on her throat. She unfastened her shorts and let them fall to the hardwood. Once Gordon kicked off his sneakers and stepped out of the athletic pants, Stephanie pressed him back to the sofa, straddled him, steered him inside, and began to gently rock. Her breathing deepened and her motion quickened until Gordon gave in to the gathering, the rush, and the deep release.

With an exhausted sigh, she collapsed on his chest, and he rolled her against the sofa's back, their legs entwined, until her breathing slowed down to the rhythm he recognized as her deepest sleep. He slipped off the cushions carefully, found his footing on the floorboards, and stood slowly. He dressed and then fetched a sheet from the linen closet to cover her from the shoulders down, despite the sticky night, where the tree frogs *creek-creeked* in the white pines and crickets violined in the quackgrass. He wondered, seeing her all-American-farmer's-daughter beauty, how he'd ever let her feel estranged or disappointed in him, and how what they had just done would not make things easier later when she awakened. He'd sleep on the TV room futon tonight. Taking his regular spot in the bed might be presumptuous.

When the morning sun blushed the sky, he made coffee in the percolator, and while it chuffed and popped, he rummaged in the cabinets for the instant pancake mix. That was a safe bet for breakfast since he wouldn't need an egg—Stephanie didn't eat eggs—and if there was no maple syrup, the canned peaches would do. The orange brew light clicked on just as Stephanie shuffled into the kitchen doorway. The sheet was wrapped tautly as a burial shroud around her chest, which she pinned to her back with a bunched fist. Her hair looked frizzy, like a perm gone wrong, and her puffy eyes squeezed to let in a minimum of light.

"Sorry, sweetie," Gordon began, "I didn't mean to wake you up."

"Who said I'm awake?" she said hoarsely. "What time is it?"

"A little after 8 o'clock," Gordon said. "I didn't sleep all that well. You?"

"I think I just kinda passed out," she croaked, smacking her lips and making a face at the morning-after taste. "What happened last night?"

"You don't remember?"

"Oh, I remember what happened," she said, "but, I mean, how'd that happen?"

"I plied you with liquor and had my way with you," he said impishly.

"I was just confused," she said, with a shake of her head. "I'm really sorry."

"I'm not."

"I meant to tell you—I mean, I didn't plan on what happened. I—"

"It's okay. I'm glad it happened."

"I was going to tell you it's over."

"What's over?" *Our time apart?*

She wiped a tear from her eye. "Us, Frankie. I thought the beer would make me brave to say so, but it made me stupid instead."

"Maybe you need to wake up a little more, have some coffee, and we can talk later."

"There's no *later*, Frankie," she said. "I can't do this anymore."

"I'm detective rank now," he said. "I'll have regular weekday hours if I want. Even your sister has to put up with her real estate broker husband who works all hours of the day and night, plus every weekend and—"

"This isn't about Caitlin and Shawn," she retorted. "I'll never be Caitlin, and you'll never be Shawn."

"I didn't become a cop for the money."

"Is that what you think?"

"It's the kid thing, huh? The fertility thing?"

"You're still not getting it, are you?"

"Not getting what?"

"Get out."

The words hit like a tactical baton. "You don't mean that."

"I said, get out."

Gordon squared his shoulders. Later, he'd recall the stance as the one he used facing a suspect resisting arrest. "It's my house, too, Stephie."

She pursed her lips, conceding. "Okay, sure," she said, her hands making a throw-away motion. "You're right. Then *I'll* leave. It's *my* turn."

She pivoted sharply and strode into the living room.

"Is there someone else?" he blurted after her.

She stopped dead. "Are you kidding?"

"Is there? Or not?"

Because there are more beer cans in the trash bin than you could possibly have had alone in one evening, unless they've been from the last few nights—

"It's you, Frankie," she said. "It's you with someone else. Always with someone else. This whole town is your mistress. But I come home every night, alone in this—in this—" she swept her hand around "—this jail."

Gordon's phone trilled.

He stood still as a gravestone.

It chirped again, like a chipmunk trapped in Batman's fangs.

"So, are you gonna answer that?" she said.

"Stephie, I—I'm on call."

"Like I said." She spun away and disappeared into the master bedroom, the door flung shut behind her.

Gordon gnashed his teeth. "Jiminy Cricket," he breathed and scooped up the phone from beside the couch on the third shriek.

"Frank, it's Lou," the coroner said. "I got the autopsies scheduled for this morning. It'll take a week or so for the full pharmacology reports, but I'll have preliminary results for both of them by mid-afternoon. Can you come in after your four o'clock roll call?"

"Lou, I—I just dunno, I—"

"I did Mr. Diedrich already. You're going to want to see this."

"I mean—it isn't a good time—"

"So, you can come later, too, you know. I don't mind hanging around."

"I don't mean that. It's just that—"

"Say, you don't sound so good. Are you sick or something?"

"I've been better."

"I didn't wake you up, did I?"

"No, Lou, it's just that I worked late and had a weird

night, and this isn't really a good time for a—"

Stephie stormed out of the bedroom, a stuffed overnight bag slung over her shoulder. She had jumped into jeans and a Chicago Bears sweatshirt and slipped into flats, laid out in advance. She rushed past Gordon to the front door, raking her hair back.

Gordon cupped the phone. "Stephie, please, not like this."

A familiar SUV pulled up to the end of the driveway. The passenger side door yawned. Caitlin beckoned from inside. That had been arranged in advance, too. It was like a burglary, with the getaway vehicle idling nearby.

The storm door slammed shut behind Stephie. *Step, stepstepstep, step, step.* The car door thumped shut.

"Frank? You still there?"

Gordon gripped the phone so he wouldn't throw it against the wall. "Hey, Lou. I'll—I'll tell the lieutenant at roll call, and I'll be there around four-thirty."

In reply, Caitlin's Buick screeched into the street.

CHAPTER 9

FOR AS LONG AS HE COULD REMEMBER, he had always wanted to be a cop. Stephie knew that. When he played cops and robbers with the neighbor kids—before it became unfashionable—he was always the cop. He'd told her so. He'd pretend he was in a squad car and make siren sounds. He'd tackled his friends and slapped on the plastic cuffs he bought with his allowance at the Dollar Time store. Then he hauled them to the tool shed, the jail.

C'mon, Frankie, you be the bad guy for a change.

I'm always the good guy. Don't you forget it.

His pals had watched cartoons, but he devoured hours of *CHiPs, Starsky and Hutch, Kojak, Baretta, Miami Vice,* and *Mannix.* In eighth and ninth grades he skipped Boy Scouts and instead trained weekends with the Police Explorers program. On the track team in high school, he leaped over the hurdles as though chasing a burglar through the streets and alleyways. He wasn't the team's fastest runner, but everyone called him "Flash" Gordon anyway, partly in homage to the science fiction hero. And on the high school wrestling team, no one was faster than Flash in penetrating the opponent's stance, then lifting and dropping him to the mat. It came in handy when Stephanie Wyatt, the straw-haired farm girl and secretary of the student council, was pressed against the lockers for a feel by Dave LeBlanc, a hulking linebacker, and Flash spun him around with a shove to the shoulder, drove forward for a single leg takedown and locked a half nelson around his neck to pin him to the linoleum until three yelling teachers pulled him off.

She said *thanks* but also said *no* to a date. The vegetarian honors student planning to teach preschool kids wanted little to do with the cop wanna-be who liked his steaks bloody.

He persisted. Two years. She finally said *Well—okay*. And despite the squad car ride-around dates, the Patrolmen's Ball, and the Pork Chop with a Cop Barbeque, Stephanie didn't fully realize until the wedding day that she was marrying into The Blue Family.

No, it wasn't Carol-Lynn Fisk, the current lieutenant's wife, suggesting that her 'something blue' be a cobalt ankle holster for a Glock 43.

It was striding into the sanctuary of St. Anselm's on Daddy's tuxedoed arm, when the first strains of *Canon in D* prompted the men in the groom's right-hand rows to rise in unison, *Leh-ft FACE*, their Class A Dress Blues smartly starched and pressed, their white gloves and gold braid in perfect order, the thin blue line, line after line, pew after pew.

And her hero, Bravo-12, in front at parade rest.

At the reception, where the men sat uneasily without being able to put their backs to the wall, Carol-Lynn seized Stephie's elbow and steered her aside.

"Raymond had to leave," she apologized, "something you'll go through often and never get used to."

"It's okay. I understand."

Carol-Lynn tilted her chignon sagely. "In due time. Meanwhile, dear, whatever you can do to make it easier to say goodbye to him, make it a ritual. Kiss him hard, kiss both hands, hug his neck three times, whatever you want. And say 'goodbye,' not just 'bye'. See your husband out the door every day like it is his last."

Two Saturdays after the honeymoon, Stephie was startled

by a loud double rap on the door. She didn't step to the floor-length window beside it to see who it was; she'd just cleared breakfast dishes and was heading for the shower without pants.

Forty minutes later, while holding a dryer to her head like an oversized pistol, she was struck by a sickening thought: *OMG, what if it was the chaplain?*

She dropped the dryer and rushed to the door. She held her breath and prayed she'd find a parcel on the porch.

She flung open the door.

Burst into tears.

A box.

Oh, thank God, a box.

CHAPTER 10

AT A TIME OF DAY when most people were getting ready to leave work, "Flash" Gordon began his shift. Shortly after the 4:00 p.m. roll call, Gordon strode from the police station that occupied part of a white cinderblock building off Main Street that also housed City Hall and a Community Food Pantry. He adjusted the black clip-on tie to his blue polyester shirt (a real tie could be used to strangle him). His black rubber-soled Oxfords squeaked on the pavement. With his ten-pound duty belt and clay vest, he creaked and jingled as he walked. He squirmed to move the vest off his belly. The gear on his belt made him hold his arms out away from his sides, and he proudly felt like a gunslinger at High Noon. He mentally reviewed the equipment he had checked out, just to be sure he had everything: the Glock pistol and ammo pouch, Taser, pepper spray, rubber gloves, cuffs, hot-dog-sized LED Light, and a tactical baton.

At the cruiser, he popped the trunk to inspect his loaded M-4 carbine and fearsome ammo magazines—just in case, you know—and then checked the evidence kit, medical kit, extra rubber gloves for blood-and-guts operations; adjusted seat belts and tested his garish light displays and radio; sounded the earsplitting sirens—always fun—and powered up the Toughbook laptop. He clipped the portable radio to his shoulder and wondered if he'd ever get a camera to clip on, too, like city cops. Come to think of it, he wondered if he'd ever get a new cruiser, considering all the budget cuts; the Impala had been in the shop twice this month. He positioned his Zeiss binoculars to the right beside him—to spot drug deals, mainly—and hand sanitizer to the left, which he'd pump frequently through his shift. He rolled down the window and cranked the AC. He tapped the accelerator and awakened all eight horses. He was now ready for, well, whatever the day threw at him. His chief objective: *get home alive.* His first stop: *the house of the dead,* Lou Willis' funeral parlor.

—⚮—

Even with a smear of Noxzema under Gordon's masked nose, the chilly autopsy room smelled like a butcher shop with some of the raw meat spoiled. Atmospheric piano played softly, the same soundtrack that soothed grieving families in the funeral parlor on the other side of Willis' house. But nothing could soften the ice-white lighting or the glint of bone saws and pruning shears. The funeral director's assistant hadn't mopped the vinyl yet, and it was streaked with blood, just like the kill floor at Richie's slaughterhouse. Willis, in a blue surgical gown and mask, glanced over his shoulder through protective glasses.

"Oh, good. You're here. Are you ready for this, Francis?" he asked.

"I never am," he replied, adjusting his face shield, his booties pulling at the sticky floor.

"At least you're fashionably late for the dissections."

"Sorry I missed them."

"Not to worry. There will be others. If you want to check out the organ slices yourself, they're in labeled formalin jars over there. Blood and fluid samples are in the usual vials."

"I'll pass."

"Suit yourself. Trooper Brandon Tate from the ISP was here to observe and collect evidence if needed."

"Guess he'll be on the task force, then. Did he take anything?"

"Nope. As soon as the Stryker Saw buzzed into Richie's skull with that dentist-drill sound and he smelled the burning bone, he ran out and tossed his breakfast. Decided not to come back in." Willis gripped his scalpel point-up as though he was about to carve a holiday ham. "Speaking of Richie: Let's talk about him first."

"Why not Diedrich?"

"You'll see why in a minute."

Willis strode to one of the two steel gurneys arranged perpendicular to the austere tiled wall. Even before the coroner tugged down the heavy translucent plastic sheet, Gordon noted those colorful tattoos on the arms, though now muted against the gray-lavender skin. At least Willis had replaced the top of the skull—minus the brain—with the scalp sewn back in place. The chest was closed, too, though Willis would dump the organs back in the cavity following the microscope exams before stitching it shut.

"I'm sure the toxicology results will prove our man was super high," Willis began. "With exactly *what* is yet to be determined. I don't expect to find alcohol in the vitreous humor I pulled from the eyeballs."

Gordon always squirmed at the thought of a syringe needle in his eyes.

"I'd safely say meth," Willis continued, "from the poor condition of his teeth, burn marks in the mouth from smoking, acne on the back, emaciated face, boney chest, severe scratching on the skinny legs to relieve itching, and the oversized heart."

"Richie had a big heart?"

"Not that kind," Willis scoffed. "An enlarged, hardened heart. I could tell even before I was done cranking the rib spreader."

Gordon gulped. The snap of the snippers separating ribs from breastbone is what usually sent him into the anteroom to retch.

"Because of where he was stabbed," Willis went on, "I focused on his coronary arteries and found calcific atherosclerotic stenosis of the vessel lumens."

"Translation, please?"

"Hardening of the arteries."

"Could be from cheeseburgers and fries."

"A close guess."

"Close guess of what?"

"The stomach contents."

"Cheeseburger and fries?"

"Chili steak burger and cayenne curly fries, to be exact."

"Ah, one of the heart attack specials they serve at Jo-Jo's," Gordon said. "Now we know where he was that night. I'll visit Joelle to be sure."

"He ate there a lot or took a lot of sausage home from the packing plant," Willis said. "He was a heart attack waiting to happen, even at his young age. My microscopic examination of the heart muscle found both acute cardiomyocyte necrosis and extensive areas of fibrosis."

Gordon stared at him, trying to figure out how that added up to a heart attack.

"The cells that make the heart contract were mostly dead."

"So, he would have died early anyway. The girl saved him the trouble."

"She did an expert job," Willis said. "Two quick jabs at just the right spots to drain the blood once hung up on the assembly line. The second stab, at a forty-five-degree angle, was meant to cut the windpipe."

"Richie said he wanted to show me how it's done. I guess he showed her."

"A guy's gotta take pride in his work. It was clearly the cause of death, but this wasn't his only injury," Willis noted. "As is the case with most slaughterhouse workers, he'd had many injuries: lacerations galore, broken bones not healed right. He's lucky; some men get limbs caught in conveyor belts, burger grinders—"

"I get it," Gordon cut him short.

"Well, I was about to say, most of these don't get reported so OSHA doesn't get involved. It's why there's a high turnover, and why some who stay want to be unionized."

"The Diedrich operations *are* union shops. They're fighting over a contract right now. There's talk of a strike."

"It won't happen. Too many of the workers are undocumented and don't want to put their names on union cards. They want to stay in the shadows, even if it means not getting medical care or injury compensation."

"Like Richie."

"Francis, I'm telling you, they treat these workers just like the animals. Sometimes worse." He pointed at Richie's tattoos. "That's why they join gangs. For protection and drug access."

Gordon peered closer at the ornate circles connected by an arrow. "Now that I get a good look at it, it's no gang sign," he said. "It's a religion. Called—what the devil was it? Espiritos something."

Willis raised an eyebrow. "You've seen this before?"

"I responded to some noise nuisance complaints a few months ago. This group in a house was making a racket with drums and ritually killing chickens and pigs in the backyard before they barbequed them. I don't remember seeing Richie there. Anyway, they all had tattoos like this: the

circles connected by arrows. I asked Father Sullivan over at
St. Mary's if he knew something about this. He said it's some
Caribbean thing—a mix of African religion dating from slave
days with Catholic saints and fortune-telling thrown in. All
legal—just noisy, and a weird way to have a cook-out."

"You want weird? I'll show you weird. Come over here."

Willis led Gordon to the other gurney. He pulled back the
opaque sheet, a magician's reveal. "May I introduce—"

"Jacob Diedrich," Gordon finished. "AKA Boss Hogg,
Chief Executive Officer and President of Diedrich Delights
and winner of this year's Most Hated Man in Sinnissippi
County Award."

The dead man's mouth gaped open to show pricey
dental work; the blank piggy eyes stared up at the ceiling
as if surprised. He was naked, and Gordon figured he'd be
humiliated if alive. With the fecal muck washed off, the
bulbous-nosed and jowled marionette face, though puffy and
purpled, was unmistakable. The thinning, receding hair, once
oiled and carefully combed back, was stringy and unkempt
from the coroner's work. Like Richie, Diedrich had been
reassembled enough to be presentable, though of course,
the organs had been removed, weighed, and inspected for
disease, damage, surgeries, implants, abnormalities, and
bullets; if bullets were found, Willis could determine their
entry points and pathways, the general type of gun and how
far away it was fired. Diedrich was now an empty hull with
no heart. Some might say he was the same way in life.

"Of course," Willis announced, "we'll have to get next of
kin to come in for a legal positive ID after I clean him up a
little and comb his hair."

"I invited the two kids yesterday. The son, Logan, is
coming in about an hour." Gordon leaned in. "So, Lou—how
come he's a darker blue, unlike our friend Richie over there?"

"Because of this," Willis said, tapping his scalpel at two spots beside each clavicle.

"They're knife wounds," Gordon observed. "Just like Richie's."

"Not quite. The length and depth differ because a different kind of knife was used," Willis explained. "The techs brought in the chef's knife that killed Richie. Pretty standard countertop tool, classic ten-inch, widens at the hilt. That girl stuck it in pretty deep, and it left a wide wound."

"And the other?"

"The neck cuts are precise and smaller. Smaller like from the Microtech Flick knife we seized from Richie."

"We'd need more evidence than that to say Richie did it. There must be dozens of these switchblades and hunting knives out there."

"Sure enough," Willis agreed. "Now, there are two other important differences. For one, Richie's livor mortis—the skin purpling—is on one side, where he lay for a while and the blood settled. But for Mr. Diedrich, the purple marbling of the skin is on both sides of his body. He was moved."

"Killed somewhere else and dumped in the lagoon."

"Not exactly flushed down the toilet, but close." Willis stepped to the bottom of the table and lifted the sheet past the ankles. The pallid skin around the lower shins looked embroidered in a line of thin blue bruises.

"So, his compression socks were a little tight?" Gordon quipped.

"They might have been," Willis said. "But someone wrapped a chain or plastic tie of some kind around the ankle area and hung him upside down."

Gordon's stomach cramped. "Good Lord. To bleed him out like a hog."

"They didn't succeed. A body this size has about five quarts of blood. Mr. Diedrich still had quite a bit, enough to pool and color the skin. Maybe a decision was made that this was going to take too long."

Willis returned to the head area. "There's no similar marking around the wrists, so he wasn't simply tied up. But there is blunt force trauma to the skull here, and here, which subdued him and may have knocked him unconscious."

"Can you tell what he was hit with?"

"Something with a small head. Could be a hammer or a tire iron. Hard to say. This blow fractured the skull but didn't penetrate the brain, this one did both."

"So that killed him? Brain trauma?"

"Might have. Knocked him out, for sure. It caused bruising, but the deep color of the skin, in general, is from the blood that didn't drain all the way out but pooled when upside down. There are no defensive cuts to the hands or arms, no stab wounds elsewhere. Except for this."

Willis tugged the sheet down to expose the porcine belly. It looked to Gordon like someone had carved a dollar sign into the flesh. A snide comment on his greed? But wait—

"Two circles with a double arrow sticking through them," Gordon said under his breath.

"Similar to Richie's tattoo," Willis said. "I took photos from both bodies, for comparison. I'll email them to you." He replaced the sheet for modesty's sake. "Espiritos, you said?"

"El Camino Espiritos, that was it. Yeah. The Way of the Spirit or Spirits, or The Spiritual Road, or—I dunno, I'll have to ask Father Sullivan again. But I wouldn't jump to the conclusion that our chief suspect is an Espiritos follower."

"Fair enough, Frank. But clearly, it was someone who knew how to slaughter a pig."

CHAPTER 11

ONCE LOGAN HAD FINISHED retching in the trash can, Gordon handed him a wad of paper towels from the men's room.

Logan wiped his mouth.

"Need a little time?" Balfour asked.

Logan waved his hand *no*. He dropped the towel into the trash.

"I'll take care of this," Balfour said, picking up the can and leaving the room. She'd bag the contents for forensics.

"So, it's him for sure?" Gordon said. He needed a verbal positive ID.

"What do you think?" Logan wheezed.

"So that's a yes?"

"Yes, it's a yes." Logan coughed.

"Water?" Gordon asked. He proffered a paper cup.

Logan took it in both trembling hands, sipped at it. Gordon rapped on the glass window partition to signal to Lou that he could pull the sheet up and store the stiff.

Officer Paul Pembroke leaned against the wall with a notebook in one hand, a pen in the other. Interviews always needed a witness.

"When we go out to the office, Logan, we'll have some release forms for you to sign so that Mr. Willis there can proceed with the arrangements," Gordon said. "Your sister already signed but we need both signatures."

"Okay, I get it. Can we go now?" He handed back the water cup.

"In a minute. Is there anyone else we should notify? Your sister said there were relatives out of state—"

"She'll call them."

"Business associates?"

"She'll call them."

"Enemies?"

"What?"

"We think someone killed him and moved the body to the lagoon to conceal it."

Logan blanched.

Gordon waited for a comment. None. He proceeded, "Did your father have enemies?"

Logan squinted in disbelief at the question. "Like, who *wasn't* his enemy? I mean, he thought *everyone* was. He said if you think everyone is out to get you, then they won't get the chance to do it."

"He was wrong. Someone did."

"It wasn't me, I swear. I mean, I know I told him to drop dead, but it was just a family argument, you know?" He cupped his ears as if trying to block out the sound of it. "I was trying to get clean, you know, really trying."

"So why did he kick you out of the house?" Gordon pressed.

"I don't know."

"Were you using in the house?"

Logan pushed away air with his palms. "No! Never! I promised I wouldn't."

"So, you used somewhere else."

"It was hard, I—"

"How'd you pay for it?"

"We have money, you know. The family."

"Were you stealing money from the family? Drawing from

an account you shouldn't? Pawning things from the house?"

"No, no, I'd never—"

"Selling drugs to get drugs?"

He snorted. "Dad's the salesman in the family, not me. We just—we just all have money. That's all."

The diamond stud. The country club. The antebellum mansion. The Audi. But this one had squandered whatever he had. Like that 'prodigal son' who wasted his family's money in wild living and ended up—ironic in this instance—feeding pigs.

"You'd get a lot more money fast if he was dead, wouldn't you?"

"Whoa, whoa."

"Wouldn't you?"

"Yeah, but—like, eventually."

"In due time, huh?"

"Yeah, in due time."

"Speaking of time, where were you between 5:00 p.m. Wednesday and 5:00 p.m. Thursday?"

He shook his head to joggle the memory. "With Bunny. Yeah, with Beverly."

"Where?"

"Where you found me. It's her place."

"The whole time?"

"Sure."

"How did you get there?"

"I walked."

"It's a long walk."

"So what?"

"Why didn't you call Beverly for a ride?"

"I dunno. I was upset. I needed to walk and think things over."

Did he have time to kill Dad and dump him? He might have gained access, being the boss's son.

"Don't you have a car?" Gordon asked. He already knew the answer. It was that clunker Cavalier parked at the apartment. He had run the plates.

"Yeah. But my license is suspended. DUIs."

That wouldn't necessarily prevent him from driving. "So that's why Beverly drives you around?"

"Yeah."

"She's waiting for us in the office." He turned to the attending officer. "Got all that, Paul?"

Pembroke wiggled the notepad.

"Good. Let's go sign those papers now."

Willis' receptionist and cosmetic assistant, Amanda, had the papers ready. Logan, a lefty, scrawled his name where Amanda had stuck the SIGN HERE arrows. His hand curled and shook, making the lettering jagged. No doubt he was sweating, too, and Gordon would bag the pen, along with the drinking cup along and the paper towel Christine had taken for DNA testing.

Gordon showed them out but stopped Beverly in the doorway. "I wanted to ask you— just routine, you understand—"

Logan turned, his face creased with worry.

"It's okay, babe," Beverly said. "Get in the car."

Logan slinked away.

"Logan says he was with you from late Wednesday afternoon 'til now," Gordon said. "Was he with you the whole time?"

"Heck, yeah," she said. "He was feeling awful."

"How do you mean?"

"Like, sick."

"From drugs, do you think?"

"No, I've seen that. Like, from a bad cold. He walked the whole way from his house when his dad kicked him out, and he was sore and shaking. And soaking wet."

"Then how did his car get to your apartment?"

"I've had it for a while. Since the last DUI. Maybe a week ago, now. So I drive him around."

"Why didn't he call you for a ride?"

She shrugged. "No clue."

Gordon shrugged back. Maybe it *was* a clue.

CHAPTER 12

GORDON AND PAUL PEMBROKE SPED OFF their separate ways, Pembroke to do traffic control where the emergency crews were showing up to contain the lagoon spillage, Gordon off to Jo-Jo's diner. Not that he was interested in food after an autopsy.

Jo-Jo's was named for Joe and Joelle Green the Waffle Queen, the long-time owners of the little breakfast and lunch hangout, whose teenage daughter Lilly hadn't come home one night, so at 3:00 a.m. Gordon got a call, and he knew exactly where to find her, watching stars with a boy on Wild Turkey Hill overlooking the Jenkins Forest Preserve— and they were really just watching stars.

Lilly was away at Illinois State now to become a teacher and get her MRS degree. It didn't work out with the boy on the hill.

Joelle worked tables and counter while Joe flipped pancakes or patties, a vet with mess hall experience and a bum leg who cooked in his old khakis. A few times Gordon had volunteered to be the substitute sergeant on the Third Shift and dropped in at 4:30 a.m. soon after the lights flickered on. Joe was scrambling eggs and Joelle was taking breakfast-all-day orders from the same four men who came every Friday to the same booth, the Romeos: Retired Old Men Eating Out.

"Be with ya in a minute, hon," Joelle called out to Gordon, and then returned to scribbling on her order pad. "Grape jelly with that, too, Petie?"

"As usual," replied Pete Crispin. He hadn't been the same since the motorcycle accident and had to leave the warehouse job early.

"Hey, Flash," Petie yelled. "Too bad about Old Man Diedrich."

So, word was out. Texting and social media had sped up the small-town grapevine.

"Yeah," rejoined his pal Horace Phelps. "This time he really bought the farm."

The men laughed. *Bought the farm, right, good one.*

"Serves him right for what he did to Horace here," Petie said acidly.

"Like what the Bible says," Horace said, raising his coffee mug as if in a toast. "The rich guy said, 'I will build me bigger barns and take my ease, eat, drink, and be merry', but God said, 'you're an idiot, this very night thy soul shall be required of thee'. Something like that."

As far as these men were concerned, justice had been done. The corporate pricing had undercut Horace's small operation to the point of bankruptcy.

"Ya know who done it yet, Flash?" Horace asked.

"We're looking into it," he said.

"Swell. When ya find him, give him a big slap on the back and say thanks for me," Horace said.

Yeah, tell him good job, right, what took ya so long, that's funny.

Joelle delivered the orders to Joe and turned to Gordon.

"Do you believe these guys?" she said.

"They've been hurt," Gordon said.

"They're not dead. Get cha something?" she asked.

"Just some information."

"Okay. Today's special is corn chowder."

"Not that kind."

"I know. Richie Valera, right? Yeah, he was here Wednesday, just before closing, of course, a little before three. It was pourin' buckets. Said he couldn't even see the road no more, so he pulled over here."

"And ordered your famous chili steak sandwich and curly fries as long as he was here."

"How'd you know?"

"Don't ask."

"Chowed it straight down, like he hadn't eaten in days."

It was likely. Meth suppressed appetite along with the need to sleep. It's why the slaughterhouse workers used it.

"Anything else unusual you noticed? The way he looked? Did he seem high to you? Something he did or said?"

"He was wired, all right. On what, I dunno. But when I say 'chowed down,' I mean he ate like an animal. Hardly chewed. Gulped it down. When he was done, he picked up the knife and gave it a look like he was looking for his reflection in it. He said, 'Now I'm ready,' and left."

"Without paying?"

"I wasn't gonna stop him, Flash. He was still holding the knife."

—⚏—

Gordon rang up the St. Mary parish office to find out if Father Sullivan was in. Rural priests traveled widely, he knew, serving the far-flung and homebound. Country churches were inordinately filled with the elderly. Home calls, rehab center and hospital visits, and the never-ending funerals kept a man-of-the-cloth on the road. The cleric had come to many an accident scene and house fire to comfort the shocked and grieving. Not that different from a cop, Gordon thought. A man in uniform moving from crisis to crisis.

But at the moment, he was moving from bush to bush with a pair of clippers.

"Hey, Father," Gordon called. It came out *fatha*.

Sullivan shaded his eyes. The brim of his straw hat didn't quite do the job. "Flash. What brings you out here this fine day?"

He wasn't exactly the young and affable Father O'Malley of Bing Crosby. More of the squat and dumpling-faced Father Brown. Gordon had never seen him in a T-shirt before, and his mottled arm sported a tattoo from his Navy days.

"I could use some help," Sullivan said lightly with a wipe of his brow. "The grounds crew members are all on vacation."

"I'll pull a few weeds, but I need your help more than you need mine," Gordon said.

"Don't tell me. It's about Mr. Diedrich, isn't it?"

"More or less."

"The poor fellow. No one deserves that."

"I'll bet most of your flock would disagree."

"Then they've forgotten their catechism. Every life is precious to God."

"He made life miserable for a lot of people."

"Love the sinner, hate the sin," Sullivan said.

"That's what I want to talk about," Gordon said. He pulled the morgue photos from the folder. He didn't worry about Sullivan flinching. Priests were accustomed to seeing people at their worst. "I thought you might recognize these symbols. They were carved into Diedrich's body."

Sullivan thumbed the hat brim higher. He bent down for a closer look. "A little messy, but clearly *El Camino Espiritos*, The Way, or The Road, of the Spirits," he declared. "Nature deities, really. Nine of them. A devotee gets a tattoo of the one to whom he or she is dedicated when initiated into their 'priesthood,' as they call it. We've talked about them before. What do you make of it?"

"Nothing yet," Gordon said. "It could be a number of things. A signature of the killer. A false lead meant to make us suspect someone from their group. Tell me: do they typically make a mark like this on their animal sacrifices?"

"So, you think it's possible they sacrificed poor Mr. Died—"

"I'm not suggesting anything," Gordon interrupted bluntly. "We're not saying someone from their group did it— or not."

"I understand," Sullivan said, repenting. "The answer is, I don't believe so. They shave part of the animal before applying the knife but a carving? As if to dedicate the animal to one of their deities? No."

"Okay. That's helpful. Does this particular symbol mean anything special that you know?"

"Could I see that again?" the priest asked.

Gordon presented the shots.

Sullivan leaned in. "Like I said, it's a symbol of one of their patron spirits, but I can't recall which one." He pinched his lips and shook his head twice. "There's so much anger here."

You don't know the half of it, Gordon thought but stifled himself.

"It comes from the harsh working conditions, you know," Sullivan explained. "Many of these workers and their families come to my Spanish masses. I've heard the anger, the frustration, the depression, the stress. I've seen how the perilous tasks in that processing plant can break a man. Injuries, physical problems. Mental health problems. Heavens, many mental health problems. Anger is just the beginning."

"Strong enough to motivate murder?"

Sullivan shrugged. "I suppose so. But Aristotle said that poverty is the mother of revolution and crime. That's why we've been fighting to secure a living wage for a decent life, benefits of basic health care, unemployment insurance, workers' compensation, Social Security. Housing, too, oh my, because there's a scarcity of affordable housing in rural areas like this."

"It's why they wanted a union," Gordon said. "Diedrich would have none of it."

"Labor protection should be a right guaranteed in law," Sullivan said, every syllable precise. His face reddened from passion, not the heat. "With all respect to an officer of the law, the law must also be amended to allow workers to challenge in civil court employers who do not provide sanitary and safe working conditions, who violate wage and hour laws, or who use dangerous chemicals."

He drew a breath. "Forgive me," he said, calming. He dabbed his forehead with a handkerchief. "Preaching comes easily to me."

"I get it," Gordon said. He replaced the photos in the folder. "If you hear anything, let me know."

"Anything, of course," he replied, "outside the seal of the confessional."

—⁓—

On his way out of town to the *Espiritos* farmette, Gordon spied a knot of young men loitering in a weedy playground. They dressed in hooded sweatshirts even though it was hot out—probably hiding grass or opioids in the pouches, though he could not search them. He pulled up. Rolled down the window.

The tallest one shaded his eyes. "Hey, Flash, what up, dude?"

"Tyler, my man, you cold or sumpin? What's with the sweats?"

"Everything else is in the wash, man. Gimme a break."

Gordon gave him a stare, a stare that could freeze water.

"I got nuttin' on me, Flash, I swear. I ain't even smoked nuttin today."

"See that you don't. Bad for your health, you know."

He sped off, keeping an eye on the rear-view mirror. The guys were laughing. Probably at the junker car. Or about the undiscovered weed in their pouches. Did it matter? Cannabis was now 'decriminalized' in Illinois for recreational use, and some days the whole town smelled like a pile of wet leaves burning in October.

—⊶—

Gordon drove the cruiser into the hilly moraine west of town, a rock-strewn remnant of a long-ago glacier, wooded and away from the stink of the river. The *Espiritos* members raised their sacrificial animals on a farmette there, a location once remote and secluded. But a developer had purchased the surrounding land, and upscale McMansions were rising near it, along with the complaints about the noise.

Gordon zipped by some brick colonials and stucco-and-timber Tudors with pasture-like lawns and split rail fences. He tapped the brakes. Paul Pembroke had already arrived, idling near the long driveway entrance. Gordon waved as he passed and then steered in, Pembroke pulling in behind.

They crunched to a stop under the shade of sprawling sycamores in front of a whitewashed farmhouse. A brood of chickens that had pecked in the dirt behind a wire fence scattered. A rooster cock-a-doodled. A trip of horned goats clustered in a nearby pen, their side-slanted eyes curious and creepy. Gordon plucked the photo folder from the passenger seat and glanced at the evidence bag next to it that contained a sample steak knife from Jo-Jo's, like the one Richie absconded with. He wondered if the *Espiritos* members would allow him to take one of their ritual knives for examining. *Maybe they sell them in the gift shop.*

Yasmani Gonzalez, a bald man with a constellation of chocolaty moles on his cheeks and an annoyed pout crimping his lips, answered the door. The horizontal stripes of his open-collared polo pushed against his paunch but could not restrain it. He folded his arms defensively across his chest. It made the belly look bigger.

"What's the problem, officers?" he said. "There's no ceremony going on. And we have the right to have one if we did. Moreno v. Texas."

"We're not here about the animals this time, Mr. Gonzalez," Gordon said.

"It's about Richie, right?" the man said. "I hear his old lady did him in. Awful."

"We have a few questions. Routine. Can we come in?"

"Why not? I got all my permits for livestock and the disposal of animal remains, if you want to see them."

"Not this time," Gordon repeated. He and Pembroke followed Gonzalez into the parlor.

Beyond the department-store sectional and mismatched end tables was what might have been a dining table. It had become an altar, with a white tablecloth and crucifix, a stack of books and notepads with sharpened pencils in a soup can, and a fishbowl of water. No fish. Hollowed-out gourds, painted in primary colors, hung from the walls. A kit of conga drums sat along the wall, beside bongos mounted on stands and brightly painted tambourines on the floor. They could make quite a racket, Gordon recalled. He tensed when he spied the life-sized black female doll in the corner, standing in a flowing dress and a colorful bandana, a half-empty bottle of Bacardi at her feet, and a cluster of battery-operated candles nearby.

"The candles meet the fire code," Gonzalez said. "And don't worry about her," he added, pointing. "She doesn't speak except in a séance."

Or drink, Gordon surmised. He found a spot where he could keep an eye on the front door and the curtain to an adjoining bedroom. "So, you've already heard, Mr. Gonzalez, that Jacob Diedrich is dead?"

"Oh, is that what you're here about? Yeah, yeah, I saw it on TV. That pig. We offered to buy damaged swine from his CAFO, you know, ones too stressed to be butchered for public sale, but he said no. They were just destroyed. What a waste."

"Did you ever get your animals from him?"

"No, no. We raise them ourselves."

"So, you weren't mad that he would not release animals to you?"

"No, no, we usually use goats and chickens, not pigs so much because pigs are expensive so—wait. Do you really think I had something to do with it?" he asked.

"Maybe you can explain this." Gordon pulled a photo from the folder and held it up. It was the shot of the carving on Diedrich's belly.

Gonzalez made a face, a mix of revulsion and curiosity. "What's this?"

"I was hoping you could tell me," Gordon replied. "It was cut into Mr. Diedrich's torso. Richie had a tattoo like it, so I figured it was related to your group. Is it?"

He wouldn't reveal that Father Sullivan had already confirmed it.

"It is," Gonzalez admitted. "When someone goes through the priesthood ritual, they are given a name and an Orisho—"

"A what?"

"A guardian or patron spirit. One of the Nine Spirits who oversee Nature and our people. These are the ones who will inhabit them and speak through them in the ceremonies. The marking is there to remind others who is speaking."

Just as Father Sullivan said. "Who is 'speaking' here?"

Gonzalez peered at it. "It's a little hard to tell. It's crude. Done pretty fast, I'd say." He tapped the photo. "But this looks like a double-headed ax. That's the sign for Shangu, the warrior Orisho who rules over the lightning and thunder, fire, and drums. He has a quick wit and quick temper. He can be funny, or fierce. That explains the double ax." Gonzalez rose up on his toes. He noticed the officers' cocked heads. "This is to acknowledge his greatness. He is hot blooded and will strike back at any follower who fails to rise at the mention of his name."

Gordon planted his heels on the floor and rummaged in his folder. "Here's a photo of Richie's tattoo," he said. "Is it the same as the one on Mr. Diedrich?"

"It's pretty close. See? There's the double-headed ax design."

"Not a double arrow?"

"No, no. Whoever did it on Mr. Diedrich just tried to make the ax handle look thick, I think. Very crude. It couldn't be one of our people."

"But it's someone who knows this sign. Would you say it's a signature?"

Gonzalez pointed at the Diedrich photo. "Are you asking because you think Richie did this?"

Gordon ignored the question. "When was the last time you saw Richie?"

Gonzalez counted on his fingers. "Wednesday. After the 6:00 a.m. to 4:00 p.m. shift at the plant."

"You mean the slaughterhouse?"

"Yeah, the packing plant. There's two ten-hour shifts. We have our meeting in between the two, to make it easy for the workers, and a lot of them are members, so about five o'clock. Good thing, too, 'cuz I wanted to go to that town hall after the mounting."

"Mounting?"

"That's our ceremony where the Orishos speak through their hosts in a trance. You remember the drums and all. I thought maybe that's why you're here. I figured the Wilsons or Old Lady Merriweather complained again. They should live across the river by the drag racing strip. Now *that's* loud."

Pembroke spoke up. "So why is it called a 'mounting'?"

Gordon wasn't sure he really wanted to know.

"When the spirits speak in a host, we say they mount them. Like on a horse. That's all."

"Was Richie—uh—mounted?" Gordon asked.

"Oh, yeah," Gonzalez said vigorously. "He had so much negativity to pour into the gourds."

"So did he—or the spirit—say anything in this state?" Gordon pressed.

Gonzalez crisscrossed his hands in front of himself. "No, no, it's not for me to repeat the messages of the Orishos to outsiders."

"Did he threaten Mr. Diedrich about the strike, or—"

"It's not for me to repeat what the—"

"—or about refusing to give you pigs for your—uh—services?"

"You should leave now."

"Are we feeling some negativity here?"

"Now."

As though it were a signal, two young men dressed in white pushed through the curtain. Gordon instinctively lifted an elbow to draw his weapon.

"*Patron,*" one said in Spanish, "*estamos listos.*"

"*Estare alli en un momento,*" Gonzalez answered. "I need to go, officers," he continued. "It is time for a spiritual reading, and outsiders are not permitted."

Gordon tugged a business card from his shirt pocket. "Okay. If you think of anything else we should know, please give me a call, huh?"

Gordon paused at the door. "One last thing, Mr. Gonzalez: Did you know Richie had a baby with his fiancée? And that he wanted custody of it?"

"That's none of my business."

"So, the girl Krystyl isn't a member of your group?"

"We don't give out information on our members."

"So, she is?"

"I'm not telling you any more."

They left the house.

"The devil made me do it," Gordon said snidely in the driveway.

"He didn't say that, Flash."

"Okay. How about this: It wasn't me, Officer, it was the warrior spirit that mounted me."

"We don't know for sure that Richie did it."

"Maybe someone else dedicated to this Chango or Shango character," Gordon speculated.

"Shangu," Pembroke corrected him and lifted his heels.

"Stop it." Gordon went on to summarize his talk with Jo Green the Waffle Queen. "So, we *do* know he was in an excited, agitated state of mind, not entirely himself, possibly drugged up, and full of grievances. He was handy with a knife, and the stomach carving is almost exactly like his own."

"Almost."

"No one said Richie was an artist."

"All we can say is that he's a suspect."

"To make him more likely, we need to establish a timeline for him between the ceremony Wednesday afternoon and the trailer park visit Thursday afternoon and find out who he was with."

"Who would know that?"

"I'll start with the girlfriend, Krystyl, who killed him. She should still be in the sheriff's custody."

Thirty minutes later, Gordon drilled his gaze into Sheriff's Deputy Anderson. "What do you mean, she was let go?"

Anderson lowered his feet from his desk. "Sorry, Francis. She asked for a lawyer before we could question her, and within an hour the DA gave me a statement—where the devil is it—I got it here somewhere. Hold on." He leaned into the desk as far as his Porky Pig belly allowed, fumbled with some papers in a tray, pulled one out, read it:

There is sufficient evidence to prove beyond a reasonable doubt that the subject believed that there was an imminent and otherwise unavoidable danger of death or grave bodily harm to the innocent, namely herself and her child. That's justifiable homicide in this county, and therefore blameless.

He dropped the paper. "So, we couldn't hold her."

"We can still treat her as a person of interest," Gordon said. "She might know where Richie was that night. And why he wanted the baby so badly. That bothers me. I'd like to talk to her."

"You know who you can talk to?" Anderson said. Nearly sneered. "Your buddy Tyler."

"Tyler Williams? What would he know about Richie?"

"Maybe he got his dope from him. I dunno." He jerked his thumb behind him. "He's been asking for you. I've got him in the cooler."

"On what charge?"

"Does it matter? He's a loiterer. A nuisance."

"That's not a crime."

"Possession with intent to sell is," Anderson retorted. "I found contraband on him after you said hello on the street and sped off. Someone had to check him out. Go ask him where he got it. He might talk to you. Tell him I'll let him go if he talks. Cell five."

Gordon firmed his lips before he said anything he might regret. The real reason Anderson hauled Tyler Williams in was to buff his record with certain white voters for keeping people of color off a small town's streets.

He punched the code buttons for access to the holding area's security passage. When it clicked, he stepped in. An officer in a bullet-proof glass booth buzzed him through to the individual cell block. Gordon found Tyler, already dressed in the familiar canary yellow jumpsuit and plastic sandals, slumped on his bunk.

"Tyler, my man," Gordon called out.

The twenty-something with the drop fade haircut sprang to his feet. "Flash, dude, you here," he said brightly. "You come to get me out?"

"I can't, my man. You're in county custody. I'm city."

"Yeah, but you all cops."

"Sure, but we all have our own turf." He figured Tyler might understand the analogy.

"But you got pull, right? I'm tellin' you, I been set up. I didn't have nothin' on me. The fat dude, he pulls a dime bag outta his own pocket and says it's mine. I didn't have nothin'. Nothin'. I swear."

"It's his word against yours," Gordon said.

"Well, he's a fat liar," Tyler said, adding a colorful expletive. "You gotta tell somebody, Flash. Tell his boss he lied."

Even if Anderson had planted the evidence, Gordon couldn't do much. There was no proof. No witness.

And there was a code of silence. Every rookie knew from day one that breaking the Blue Wall by ratting on a fellow officer meant losing your career. Tyler wasn't worth that.

"I can't do that." It wasn't a lie.

"Flash, you gotta," Tyler insisted. "You're one of the good guys. Am I right?"

"Listen," Gordon said, "Let's say it *was* yours. Who would you say you got it from?"

"I didn't get it from no one, I'm telling you—"

"Let's just *say* you did."

"I ain't saying that. I'm not gonna be known on the street as a rat."

"You want a hint, huh? How about a guy named Richie? Know anyone named Richie?"

"I don't know no Richie."

"Let's say you did. Could you say you got it from Richie? Richie Valera?"

"Richie who?"

"Valera. Richie Valera."

"You can say I got it from Little Richard," Tyler sniffed with a dismissive wave. "Will it get me outta here?"

"Little Richard. Good one. Okay, I'll tell him. No guarantee, huh? But Deputy Anderson said he would spring you if you cooperated and named a source, and since other guys heard him say it, to save his own butt, he'll live up to what he said."

"Fine. I believe you. You're okay."

"I should tell you that Richie Valera is dead."

"You don't say? Then it's not a snitch, is it?"

"Nope."

"That's different, then. That's good. Richie. Richie Whatever."

"Valera."

"Yeah, yeah. Richie Valera."

"Good to see you, Tyler, my man."

"I can't say the same. But thanks anyway."

Gordon passed through security and found Anderson.

"He says he got it from Richie Valera." Gordon said it loud enough for the staff to overhear. "As you suspected."

Anderson guffawed. "That's horse manure."

Of course it is, Gordon thought. *Because you planted it on him.*

"He doesn't know Richie from dirt," Anderson argued.

"It's a small town."

"Richie's dead," Anderson said.

"Then you can't arrest him. I guess you'll have to spring

Mr. Williams, Deputy, as per your bargain," Gordon again said louder than necessary. "He revealed his source. Your prisoner is now your CI."

Anderson scanned the room, noted the eyes on him, and scowled. He couldn't keep a Confidential Informant in jail who was promised immunity in exchange for information. He lowered his gruff voice. "Watch your back, Gordon."

The phone jangled. Anderson snatched it from the cradle. "Anderson," he gruffed, then softened. "Yes, Lieutenant Simms." He held up an index finger, indicating Gordon should not leave yet. "Nine o'clock. Of course. Yes. See you then." He parked the handset. "Your boss," he said. "Expect a call from him any minute about a war room tomorrow morning. We'll probably decide then as a team who should talk to the girl. I'll argue it shouldn't be you."

CHAPTER 13

Yasmani Gonzalez took his seat at the table near the crucifix, prayer books, pencils, pad, and fishbowl, there to cleanse the spirits from negative to positive. They were surely present, the room chilling quickly, now that their ornately painted gourds were filled with the shells and stones that they liked. He cupped the bowl of water himself, to empty his own negativity. He must not allow the policemen's meddlesome visit to trouble him now.

Gonzalez's five assistants, all in white, were already goose-bumping in their seats. Before proceeding with the sacrifice, they needed a go-ahead from one of the Orishos. It wouldn't be long. One rubbed his arms against the chill. Already, another one of the saintly ones at the table contorted his face, his eyes squeezed and mouth downturned, grunting, taking short, frosted breaths. His Orisho was taking hold of him.

His eyes popped open, and his surprised gaze roamed the room as if he'd never seen it before. He tried to speak, but it was as though he had not yet learned to coordinate his tongue, lips, and breath. He huffed, took control, and asked for rum. A woman handed him a gourd brimming with white Bacardi. He quaffed it in loud gulps. Smacked his lips.

"*Deja que comience,*" he said deep in his throat.

Gonzalez wrote down the message on the pad, dated it, gave it to a female assistant, and rose. The others followed, except the "mounted" man, who had fallen into a heavy-breathing sleep. Gonzalez strode to the inner shrine's entryway, threw back the curtain, and smiled at the attendants waiting there, a circle of men and women in white hats, bandannas, dresses, trousers, shirts, socks, and shoes—all white. They had arranged a cluster of ceramic pots, brightly painted and filled with shells, colored stones, and rooster carvings, the physical and portable dwellings of their Orishos. Fruits, sweets, and cigarettes filled the gaps between the pots, pleasing offerings to the spirits. The initiate, standing in the middle of the circle, dressed in yellow satin and wearing a crown, needed to invite these spirits into new pots to bring home to her own shrine. But first, her empty pots needed to be cleansed with animal blood.

Gonzalez clapped his hands and shouted, *"Ahi va el primero!"*

The first goat, a brown and white male, was carried by a burly man to the circle of pots and placed on the white tile. A woman bent to lift its front legs in the air, presenting it to the initiate.

The goat relieved itself on the shoes of the woman. The mess was mopped up quickly— it was not the first time a frightened goat had let loose. The big man scooped up the bleating goat, the animal's front legs crossed with the rear legs to stop it from struggling.

Gonzalez, after being handed a sharp blade, braced the head of the goat. He pinched the skin of its neck and shaved a line of fur, allowing the hairs to drift on the pots, on the heads of the spirits, to awaken them to the coming of blood.

"Are you ready?" he asked the initiate.

"I am r-ready," Lucy said with a shiver.

CHAPTER 14

THE SKIES HAD BEGUN TO BLEED. What was that saying: *Red sky at night, sailor's delight.* A high-pressure system was muscling in from the southwest, shouldering storms and the stink of the spill away, northeast toward Chicagoland. That made sense to Gordon. After all, the indigenous peoples' name for *Chicago* originally meant *it smells*.

While cruising the town, running license plates at random, Gordon got the call from Lieutenant Simms.

"We'll have the preliminary toxicology reports and video surveillance," the Lieutenant said. "The canvassing interviews came up empty. But we'll want to hear what leads you've turned up so far."

The devil made Richie do it, Gordon wanted to say.

"Expect to be named head of the investigation," Simms said. "Sheriff's Department is in over their heads with the manure spill—in a manner of speaking—and ISP is fine with a supporting role."

State troopers probably also wanted to avoid stepping into the local politics. The sheriff's department was also in over their heads with the upcoming election that had already turned ugly. Otis Anderson was right to be peeved with the current sheriff, Daryl "Bubba" Bannon, sliding from election to election without accountability for the small number of officers on the roads, fixing tickets for his family members, friends, and donors, and collecting fines from motorists that ended up in his own pocket. And when he and other deputies were ordered to hand out "Bannon for Sheriff" cards while on duty, well, that was it. Anderson let it be known that Bannon had used his position to protect a drug-dealing nephew from law enforcement action. And when questioned by a reporter, Anderson refused to suppress a rumor that Bannon had a criminal domestic violence incident with his wife in their home and had repeatedly come on to female deputies. That's when the first campaign signs for Bannon were defaced with "WIFE BEATER" scrawled in black felt markers over his name. Anderson didn't object. Bannon didn't suspend or fire him, lest it look like the accusations were true and he was out to silence his own deputy.

The manure slinging was likely to get worse. As if there wasn't already enough of it stinking up the countryside.

Paul Pembroke parked the black-and-white at the boat launch gate where a red CLOSED sign hung by a rusty chain. Two utility trucks and an RV-looking bus from the Illinois Department of Natural Resources told him that techies were setting up a command post in the asphalt lot. A worker in lime hazmat suit pants and a respirator approached. When Pembroke lowered the window, the hellish heat and rancid smell poured in.

"You'll need one of these," the man said, dangling a face mask by the ear loop. "It's an N-95. Won't help the eyes, though. You got goggles?"

Pembroke coughed acidly. "In the back, yeah."

"Good. Thanks for coming. The county highway guys already set up the detour signs. We need you to enforce it and keep the peepers away from my crews."

"No prob."

The man patted the door twice, a gesture of gratitude or dismissal, and returned to the RV.

Before he took his post, Pembroke studied the team at the

shoreline loading a large raft with containment tubes, pipes, nets, and instruments with dials. He remembered how, in his first week as a rookie, Frank and he had driven here near the end of a shift around two in the morning. Frank told him to go ahead and catch a nap while he typed up the report. He was jolted awake by Frank's shout: "Foot race! Foot race! Suspect on the run! Go, go!"

Frank ran out. Paul threw his door open, swung out, and stepped knee-deep into water. Frank had parked the cruiser with the passenger side dipped into the river.

Belly-laughing, Frank snapped off photos to show the guys at the station.

At the next briefing, while they were all yukking it up, Paul left early and took out the floor jack from his trunk, the one for the many flat tires he changed. He positioned it under the rear differential of Frank's Impala and jacked it up so that the rear tires were barely one-quarter inch off the pavement. When Frank emerged from the briefing, chuckling, calling out *No hard feelings, right, Rook?* he slid into his seat, put the car in drive, and punched the gas. The wheels spun and smoked.

Frank held up two index fingers side by side with a grin to say: *One-to-one. Now we're even.*

—⁓—

When the blood had drained from the sky and the shredded clouds mopped up, Gordon cruised by the library to make sure the transients were leaving peaceably. He wheeled into the QuikStop for a jolt of iced coffee, where Pembroke had already parked. Gordon drew alongside.

"The spill workers are gone for the day," Pembroke explained.

"Think it'll take long to clean up? Did they say?"

"Nope. Didn't say. They were doing mostly surveillance

today, to figure out where to start the dirty work tomorrow. Oh, speaking of tomorrow—"

"War room."

"Lieutenant Simms called to invite me. Not sure why. Maybe because I was with you for a couple interviews today?"

"Likely."

"Any theories yet?"

"Richie carved a signature into his vic with a stolen knife and hoped it would frame Jo-Jo for the crime."

A pause.

They laughed.

"Case closed, huh?" Pembroke said.

"On to the next one," Gordon agreed.

Their radios crackled with a 10-52, *Ambulance needed.*

"I'll take this, Paulie," Gordon said and sped off.

He raced to the Sinnissippi Clinic, bars flashing, no siren. The nearest hospital was nearly twenty miles away, but this place was open late to handle the accidents, heart attacks, drug overdoses, battered women, and bar fights that Gordon dealt with. He'd spent many a night here and made it one of his regular last stops on patrol. *What's Suzie got now?* he said out loud to himself.

At the Charge Nurse Station, Suzie Pendergrass tapped at a keyboard. She hadn't changed much since high school— the bangs, the braid. The cute crease at the corner of her smile. The raspy voice. Even without the cigarettes. Gordon had dated her twice before she met Eddie, with the white 1971 Ford LTD convertible. That was the end of that. Suzie softened the breakup by telling her friend Stephanie that Flash was an okay guy. A real gentleman. Maybe that was the problem. Suzie had a thing for bad boys. So, she eloped to marry Eddie—and the car—at eighteen and popped out two kids before Eddie took off in the car with a roller derby star named Bambi who was passing through town. Gordon was just finishing his criminal justice program at the community college when she entered the nursing program there, trying to get her life back. She dropped the married name and went by Pendergrass again, starting over. Gordon was serious with Stephie by this time. So that was *really* the end of that.

"Suze," he said. "Hey. Busy night?"

She glanced up. Her face lit up. Maybe it was just the glow of the computer monitor. There was that cute crease.

"Nothing for you, Flash. No one to arrest this time."

"I heard the call—"

"Emergency baby delivery. Traci Perkins."

"Ol' Man Perkins' little girl?"

"Little? She's sixteen."

"Sheesh. Who knew?"

"Everyone but you." Suzie shook her head. "Kids having kids. It's not right."

Gordon pinched his lips. No, it's not right. It's not fair. One try, one adolescent mistake, and *boom*. He hoped he looked sympathetic, not angry.

"Yeah, yeah, I know," Suzie said. "I was only eighteen myself. Eighteen and stupid."

"So how are they?"

"My boys? Seventeen, eighteen, and stupid." She laughed, a nervous chitter. "Say, you and Stephie—still trying?"

"Taking a break, let's say."

"I get it." She beckoned to a passing nurse. "Lori, could you mind the store a minute? I'm gonna step outside for a break."

Gordon followed her out to the parking lot where she shook out a Salem cigarette, thumbed a lighter into flame, and puffed the tip into a glowing cherry. She blew out a plume and said, "It'd be tough having kids, anyway, being a cop and all."

"Everyone I work with has kids. Except Paulie Pembroke. He's a kid himself. But everyone else, yeah."

"Sorry. I didn't know. They putting pressure on you?"

"Nah, they're good about it. Some offer to help out, you know. Hey, Flash, lemme give it a try, they say."

"Cop humor."

"They mean well."

Suzie took a deep draw and exhaled slowly. "I know a fertility expert in Rockford who can maybe—"

"Suze, we've probably seen him or her already. We've seen them all."

She tapped ashes. "Sorry."

"It's okay. Look, everyone's got to live life and move on. This is our life right now."

But it wasn't like the lives of their friends, including Suzie, all of whom had kids in Scouts and soccer and softball and band and the Y and piano lessons and camping trips and parties where all the other parents with kids talked about their kids and shared photos of their kids on their phones *omigawd how cute* while Frank and Steph felt left behind and somehow broken, marginalized and malfunctioning. But the doctors in River Falls, Dixon, Rockford, Springfield, and Chicago—all the way up the medical food chain—couldn't find anything wrong with Stephie, even after the ultrasounds and the painful laparoscopy for endometriosis, and all the hormone shots Franky had to give Stephie in the butt cheek didn't do much but make Frank feel even more squeamish about needles. The worst time was when she had to come into the station for the shot and they went into the cramped Patrol Sergeant's office for privacy, but in his nervousness, Frank forgot to lock the door and patrolman Ross Davidson walked in when Stephie was bent over, elbows on the desk with her pants down and Ross covered his eyes and said, *Geez, Flash, do it at home.*

Suzie crushed her cigarette in the sand bucket. "So, tell Stephie I said hi, okay?"

"Sure." No need to say he wouldn't see her tonight— maybe not ever again.

"Bravo-12," the radio buzzed.

Gordon pressed the call button. "Bravo-12, copy."

"10-14 at two-two-six Harlan Circle."

"76." Gordon pivoted to leave. "I gotta go. See ya later, Suze."

Her eyes widened in distress. "Harlan Circle? Isn't that where Hazel Hirsch lives? What's the matter?"

"10-14 is a prowler call—"

"Omigosh."

"It's no prowler," Gordon said. "Once a month she calls to say there's someone with a bright light outside her window. It's the full moon."

—⁂—

When Gordon pulled up to the curb on Harlan Circle, the moon had faded to a hazy disk; a loosely woven cloud had begun to wrap it like an old shawl. Mrs. Hirsch rocked on the porch. "Frankie, I think I scared him off," she called out, raising her glass of white zinfandel. "I should have called to say so."

"That's okay, Mrs. Hirsch," Gordon said. "I'll check around the house anyway."

He drew his LED flashlight and clicked it on. He swept the bushes and trash barrels with the beam. He stepped to the rear and traced the light along the foundation and fence. Just like the previous times. He'd been coming since Fred Hirsch passed away the year before, from some rare cancer he probably got from inhaling the chemicals at the metal finishing plant for over thirty years. Gordon suspected that

Hazel Hirsch knew the intruding light was the moon and just needed someone to talk to.

"So, as long as I was out, I thought I'd look at the lightning bugs," Mrs. Hirsch said once he returned to the front lawn. "They're out longer this year."

"It's because of all the rain," Gordon said.

"I couldn't go grocery shopping the other day with such a rain," she complained. "And, Frankie, can you believe the price of lettuce at the Jupiter Fresh Market? Is California getting the same rain and flooding them out, too?"

It was wildfires, but he refrained from saying so.

"I'd grow my own, but *oy*, my knees."

"I don't have a garden, either."

"Who has the time?" She sipped from the glass. "Speaking of planting—someone planted a sign in my yard this week."

"A sign?"

"You know, a yard sign. Anderson for Sheriff. I threw it out. Maybe they didn't know that was my property over there by the ditch."

"Probably not." It was still illegal.

"You know him? This Anderson?

"We've met. We've worked together."

"Be careful, Frankie. If you lie down with dogs, you get up with fleas. I saw this Anderson on the TV. He has as much sense as a church has mezuzahs, if you know what I'm getting at."

"I think so."

"I mean it. I'm getting mailings and calls already, and the election isn't for—what? Eight weeks? Empty barrels make the most noise." She placed her fingertips to her chest and tapped twice. "So, look who's making the noise now. I'm keeping you from your work. You're busy, am I right?"

"I'm working on the matter with Mr. Diedrich that you may have heard of."

She sucked in her breath sharply. "Oh, that man. Show a pig a finger and he'll want the whole hand."

"I'm still going to try my best, Mrs. Hirsch."

"Oh, I know you will, Frankie. Your father, bless his soul, would be proud of you."

"It won't be easy."

"Nothing is too difficult; you only need to know how." She swirled the wine in the stemmed glass. "You know how to change a light bulb, right, Frankie? Before you go, can you change a bulb for me? The kitchen light, in the ceiling fan? I'd get up on the step stool myself, but—"

"I've got it."

"The bulb is on the table. And the house screwdriver. And the stool. That's a good boy."

He finished in five minutes and folded up the step stool.

"Thanks for fixing my light," Mrs. Hirsch said when he emerged and pressed the sticking screen door shut with his knee. "And speaking of light: look at these lightning bugs. Still lighting. Still looking for mates. And how's yours? How's little Stephie?"

"She's fine, Mrs. Hirsch, just fine."

"She was the smartest little girl in my class. She was smart to marry you, that's for sure. Give her my love, will you?" She raised her glass in salutation. "One more thing. You and Stephie. Makes me think: Why did Adam and Eve cover their business with a leaf if there was nobody to see them?"

CHAPTER 15

IN ANOTHER JOB, he might have found some diversion to decelerate on a Friday night, to get some distance. It wasn't high school football season yet, so he wouldn't be pulling traffic control duty for a game. He had stopped going to the movies because if any kids he had arrested were there, they sat a few rows behind him and threw popcorn at him. He stopped going out to dinner when he realized he could only sit with his back against a far wall where he could see the door. There wasn't a place in town where someone wouldn't recognize him and make some comment: a criminal, a victim, a high school acquaintance, an ordinary Jack or Jill who had once needed his help. So, after the paperwork, he returned to the apartment pining for a hot shower and a cold beer. The shower he could do. The beer he couldn't, being on call.

He lifted weights, took that shower, made a sandwich, and watched TV with Batman until he dropped into bed and tried not to think of Stephanie bent over with her elbows on the Patrol Sergeant's desk and her capris around her ankles.

When the alarm jangled him from a brief and fitful sleep at 5:00 a.m., he fed Batman, dropped forty push-ups, showered, and shaved. When he dragged the blade across his throat and windpipe, he wondered with a wince how anyone could cruelly slit a man to bleed him out. He shrugged into a snug business shirt and clipped on a tie. The Brass and the Smokies would expect it of a detective at the 9:00 a.m. war room conference. Still, he missed wearing the uniform—a patrol officer at heart. On the other hand, with today's temps likely to be in the steamy nineties again, he was glad not to be wearing the wool outfit and clay vest as he did when working traffic. He deserved the tie, anyway. It had taken him five years to get to the Detective Bureau, ten years to make Sergeant, and eleven years to make Detective Sergeant. Come to think of it, he'd actually been in the department since ninth grade as an Explorer when he showed up twice a week to do a shift at the front desk.

He filled his travel mug with fresh supermarket-brand coffee, strapped on his sidearm, and drove to Wild Turkey Hill in the unmarked Corolla he had switched out last night (the Impala was in service—again) to catch the sunrise in the heartland.

Gordon had worked midnights when he started, and while Stephie and the whole town were still asleep, he'd drive the cruiser out Old Towne Hall Road to this secluded outlook, up a graveled way hidden by chokeberry and spicebush that only farmers and lovers'-laners knew. The burr oaks met here for a conclave, their gnarly arms in a thousand gestures. The robins awakened, irritated at first light. A wide V of geese gronked toward the river, their wings beating a united and steady *shuff shuff shuff*. From this familiar clearing at the top, the whole Sinnissippi Valley spread out before him, and with his coffee cupped in both hands, he watched how the mounting sun pinked the prairie made of fudge-dark earth, the most fertile in the world, and seemed to create the town anew out of darkness. Once the brassy rind of the sun showed, the prairie fleabane glittered, and the green sea of corn gilded.

Under a marmalade dawn, a parade of yellow school buses coughed down the road and pulled over, parked with a sigh of brakes, and disgorged the corn detasselers to do one of the sweatiest, dirtiest of summer jobs. The month-long detasseling season had been delayed for nearly two weeks by a drenching spring and then by the Gulf hurricane that had metastasized over the Midwest and flooded every river and stream.

Like thousands of other Illinois teens, Frank had spent many such torrid days when he was thirteen and fourteen moving row-by-row-by-row-by-row through the corn fields, yanking the tassels from the tops of the plants and tossing them to the dirt. As the young workers disappeared into the plants that grew far over their heads, a season of scarlet tanagers flew off like fanning blood spatter, and Frank could hear the shouts of bull-horned managers urging speed. After all, the detasseling company would soon lose its workforce to the annoying schools that these same buses served and be left with skeletal weekend crews. Even so, for just a couple of weeks of work, these kids would earn more money than they could all summer bagging groceries or flipping burgers or scooping ice cream. But it was hot, clammy work, with paper cuts from the leaves and the salty sting of sweat in your eyes.

A mechanical cutter had already snipped the tops of the stalks, but every tassel had to be seized and pulled by hand. Gordon remembered being told why this tedious task was needed: *The tassel is the male part of the plant that has the pollen in it, so when it drops, the pollen spills on the female part of the plant, the silk. Then the pollen travels down the silk and makes the corn kernel. That's why we have two breeds of seed corn separated by rows, since pulling the tassels from one breed prevents it from self-pollinating, and that means we'll get a hybrid seed.*

And Frank could still hear the other boys' cupped-hand giggles. It was, in a way, the sex talk their parents dreaded. *The tassel and the silk, hee hee. Spills his pollen on her, hee hee.* But this was big business in Illinois. And it was serious business for Frank and Stephanie: was their problem with the tassel, or with the silk?

And maybe it didn't matter anymore. All of a sudden, the reality of what was coming, a loss beyond bearing, struck him in the chest, and the heartache spread down to his gut and up to his eyes where a mist gathered like a fog in March. He couldn't see a foot past the thickening grief. The death of a marriage took two lives, and he had caused it. How could he remain stoic and do his job when the whole world was about to change?

The day was already preheating slowly like an old oven when he pulled into the police department's fenced lot. Just as well he had the unmarked beater; he had to pass through a gauntlet of TV trucks bristling with antennae and satellite dishes and a swarm of reporters setting up stand-up spots with umbrella spotlights and boom mics. Even WGN and WBBM Chicago were here. *Here comes the circus.* At least the area B&Bs and restaurants would be busy, despite the manure spill. One reporter was already interviewing Gloria Bickham, the buxom badge bunny who often showed up at Paul Pembroke's calls, who brought him brownies at the office and once called him to her apartment on a flimsy pretext and met him at the door dressed in something even more flimsy. He cited her for a false alarm. Smart kid.

After parking, Gordon got buzzed into the headquarters. The scuffed and yellowed linoleum floors mopped easily, and the plaster walls were empty—nothing to grab and use as a weapon. The only décor were a few fist-sized holes now poorly patched, remnants of difficult arrests.

Mitchell McWhorter, working the front desk, offered a perfunctory salute. "Morning, Flash. Some idiot broke into a dozen cars in Alton Estates last night," he said.

Great. Twelve new cases in the inbox.

"Two more bikes stolen from the high school racks."

There had been a spate of these.

"Sexual assault in the parking lot behind Safe Haven."

The women's shelter. Not so safe.

"The offender's in cell six."

"On it." Actually, with a high-profile homicide investigation in progress, he'd pass along the auto break-ins, a class one felony, to a patrol sergeant; a sexual assault with a known perp could wait since he was in custody and waiting for a court appearance; the bikes? He'd hand those on to Paulie for the legwork. The kid was barely out of Sinnissippi High School himself.

He decided not to refill his travel mug with the office coffee, which looked like driveway sealant. He checked his voicemail. It should have been full of messages from family members of the victims, anguished and desperate for answers, calling with what they believe are useful leads and evidence. Instead, there were calls from reporters from every paper and radio and television station in Illinois and two from North Carolina. Those parasites outside. Vultures looking for a story. He deleted them all. Let the lieutenant or the chief handle this. No one was going to give information that might help the bad guys.

He pushed away from the cubicle desk and its shelf of binders covered in post-it notes with court schedules and reminders to check lab results or to call witnesses. The framed photo of Stephie was gone, buried in the bottom drawer beneath some *First Tactical* and *Streicher's Police Supply* catalogs. He surveyed the open-concept office. On TV, squad rooms like this were busy and noisy. But here, days were dull and staffed by cops biding their time for a full pension, RIPs, Retired In Place, just driving around in the patrol car. On the way to the staircase, he passed the patrol sergeant's office, that cramped office off Records where clerks ruled by day and sergeants by night and where Patrolman Ross saw Stephie bent over with her elbows on the desk and her capris around her ankles.

The task force convened in the second-floor conference room. Lieutenant Kevin Simms liked his meetings here because it was cold and practical, like him. The chairs were hard, the table plain, the cinderblock walls a humorless gray. There was no flashy digital display of glass screens as in TV cop shows, just a pull-down screen with a ceiling-mounted projector and a laptop on the table. There was no "crazy wall" as the Brits called it, either, with push-pinned photos and paper maps marked by tacks and colored strings. TV dramas loved them as a way to visualize the plot and remind viewers of the suspects, often *crazies* like stalkers and serial killers who kept "crazy walls" of their own. But here, a chipped whiteboard, a city map, and an oversized calendar sufficed to make lists, to track movements, to determine timelines. It was not a room for casual banter or light-hearted jest. No one would hang out after the meeting to gab about the Cubs or the Bears over donuts. It was *get in, get out, and get going.*

There were seven steel chairs and every one taken but one. Simms, presiding at the head, peered at Gordon over his blue-framed glasses. On his right sat Sheriff's Deputy Otis Anderson who gave Gordon the stink eye. Probably because he had bested him with Tyler. Or was he late? Gordon glanced at the wall clock. *Nope. On time.* Next to Anderson, Deputy Chief of CID Jack Holden looked up from some notes, and beside him was Paul Pembroke. Why hadn't he seen Paulie in the squad room? *I guess he came straight up here for some reason.* To Simms' left sat State Homicide Detective Gerald "Jerry" Davis. He was whispering something to his state trooper partner, Brandon Tate, who had visited Willis's autopsy room and had emptied his stomach in the trash can.

Everyone had a stack of field report copies in folders, along with crime scene photos, Willis's autopsy report, the state forensics report, and photocopies of Gordon's report and his crude sketch of the crime scene. The County Crime Scene Unit would have a neater diagram somewhere in the pile. Gordon pulled out his chair with a squeal.

Simms' cell phone pinged. It was a timer. "Let's get started," he said. "Chief Fisk will join us later for a briefing before he meets with the press. You may have noticed them gathering outside. Needless to say, no one should be talking to them apart from Chief Fisk or myself." He tugged off his glasses and continued:

"Before we get started, you should know that Tommy Arden over at Crime Stoppers is launching an ad campaign for the anonymous Text A Tip Line and the Communication Officer from the Diedrich plant sent me a press release in advance—" he picked it up and waved it— "announcing a fifty-thousand-dollar reward for information leading to a conviction. That'll get the tips coming and the phone lines burning. Detective Gordon—"

"Sir?"

"You'll be the lead on the case since you were first on the scene. The sheriff's office agrees. Isn't that right, Deputy Anderson?"

Anderson ran his palm over his jarhead haircut and jut out his chin, clearly miffed. "Understood."

Gordon's stomach suddenly flipped. What *he* understood was that Simms favored the current Sheriff "Bubba" Bannon in the elected position. Simms, an old friend of Bannon's, didn't want to give Anderson a feather in his cap that would allow him to run successfully against his pal the sheriff. No wonder Anderson gave him the stink eye when he entered the room. It wasn't just because Gordon had embarrassed him into springing Tyler Williams. Everyone knew the county sheriff's office normally handled a major crimes case. They had better-trained investigators and technicians; they wielded a higher authority and could coordinate things better over a large geographic area. But that was the problem: the environmental crisis of the lagoon flooding was sucking up their resources since all the unincorporated townships had no cops of their own.

"That means," the Lieutenant continued, "that everyone reports to Detective Gordon, and he reports to me."

Simms paused to read faces. The state troopers shrugged assent, though a case like this usually bumped up to them. The lieutenant was sending a message to them, too: *We welcome your cooperation, but this is a local matter.* "All right, Detective Sergeant Gordon. It's all yours."

Gordon picked up a yellow pencil and wiggled it in his fingers. "Let's start by sharing what we know, huh? I guess I'll go first, huh?" *Stop with the tic.* He ran down his interviews with Chelsea and Logan Diedrich, with Paul filling in while referring to his notebook.

"They're each a piece of work," Gordon concluded, tapping the eraser on the table. "Chelsea seems glad Daddy is gone, partly because he was controlling of her, but also because he was controlling in his business, especially in the negotiations with the Chinese looking to buy into his operations. Chelsea, the main negotiator, disapproved of the bullying tactics. So did the Chinese."

"When you say 'the Chinese,' Francis, do you have names?" Holden asked. "Do we know where they are?"

"No."

"I'll track that down," Holden volunteered.

Gordon continued: "And Logan, while upset, had an ongoing spat because of his drug use. Each had an alibi, although Logan had a couple of hours unaccounted for when he left the house in a huff on the night of the killing. But he had no car. He showed up at his girlfriend's place alone and soaking wet from apparently walking about an hour, maybe close to two, in the rain. That accounts for the time from leaving the house. Besides, I doubt they'd do the deed; they'd hire it out."

"If it was a hit," Anderson blurted, "why not just shoot the guy? Why the bludgeoning, the bloodletting, the lagoon? All that trouble. That says rage. That's out of control. That's mob action. People going crazy in a group."

"We'll consider theories later," Gordon cut him off. "Let's lay out what we know first. Let's start with the canvassing. Jack?"

Jack Holden summarized the canvassing of the shift workers at the CAFO. No one wanted to talk, and many actively avoided the officers.

"Probably undocumented," Gordon said, "though we have no authority to arrest anyone on that score. Only the feds do."

"They don't know that," Holden responded, adding that the few they spoke with on a shift separated from the incident had not seen or heard anything odd such as an argument of a threat. A team of day shift officers had interviewed CAFO workers from earlier in the day, with similar reluctance and results. Solid alibis. No strangers on the premises. Nothing out of the ordinary. No one saw a thing.

Then again, maybe *everyone* did and didn't lift a finger.

"Maybe we're talking to the wrong people," Gordon said. "We need to talk to workers in the slaughterhouse. Some of them work probably at the CAFO, too. Maybe someone there heard something or saw something. Okay, speaking of seeing, let's hear about video surveillance."

It was Davis's turn. "The video didn't see anything, either. We downloaded twenty-four hours' worth of files from all the cameras and—well, let's run some of it."

He leaned over to the laptop, tapped the keyboard, and palmed the remote mouse. The projector blinked on and hummed; a watery view flickered on. "Can we dim the lights? Thanks, Jack. Okay, then, that's the lagoon from 9:00 p.m. Wednesday, when the town meeting adjourned, to the report of the body, about 3:00 p.m. Thursday. So, eighteen hours. I'll speed it up."

Water drops and snaking ripples obscured the view. Shadows played back and forth, but it could be shifting clouds. It went entirely white for a few milliseconds and then cleared.

"Can't even tell it's the lagoon," Anderson said.

"It is," Davis said. "The files are clearly imprinted with the camera location. As you see, that storm is a real problem. The high winds drove the rain into the lens even though it was under the eaves. We got nothing."

"What about the front gate?" Gordon asked. "Cameras there would pick up everyone coming and going."

"Company trucks," Davis said. "Livestock carriers. Service vehicles operating on schedule. Some salesmen. Nothing out of the ordinary. Not Diedrich's children, in case you're wondering."

"I want a list of every vehicle," Gordon said, "when they arrived and departed, and the drivers and anyone that may have been in the vehicle."

"I'll get that," said Davis. "I'm sure they keep a careful log."

"And a list of every visitor," Gordon added. "The PR guy told me Human Resources would have that."

"On it," Davis replied.

"What else do you have?" Simms asked Davis.

"The rain washed away anything that might be useful," Davis complained. His review of the victim's bank records showed that deposits were in statistical keeping with past patterns of earnings, and there were no unusual withdrawals of any substance. A search of the home, especially Diedrich's room—to Chelsea's great consternation—produced no controlled substances, hidden cash, weapons, or a diary. "The guy had a lot of framed photos of himself posing with important people, state politicians, members of Congress, and business people. We made a list. Three of them were at the town meeting: State Senator Ron Michelson, State Rep Jeb Harmon, and his business partner County Commissioner Terence Sellers. And the desk had a calendar, kind of an appointment book. The book showed appointments with the three I just mentioned for that evening."

"To coach them?" Holden said.

"To pay them off?" Tate suggested.

"Even so," Davis went on, "his assistant, who managed the appointments, a Carole Wakefield, was one of the last people in touch with him. When we told her about Diedrich, she fainted. Had to revive her. Anyway, the phone records confirm she was one of the last to talk to him. The last cell phone tower pings locate him along River Road, on the way back to his house, at about nine-fifteen. The uniforms are checking every route a car could take."

"Diedrich had a driver, named Lo Phat. What about him?" Gordon asked. "He would actually have been the last person to see Diedrich since Diedrich never made it home."

"No way," Anderson said with a muffled laugh.

"No way?" Gordon echoed. "Why not?"

"I mean, no way is the guy named Lo Phat. It's a joke, am I right?"

"It's what Diedrich called him," Gordon clarified. "Bullies love to use nicknames. It's really Lo Phan, I think."

"That's right," Davis said. "And there's been no sign of him since Wednesday night. Neighbors and relatives haven't heard from him. We can't find him."

Gordon tapped his chin with the pencil. *Curious.* "No one filed a missing persons report?"

"The guy stuck to himself," Davis said.

"What about the car?"

"Not at the guy's apartment, where he usually parked it," Davis answered. "Not at the plant, either, where he was supposed to park it. Not in any repair shop locally. We checked."

"Sounds like we need to put out an APB on the car and the driver," Tate said. "I'll get on it."

"The Chinese would probably know how to stick a pig," Anderson offered.

"Let's talk about the sticking," Gordon said. "Jerry, you're on again. Autopsy summary."

Jerry Davis licked his thumb and pulled open the coroner's report to consult the summary while Tate spread out Willis's autopsy photos across the table. "Mr. Diedrich was rendered unconscious, no doubt, by twin blows of a round-ended blunt instrument to the anterior region of his skull, inches apart, just above the forehead," Davis began. "One blow nearly breached the skull, causing a serious third-degree concussion. The imprint of ties around the ankles and the two precision knife cuts in the neck area suggest he was hung up to be bled out like a pig. But he wasn't. The offender, we're guessing, decided it would take too long and he'd risk discovery. We have not yet found a rope or chain that would have made this possible."

"Maybe it's one routinely used in the slaughterhouse," Gordon conjectured. "The offender would have to have access to the slaughterhouse to do it."

"With all the workers looking on?" Paul asked with a doubting shake of his head.

"Sure, and cheering," Anderson said with a laugh.

Gordon didn't think it was funny. "We haven't found the blunt instrument or the knife," Gordon said.

"No," Anderson admitted, "but there's a huge stock of knives of various kinds in the slaughterhouse that is carefully cleaned and sanitized, wiping away any evidence. I guess we could ask if any are unaccounted for."

"But," continued Gordon, "we do have Richie Valera's Microtech knife, and the cuts are consistent with the kind that would be made by it. And Richie knew how to use it. It was his job. He told me he was good at it. Here's another thing: Richie was in Jo-Jo's Diner after his shift and before the town meeting. He acted like he was wired and stole a steak knife, announcing that he was 'ready.'"

"Speaking of knives," Davis put in, "there's the body carving. It's consistent in design with the tattoos used by followers of *El Camino Espiritos*, a religious group that sacrifices pigs and goats and chickens. Tattoos just like the ones on Richie Valera, as you see in the photo there."

"I confirmed that with Reverend Sullivan over at St. Mary's church before I visited those folks with Paul," Gordon reported. "It's one of their designs, all right, and it's close to the one that Richie had, but obviously made in a hurry by an amateur."

"Well, just a sloppy job in a hurry and in a rage," Anderson said. "No one's gonna do a work of art under those circumstances."

"So, what I'm hearing is that we need to find out where Richie was that night," Gordon said. "He was amped on meth and full of anger. He'd vent it on the boss who made his life hard, and he'd have the gorilla strength from the drugs to overpower him and his bodyguard. He had access to both the slaughterhouse and the CAFO. We should check his truck out."

"I'll impound it," Anderson said.

"CID will give it a look once you have it," Tate said.

"And I'll go back and talk to Richie's girlfriend, Krystyl," Gordon said. "She knows me. She'll talk to me."

"So," Simms said, straightening, "do we have a list of suspects?"

"I do," Trooper Tate said. He tossed a phone book on the desk. "Start anywhere."

"C'mon, Tate," Holden said. "Let's start with any threats we know about."

"I hear there's lottsa nasty comments on social media," Anderson said. "But there's only one real threat everyone heard out loud."

All eyes turned to Gordon.

"Sheesh, really?" he said. "Stephie was just worked up, you know? She said what everyone in the room was thinking."

"The open threat makes her a suspect," Anderson said. "You might need to recuse yourself, Francis."

Gordon's blood boiled. "That won't be necessary. Stephie didn't belong to *Espiritos.* Someone else who knew their tattoos had to carve the sign into him. And she doesn't have access to the manure lagoon. Security would recognize her as an activist who was there a lot with a protest sign. They'd toss her out on her can."

Anderson made air quotes and falsettoed his voice: "You should be bled out like a pig."

Gordon sprang up. "There's no need to—"

"Francis, sit down," Paul said.

"—bring my wife into this. I saw her the night after. She didn't know anything about this. She's clean."

"I thought you two were separated," Anderson said.

Gordon curled his right fist into a hammer.

"Did you ask her where she was the night before?" Anderson pressed. "The night of the murder?"

Gordon drew his fist back. Paul grasped his forearm. Gordon shook it away.

"Detective Gordon," Lieutenant Simms growled, "sit down. Right now."

Gordon opened his hands, brought his palms to the tabletop, took a deep breath, and sat. "You know what, huh? Stephie is a farmer's daughter, and she knows how to slaughter a pig. That's for sure. But you know what else, huh? It wouldn't be a pig farmer who did this. He—or she—would have fed the body to the pigs. They would have eaten all of it, including the bones."

"Well, then," Anderson said, "someone else took her up on the suggestion."

Gordon's biceps bulged.

Paul noticed and leaned forward to get between them. "Look, let's be logical here: it's gotta be a strong male worker or group of workers, maybe hired by someone, who stood to gain by it."

A pause.

"The kids." Davis.

"The Chinese." Anderson.

"Or someone who had a grudge," Paul added.

"Logan." Gordon.

"The union." Tate.

"And who knew where Diedrich was that night, and who can come and go at the CAFO and the slaughterhouse without being noticed, and who knows how to kill pigs with a knife. Who has a mean streak. And who knows *Espiritos* signs," Paul concluded.

Another pause.

"Richie," three voices said.

"That was easy," Anderson said.

"Let's not jump to conclusions too fast," Simms said, aiming his glasses at the table. "Any other operating theories? Any at all?"

"How about the driver, who is conveniently missing?" Holden asked. "Sick of low pay and poor treatment, he drives his pig of a boss into a planned ambush where other disgruntled workers, peeved about the stalled contract talks and other abuses, do what they do best," Holden said. "So, it's a group, not Richie alone. If the driver was ambushed and Diedrich was killed or dragged away, wouldn't he have reported it right away if he wasn't part of it? Instead, he disappears into the shadows, like so many undocumented workers."

"Sounds like a TV plot," Davis said.

Holden laughed. "Well, if it's anything like TV, we'll be done in an hour."

There was a rap at the door. Chief Fisk poked his head in. "We found Diedrich's car and the driver," he announced.

"There goes my theory," Holden said, splaying his fingers *poof*.

"What's he got to say?" Gordon asked.

"Nothing," Fisk said. "He's dead. The hazmat crews just found the car at the bottom of the Sinnissippi River."

CHAPTER 16

THE ASSIGNMENTS WERE DISTRIBUTED quickly: getting a list of all the visitors from HR and a log from Shipping and Receiving of all vehicles and drivers who came and went on the surveillance video between 9:00 p.m. Wednesday and 3:00 p.m. Thursday, a canvas of slaughterhouse workers on second shift, tracking down the Chinese to notify them of the driver's death, ID the body and check their alibis, getting a record of Diedrich's phone calls and locations to track his timeline and movement.

Gordon tapped the pencil. "I'll go check on Diedrich's car and driver—"

"County Crime Scene Team is already on location," Anderson interrupted, smiling in triumph.

Gordon's fist hardened. "Why didn't you mention it before?"

"They were called when the meeting started," Anderson said curtly, feigning offense. "I just got the text, just now."

Sure you did, Gordon thought. *You knew the whole time. You wanted a head-start to look good for the election.*

"I'll join them after we're done here," Anderson said.

"No, I'm going," Gordon said. "it's on the way to the trailer park, so after that, I'll visit Krystyl there. Maybe she can help us backtrack Richie's movements and timeline. Otis, you can go ahead and take a county team out there to impound Richie's truck. Maybe we'll find some clues in it. And it'll keep Krystyl there."

"I'll talk to Krystyl while I'm there," Anderson said.

"No. Like I said, I think she'll trust me."

"Fine," Anderson said with a pout.

"What about me?" Pembroke asked.

Gordon turned to Lieutenant Simms. "Sir? It's your call."

"Appreciate your back up here, Paul," Simms said. "But we need you to stay on patrol."

Pembroke nodded resignedly.

"Some stuff came in overnight that I need you to look into, Paul," Gordon said. "And I'd appreciate it if you monitored the tip lines. Okay with you, Lieutenant?"

"All right, fine with me," Simms said. With a single clap of his hands, he ended the meeting. "Keep Gordon informed, everyone. Gordon, keep me in the loop. The chief and I need to go to the shark tank now."

—⁂—

Gordon assigned Pembroke the follow-up to the burglaries and then they slipped out a back way to avoid the press conference in Public Room A. But as Chief Fisk and Lieutenant Simms opened the bullet-proof door to the small auditorium, the clatter of camera tripods and folding chairs, the blaze of overhead lights and the rustle of reporters tumbled out.

"—and thank you for coming today. Mayor Ami Pratt has opening remarks, and Chief Raymond Fisk of the River Falls Police Department has a brief statement, and then he'll take a few questions. General information will be given because this is an ongoing investigation, so we thank you for your patience as we—" Christine Balfour was always a calming presence.

"Shouldn't you be in there?" Pembroke asked Gordon in the motor pool.

"Nah," Gordon said as he beeped open the squad car lock. "I got a face for radio."

—⁓—

By the time he pulled up twenty minutes later to the bluffs of Castle Rocks Park overlooking the river, the fire and rescue team was packing up inflatable watercraft. A Sheriff's Department pickup idled nearby. Two black-and-yellow striped sawhorses reading POLICE LINE DO NOT CROSS had been set up; two extras sat in the back of the truck. The county crime scene unit was still unrolling yellow tape, and Donny Arnold of Don's Towing was clanking chains on the flatbed holding a white Lincoln Continental, dripping a viscid sludge.

A blue body bag on a gurney was being slid into Willis' hearse at the coroner's direction.

"Hey, Lou," Gordon called. "You got started without me?"

"The Unit got a call from Sheriff's Deputy Anderson to get moving," he replied.

Just as I thought. He's trying to take charge already, Gordon fumed. *He wants to take credit for this for his sheriff's campaign.*

Sheriff's Deputy Lee Sherman had stepped from the pickup, peering over his sunglasses with a *what's he doing here* look. "Hey, Flash. Good to see you."

"Did Otis tell you I've been assigned the lead on this?" Gordon asked bluntly.

"No kidding?" Sherman said. "I thought the county sheriff was supposed to—"

"Not this time."

Lee Sherman shrugged. "Who knew?"

Anderson knew, Gordon answered silently. *And so did you.*

"So, Francis, you wanna check out our latest customer before I load him up?" Willis asked.

"Let's have a look," Gordon said. "If that's okay with you, Lee."

"Be my guest. He ain't pretty."

"Thanks. And I'll need a copy of your notes."

"I was typing them up just now. I'll cc you."

"Appreciate it. Okay, Lou, give me the tour."

Willis secured the gurney legs and then tugged at the bag's vinyl zipper. "He's not ripe yet," he said. "Being in the water for two days slowed the rot. He was still in the seat belt." Willis folded aside the bag edges like two flower petals. "He didn't drown."

Half a face stared up at Gordon. The other half—spaghetti.

Gordon turned away, as much from disgust and shock as from offering the victim a little dignity.

"He didn't feel a thing," Willis said.

Except terror. Or puzzlement. He can't possibly mean to shoot that thing BLAM. When Gordon had the stomach to turn back, the puckered, pruney, and pock-marked half-face of the driver, one Lo Phat, grimaced up at him. The greenish skin showed some bloating from gasses, but he hadn't been in the water long enough to form the waxy adipocere film that usually lined the nose and mouth. But Lo Phat had no nose, only one eye, and half a jaw remaining.

"Was the car window down or up and shattered?" he asked.

"Down. No shattered glass beads in the body or in the cabin. He might have had a word with the assailant. Maybe known him. Stopped the car, rolled down the window."

"And faced a shotgun. Practically point-blank range. Even with the river current, the cabin will be sprayed with bone, blood, hair, brain, and shot," Gordon said. "How about Diedrich? Wonder why there wasn't there anything on him? He was in the back seat, no doubt."

"It all might've washed off in the lagoon or when the EMTs power washed the gunk off the body," Willis replied. "I would've found imbedded shot, too, but there wasn't any."

"Then he must have been removed from the car before the driver was popped," Gordon guessed. "Pulled out or forced to step out."

"Lee took some tire imprints over there, where it looks like the car was stopped and made dents in the dirt softened by all the rain," Willis said. "He took some other impression of tires, too, that looked about the same age."

"I'll ask him about it," Gordon said. "So, you think Diedrich stepped out of the car or was dragged out. Wonder if Lee got shoe prints or marks of a dragging heel?"

"Not good impressions, he told me. You'll have to ask him and see the photos. But the rain didn't wash away all the evidence this time," Willis said with a grin. "Lee found a Remington game shotgun shell casing down that-a-way. I bet if we compare it to the ones recovered at the trailer park—"

Gordon finished the line. "It'll be from Richie's shotgun."

"Even if he had cleaned up and took the casing, we could have identified the shot left in Mr. Lo Phat's face. Well, what's left of it."

Sheriff's deputy Lee Sherman stepped into their circle. "You talkin' 'bout this?" He dangled a sealed baggie with a spent shotgun shell casing. "Lead game load two-and-three-quarter inch for a twelve-gauge," he announced. "Easy to tell, even with the burns. I use them myself."

It would likely match Richie's gun and any leftover ammo used for geese and pheasant.

Sherman pointed to the roadside. "And I took photos of track imprints over there, where it looks like the car stopped and made dents in the dirt softened by all the rain. I took some other shots of tire track and tread nearby."

"So, you think there were two vehicles stopped here."

"Oh yeah."

"Only two?"

"Far as I can tell."

"Do you think Diedrich stopped here on his own, or was stopped by someone else?"

"No way to tell, really."

"Are you sure?"

"All I know for sure is that one of those tracks matches the tracks rolling down into the river, and it's Diedrich's car."

"When you send the photos to the state lab, could you cc me on those, too?"

"Will do."

"Why don't you show me where these tracks are."

"This way."

Sherman led Gordon to the gravelly shoulder where rain had washed away the stones and left muddy puddles and trails. The weedy grass and clay had been crushed into imprints in a couple of spots, long enough to recognize a pattern. A canopy of trees had prevented the tracks from being completely obliterated.

"Those there are Diedrich's," Sherman said.

"Looks like his driver pulled over. Are these the other tracks?"

"These two. They're wider. And angled in front of the car."

"Looks like someone in a bigger vehicle pulled him over," Gordon said. "Maybe forced him off the road and blocked him."

Gordon squat on his haunches and eyed them closely. The marks were flat but deeper, with ridges on the sides. Rain hadn't washed away the tread details. There weren't any to begin with. "It's a truck, a pickup, about five thousand pounds curb weight, and the tires were old. Owned by someone who didn't have the money to get new ones for a long time."

Richie, he breathed. *He kept the shotgun in the truck's gun rack.* Gordon arose and surveyed the shoulder. Any footprints had been muddied, flattened, and obscured by the downpours, and he didn't see a long rut to indicate a dragging heel. He checked the trees to see if there was any sign of a body being hung from a limb—a rut from a rope, stripped branches. Nothing. No pool of blood. Gears spun in his head: Even with all the rain, there might be traces of it. There? Nope. Just mud. He wasn't bled out here. He was taken somewhere else. A remote barn. A deer rendering cabin. Or the slaughterhouse, where there's already a chain and pulley system with hooks to hoist a heavy body and plenty of knives to choose from, then to clean and to sanitize, then replace in its proper rack, hidden in plain sight. *But why all the trouble? Just shoot him. Leave him in the car like the driver.* Some twisted sense of justice. And wouldn't there be dozens of witnesses in the slaughterhouse? Or was the layout of the place such that something like this could be out of sight?

"Okay, thanks a lot, Lee. Carry on."

"Sure thing, Flash." He plucked at his ear lobe. "Hey, uh— I'm sorry about, you know, about you and Stephie."

About what? Gordon stopped himself from asking. The separation? Or what's causing it, the infertility? Who *didn't* know, after Patrolman Davidson walking in on Stephie assuming the position? Or the big-mouthed receptionist at Dr. Fallon's calling out to the waiting room "Whose semen analysis is this?" and wiggling the collection cup where the label had fallen off and Gordon having to claim it in the view of all the small-town whisper-behind-their-knuckles ladies (including Mrs. Huddleston, his sophomore-year English teacher) whose noses jerked up from their magazines and now understood why he'd taken so long in the rest room, I mean, who *didn't* know about him and Stephie?

CHAPTER 17

"Stephie, turn that off."

Caitlin strode from the kitchen, flung the dish towel over her shoulder, snatched the remote control from the end table, and clicked off the TV.

Stephie blinked her bloodshot eyes. "He deserved it," she said.

"Don't say it too loud," Caitlin cautioned. "You're probably the chief suspect as it is, after what you said in that meeting."

"He still deserved it."

"No one will disagree with you, sweetie," Caitlin said, returning to the kitchen. "Not even Frank, who probably has to find the public servant who did this, haul his can off to jail, and call it justice."

"He wasn't there. At the press conference. Well, I didn't see him."

"Standing in the back, or already in the field," Caitlin said. "Like you say: always working. What was it you said once that he's married to the whole town?"

Stephie thought she'd only said *that* to Frank. She had told Caitlin that she didn't plan on ever having him home for supper because after ten years it was hit or miss so she ate cereal when he was on duty because it was easier to fix something for one person. She'd stopped calling to find out why he was late a few hours after she expected him and often got into a 415—an argument—about all the overtime he worked and hadn't put in for. Even on house errands, like going to the supermarket, he came home much later than expected because he saw someone who had an outstanding warrant stealing beer. Sometimes when he came home, he smelled of weed and told her not to touch his clothes because of something gross on them. He didn't explain, perhaps to protect her, she thought at first. But then he kept saying "It's not a big deal." Soon he stopped talking altogether. "I want to *do* it, not *talk* about it, okay?" Sometimes she'd listen to the scanner for company and to hear his voice now and then.

"I don't think I ever said that."

Well, like Frank once said: everyone lies. He had even stopped believing everything she told him.

"I need to go," she said. "I stayed too long. I'm really sorry."

"It's fine, sweetie. Anytime. You just needed a little space. Shawn did a drive-by this morning on his way to the office and the car's gone from the driveway. So, Frank's back at work, obviously, and the house is free. You'll be back at work soon, too. You must have things to get ready. This Monday, did you say?"

"Yeah. Monday." Monday-Tuesday-Wednesday used to be Frank's "weekend" and it caused her to lose track of the days. Monday, yes. It would be a welcome distraction. The three-and-four-year-olds were still too small to know that someone in their family had probably been arrested by Frank at some point for something or other.

For a moment, she considered going to her parents' farm, where they lived quietly in retirement while the hired help managed the business. But Mom and Dad didn't know about their separation, and so they might get the wrong impression about Frank; he wasn't abusive, just, well, absent, and the strain of their failure to "make a baby" was taking its toll. Frank had even lost interest—no, that wasn't quite it—lost the ability to rise to the occasion, as it were, from the fear of failure and the frustration that followed each failure, month after month. But she, too, felt that her body didn't work; she didn't feel like a woman; their attempts were becoming more futile, less hopeful, fewer between, and beginning to feel more like a chore. Speaking of chores, if she went home, Mom would ask too many questions about her and Frank trying to get pregnant, and Dad might set her to some chores—and she would have none of it after the last time, when her folks had gone away for a weekend vacation and the pregnant Hereford went into a difficult labor.

Stephanie had flung the barn doors open and hustled to fill the steel pail at the cement sink with water and Formalin anti-bacterial solution. Snatching the chains from a hook on the wall, she dropped them into the bucket and bolted through the door lugging the supplies, water sloshing. She fell to her knees on the firm ground behind the suffering cow, took a deep breath, and prepared to pull. The cow was not calving properly, and she needed to act fast to avoid losing her and the calf.

She hauled the chains out of the water and reached inside the writhing female. The beast let out a plea for help and a groan of protest as Stephie wrapped the chains around the struggling calf, trying urgently to free itself from the mother's womb. She hooked the chains to the infant's front legs, and then leaned back on her heels. She wrapped the chains around her wrists, gripped them, dug both her heels into the dirt, and after a huge breath, yanked with everything she had. She prayed fervently for a contraction to help.

The cow threw her head up into the air and landed back on the ground with a heavy thud. She bellowed, an agonizing cry that ripped Stephanie in half. Her muscles were as taut as the chains. The cow tensed, pushed, and delivered halfway. When Stephanie pulled, the cow tried to get to her feet, and the calf retreated to the womb. *No, no, no*, Stephie pleaded, *not that way.* It might cause internal bleeding. She pulled harder. Slipped and bumped to the dirt.

Oh, God, I wish there was someone here to help me.

She couldn't let go now and call Frank. He could come howling in the cruiser, lights blazing, but he might still be a good thirty to forty minutes' drive away, and besides, the phone was inside, and she couldn't stop now.

So, she tried again. Again. And again.

Deep breath. A bellow. Again.

Thirty minutes later, she relaxed her aching arms, sweaty, muddy, covered in manure and blood. *This isn't working,* she thought. She blinked away tears and perspiration. *This birth is a loss. A loss.*

The mother screamed. Stephanie jerked back to the moment. She pulled the chains to her chest, grimaced, and with her grunting, groaning effort, the baby calf slid out of the huge, helpless animal.

The cow lay still, exhausted.

The calf was limp and cold. It did not move. It looked lifeless. Stephanie patted the ground, looking, feeling for anything to invade the mouth and nose of the calf. She scrounged up a piece of straw and tickled the inside of the baby's nose while wiping out the mouth with her other hand. The cow awkwardly tried to stand up and assist with the newly-arrived miracle. But she was useless and slumped back to the ground. Stephanie continued to tickle the infant's nose when suddenly a sneeze that sounded like a trumpet trilled from the still body and shook it. The calf mewed. Stephanie shouted *"Halleluiah!"* The mother jumped to her feet.

Despite her excruciating strain, the cow turned about and looked at Stephanie with grateful eyes. Stephanie tried to smile. But she knew the worst part was coming. The mother was unaware that her new child would be taken away from her before the end of the night.

Stephanie robotically attended to milking the rest of the herd and prepared the little house-like structures filled with straw called hutches. She hosed herself off and daydreamed about having her own child: would she suffer as much as her cow? Would she regard her flesh-and-blood as adoringly? Will someone be there to help? *Was the cow afraid? Will I be?* The mystery of life, of bringing a new member into a family, surely brought wonder, but also fear: *What if I make a mistake as a mom? What if there's a problem? What if my child is stolen from me like how I'm going to take the cow's child?* How many times had she seen the tear-stained faces of fathers and mothers on the TV news begging for the return of a missing youngster? What if you could hear your child calling but you could not get to her? What if you could not protect her? Unthinkable. She swiped away the cobwebs of her daydreaming and reluctantly prepared for the final chore. The guilt of it crushed her.

She entered the corral to approach the waiting mother. Stephanie gripped a weapon, a two-foot-long steel bar, for her own protection. The mother cow, suspicious, turned hostile. She lowered her head in a challenge. Stephanie wished she could turn around and forget it. Could she ever forgive herself for this grave sin? How could she ever explain it to a cow?

In the pause, the mother turned to lick her prone calf tenderly until it was clean of all the dirt and dust from the last few hours. The calf attempted to stand up, wobbly. The thousand-pound mother, still with a wary eye on Stephanie, pushed her broad nose under the little belly and nudged the baby to her feet. Yes, it was a *her*. The baby girl slid back to the hard ground. The mother's big brown eyes filled with pride, wonder, affection.

It was now or never.

Choking back her regret, Stephanie strode resolutely to

the cow and raised the steel bar. The cow, chased backwards, chuffed and glared, confusion in the limpid eyes turning to anger and building to fury. *She wants to kill me. I want to give her the baby back. I can't.* Stephanie waved the steel bar menacingly again.

Once the mother had retreated to a safe distance, Stephanie bent down, expertly grasped the hundred-pound newborn, hefted her up, and carried her through the gate. She kicked the gateway shut behind them with the heel of her boot and listened for the latch to click. She took the calf to an empty hutch.

Completely spent, Stephanie plodded into the house and settled into a kitchen chair, laying her head on her crossed arms atop the table. She closed her burning eyes. It's a chore, she told herself. Had to be done. Saved the cow and her calf. Mom and Dad will be pleased with their daughter.

That's when she heard the anguished cries of the mother and daughter. She opened her eyes, stood, and pulled aside the kitchen window curtains. The mother, at the gate to the dairy cows, had spotted her baby in the hutch across the yard. The baby, unable to see the mother, responded to the sobs anyway. The mother desperately butted her massive head against the steel fence and screamed again. Back and forth, they mourned for each other.

Unable to stomach it, Stephanie ran to the car. Slid in, started the engine. Ignored the seatbelt. Punched the gas.

A quarter mile down the gravel road, she heard a final low of loss.

The next day, her parents returned with shocking news.

"We're selling the herd."

Stephie blinked at her father across the kitchen table twice, hard, in disbelief.

"Daddy, you—you can't mean it," she sputtered. "What will you and Mom do without the herd?"

"Don't you worry, punkin. We'll semi-retire. We'll invest the money and stay here." He tapped the sugar spoon against the cup rim. "It's been getting hard to take care of things ourselves, anyway. The Mason boys can manage the beans and the corn. Mom is going back to helping at the community college in their Learning Skills, Tutoring, and Testing Center, and I'll be at the feed and tractor supply store. Bo Michaelson promised me a spot last year once he heard that CAFO was coming. He knew what it did to small farmers over in Iowa."

"But this has been your life," Stephie protested. "*Our* life."

"If we don't do it this way, that life will be over for good, just like with the MacKenzies and the Dales. Diedrich's trucking and rendering fees broke their profitability and they took his offer to buy instead of falling into the bankruptcy he caused. Their kids weren't going to continue the farm, anyway."

"They could have fought," Stephie said, banging a fist on the table. The coffee cups rattled in their saucers.

Her father sighed. "Punkin, we all talked about it. But their lawyers made it clear: if we threatened to raise a stink about the hiked fees as a kind of racketeering to the State Ag Commission, Diedrich would sue us for defamation and the court costs would drive us all out of business. It was pay the fees or sell the farm or do what we're doing. We keep the house and the land. And our dignity."

"We can't let him do this to us."

"It's all right. We won't starve. We'll keep enough pigs for our own freezer. We won't do what Charlie Ketcham is doing: turn his farm into a tourist attraction."

"What's that mean? Hayrides and Pick Your Own?"

"Not quite. Almost. It's the darndest thing. He's selling people what he calls 'a pork experience'. The customers show up by appointment and butcher a pig they buy, which gives him free labor. They bring coveralls, rubber boots, and a cooler for their meat. 'Course, they bring their phones for taking souvenir photos. He shoots it, rolls it over and sticks it, and the customer helps to drag it to a hoist. After the customers watch an instructional video, they skin it and cut it up into primary pieces. Then they see another video, get a table and gloves, and then cut the primaries into chops and such at $3.00 a pound, liveweight. Because they buy the pig, it's their property, and the USDA stays out of it."

"That's slaughter for entertainment," Stephie said with a disapproving head shake.

"No, punkin," her father said. "That's survival."

There was another word for the whole situation:

Injustice.

CHAPTER 18

ON THE WAY THROUGH TOWN, Gordon beeped at old friends, honked at parents of old friends driving by, and waved to Mike Castillo, an old high school classmate staggering on the sidewalk. He clasped a paper bag with the top twisted around a wine bottleneck. Gordon slowed down and clicked on the PA. "Hey, Mikey! Don't be stupid! Go home, man!" Mike flipped him off. Poor Mike, who once ran a decent twelve second hundred-meter sprint, didn't have a steady job since the car accident five years ago that gave him seizures and that wobbly walk. The wine didn't help. Arresting him for public drunkenness—again—wouldn't help much, either. Let him be.

Gordon passed the Thirsty Horse Tavern and turned onto Route 251. Funny how he was observant about people on the street but hadn't a clue about Stephie. Sure, she was unhappy about the fertility thing and frustrated with how nothing seemed to work: the hormone shots, the pills for ovulation induction, the intrauterine insemination.

Why not in vitro? he had asked. Stephie had snapped, *No way. Producing multiple eggs and embryos might work for Diedrich's farrowing operation, but I'm not a sow.* Is that when it crossed a line? When she thought he might be open to surgically removing her eggs and fertilizing them in a whitecoat lab from which one is chosen and the others are frozen or discarded like a cracked egg from the supermarket?

What made such a lab different from a CAFO? The main difference, it turns out, is that a CAFO is more successful. All of their inseminations work. Breeding is their business. In the human IVF labs, half of the eggs survived. A third of those were fertilized. Only twenty percent of the fertilized embryos, the blastocysts, made it to day five. Two-thirds of the remaining ones perished. And from whatever embryos remained, only one or two were chosen for implantation. Which one? Which two? Who made that decision? Who got to play God?

He drove into the gravelly circle of the trailer park. The single-wide where Richie died was boarded up with scrap plywood and a shredded banner of yellow crime scene tape fluttered from a nail. So, where was Krystyl?

She could be inside. People lived in boarded up trailers and ramshackle shacks all the time. But she probably would not, given the gruesome memory and the stain on the carpet. Gordon stepped out, chirped his car's lock and checked the crudely repaired door.

A woman called from the trailer next door. "You looking for Krystyl?" It was the red-haired sister, Lucy, who had taken the baby. "She ain't there."

"Can you tell me where she went?"

"She under arrest or somethin'? She said she was let go."

"I just have some questions. Routine."

"Ain't nuttin' routine 'round here no more."

"Did she take the truck?"

"Richie's truck? Heck, no," Lucy said. "Your cop buddies took it not a half an hour ago."

"So, how'd she get anywhere, especially with a baby?" *Seeing as how the River Falls subway system doesn't have a line all the way out here.*

"Buck come and got her."

"Buck?"

"Buck Carter."

"Rod Carter's boy?"

"The same."

"Didn't know they were friends."

Lucy laughed. "Neither did Richie. They been—well, seein' each other a long time. If you catch my drift."

—␣␣—

Buck Carter's fishing cabin balanced uneasily on stilts, a house-that-Jack-built using salvaged planks from his father's old barn and, allegedly, frames and timbers stolen from local construction sites. A rickety pier jutted into the Sinnissippi River like a long tongue lapping at the water. It was luckily upstream from the CAFO spill and didn't smell like a cesspool. A rowboat moored there, nodding in the wake. The roof sagged where moss had curled the tar paper and shingles; a tangle of honeysuckle vines clutched at the mildewed gutters. A scold of blue jays, hearing Gordon's footfalls on the rutted gravel driveway, complained in a bark-stripped ash tree cursively etched by emerald ash borer beetles. Under a corrugated steel-roofed carport sat a Nissan Frontier truck. It was too small, and the tread showed too clearly to have made those tracks.

Gordon stooped under the rusty carport and rapped on the aluminum storm door. Stepped to the side.

A radio inside snapped off, "Gusty winds expected ahead of the storm front that will—"

"Who's there?" Man's voice. Unhappy.

"River Falls Police. Looking for Krystyl Valera."

"No one by that name here."

"Shut up, Buck," a woman said.

The door swung open. Krystyl brushed her hair back. Plucked a Doral One Hundred from her lips and blew out the smoke from the side of her mouth. "The name's not Valera."

"Forgot," Gordon said. "You and Richie weren't married, huh?"

"We wasn't even together," she said. "So, what do you want? They let me go. They said, like, I had no choice but to stick him."

"I know that."

"So why are you here? Did you find something in the truck?"

"Am I supposed to find something?"

"I dunno. Why else would you guys take it?"

"The truck won't tell us where it's been," Gordon said. "I thought maybe you could."

"How should I know that?"

"Let me put it another way," Gordon redirected. "We'd like to know where Richie was and when from last Wednesday into Thursday morning when you had your altercation. Since you two were close, we thought maybe you would know."

"He was at work, of course," Krystyl said. "Ten hour shifts every day and sometimes a couple more if the line got slowed down. And he was sure out and doing drugs in between. Remember how amped up he was?"

"Okay, but where?"

"Wherever he was getting it from, I guess."

"Did he get it at work?"

Buck spoke up. "That's likely. It's all over the kill floor."

"You mean the slaughterhouse?"

"Yeah. So, you, uh, wanna come on in? You're letting in all the bugs." He smacked one on his arm below the barbed wire tattoo.

Gordon leaned forward for as much reconnaissance as he could get for personal safety before stepping into the confines of the linoleum-floored kitchenette. Checkered curtains filtered the amber light falling on the chipped

Formica-veneered table where a can of Budweiser and a glass ash tray full of crushed-out butts sat. The place smelled like the Capital Tap Room at 2:00 a.m., where Buck liked to pick fights.

"How's the baby?" Gordon asked.

"The baby?"

"Your baby." *Thirty inches tall, about twenty-four pounds, brown curly hair, leaks from the eyes, last seen wearing diaper.*

"It's with my mom," Krystyl said. "She gets grandma time; I get a break."

"Close by?"

"Joslin Corners," she said, taking a deep draw and spewing it up at the stained popcorn ceiling. "Say, why would you need to know about where Richie was, anyway? What other trouble was he in?"

"Ain't it obvious?" Buck said as he plopped into the vinyl couch with the beer can. The cushion's rips yawned open with his weight where the duct tape failed. "The time you're talkin' 'bout is when Old Man Diedrich got popped."

"Geeze Louise," Krystyl said with a whistle. "You guys think Richie done it?"

Gordon shrugged. "We're just following all leads," he said evenly. "Was he with you at all that day and night? Between his shift ending at two o'clock and the time when I showed up?"

"Nope. Didn't call or text, neither."

"Was that unusual?"

"Nah. He'd disappear on binges all the time."

"Where did he sleep?"

"In the truck. Sometimes at the *Espiritos* house. You know, those whackos that sacrifice pigs and such." She pulled on the cigarette again, blew out the smoke through her nose, and then leaned across the table to tap ash into the tray. "Come to think of it, he musta been there Wednesday for one of their seances or whatever they call 'em. And you know what?" she added, pointing at Gordon with the smoldering butt. "That's prob'ly why he wanted the baby so bad. To sell it to them for a sacrifice. I betcha his so-called warrior spirit told him to."

"Did he tell you that?"

"Not in so many words. But he needed money for speed. He'd sell the baby for it. Heck and high water, I wouldn't put it past him."

Buck laughed explosively, and Bud sprayed from his nose. He swore and sputtered, wiped his nose on his sleeve and said, "Sorry. Sorry, but that's too much, even for Richie."

"You know he didn't want the baby in the first place," Krystyl said, eyes narrowed. "He told me to get an abortion. I didn't, so he sure as shinolah wasn't gonna get it to sell for drug money."

"You sure 'bout that?" Buck asked.

"Did you know him well?" Gordon asked.

"Well enough," Buck said. "For a while we had the same early shift at the plant, but I been moved to second."

"You a sticker like him?"

"Oh, heck no," Buck said, crossing his hands, palms forward. "That there's real dirty work. It's hid from everyone else by a curtain. I'm on the other side. A stunner."

"What's the difference?"

Buck sat up straighter. "I make it humane. Quick. One zap from the two prongs behind the ears and it's over. Four-hunnert-fifty volts and whammo, they're out cold. Ya better be in rubber boots, or you'll get shocked bad, too. But I haven't killed it. I'm no killer. They're hung up right away, and the conveyor takes the product to the kill floor where, in just fifteen seconds, they're stuck twice and bled out."

"What happens if the zap doesn't work?"

I stick 'em even when the stunner screws up, Richie had said.

"Stunner's supposed to stun the heart, but there's never

any time," Buck said. "I mean, I *could*, cuz the stunner don't need no cord, but ya gotta do the next one real quick and not chase after the other one. So, the sticker sticks 'em anyway. Sometimes Richie used the gun."

"He shot them?"

"Not that kind—" with a gesture to Gordon's sidearm "—he used whatcha call a captive bolt gun. A cartridge blows a bolt into the brain, and it retracts back in the barrel to do it again. I never liked using it."

"Why not?"

"Pig skulls are thick, man. It don't work as well as the 'lectric wand. It's hard to find the right spot, 'specially if they thrash around. It might take a couple tries."

"Buck, stop it," Krystyl scowled.

"Plus, cleanin' it's a pain. And even with all the noise in there, you can still hear the skull crack."

Krystyl grimaced. "Are we done here?"

Buck tipped the can high and drained it. Self-medicating. How else do you deal with death all day? He crushed the empty can in his fist. It sounded like a skull cracking.

"Yes, I'm done," Gordon said to Krystyl, "except to say no one has claimed Richie yet or made arrangements."

"Don't look at me," Krystyl said. "We wasn't married."

"The Illinois Department of Human Services will fund a burial for those who can't afford it—"

"I'm not kin. And he can rot there for all I care."

Gordon pinched his lips to prevent a comment from slipping out. "Does he have family?"

"Sure," she laughed. "The other stickers at the plant."

Gordon reached into his shirt pocket. "All right. If you think of something else about Richie's whereabouts during that time I mentioned, please call me." He snapped a business card on the table.

"Don't call us, we'll call you?" Buck joked.

Krystyl held open the storm door with a *shut up, Buck* look on her face. "You have a blessed day, officer," she said.

Gordon stepped down to the spider-veined driveway. He glanced inside the truck's cab. Tapped the window. "You realize that Illinois law requires children who are younger than two years old and under forty pounds to be properly secured in a rear-facing harness system. I don't see one."

"Momma took it."

"Okay. Makes sense."

But it didn't.

He returned to his car wondering if Momma had taken everything else along with the car seat: the baby bag with wipes and diapers, the floor seat with a tray, swing seat, teething rings, pacifiers and bottles, stacking cups, and plastic donut rings. The cabin had nothing that said "infant." Maybe it was all in the trailer.

He was thinking that he might not ever see those items around in his own house either when his cell phone trilled.

It was Anderson.

"The lab guys are finished with Richie's truck," he reported.

"Is there an infant seat in it?" Gordon blurted.

"A what?"

"Never mind. Go ahead."

"All right, well, first of all, the treads—what's left of them—match the tracks at the scene. The dirt splattered on the chassis and wheel wells match the clay and dirt at the scene. There's a mean dent and a deep scratch behind it on the right front fender. I called to ask about the Lincoln. The left door has a heckuva dent and there are traces of red paint on it matching Richie's truck."

"So, we were right about that."

"Listen. What was *inside* is what's even more interesting. A tie clip with a diamond chip was in the glove box."

"Diedrich wore one at the town meeting. Gotta be his."

"I doubt Richie ever wore a tie. Then there was the knife from Jo-Jo's, with dried blood on it. I'll send it to the state lab for analysis. A box of shotgun shells, Lead Game Load two-and-three-quarter inch for a twelve-gauge, just like the spent ones found at the scene and the trailer. Matches the shot in that driver's face. And a weird gun."

"Weird?"

"Looks like a hand drill. It's a captive bolt stun gun, the kind used in the slaughterhouse. I'd say the bolt diameter matches the wounds on Diedrich's skull. Was Richie a stunner or a sticker? I thought he was a sticker."

"Yeah, a sticker," Gordon said. "But a stunner who worked with Richie told me today that sometimes Richie used a gun like that to finish off a stunning job that didn't work."

"Well, I think you should see it before I send it off to the state lab. And you ought to see the photos of the truck. Can you meet me at the rest stop between Exits 4 and 6 of the toll road in about fifteen minutes? You're not far from there, right?"

"All right."

"So," Anderson said, "everything says Richie."

"Yup."

"Easy."

Too easy, Gordon thought.

CHAPTER 19

PAUL PEMBROKE SWIGGED a Mountain Dew and tapped his laptop screen to life. Did they assign him the tip line monitoring because he was "The Kid"? Sometimes Frank Gordon acted as though he was his father. Maybe it was hard to be taken seriously if you didn't have to shave twice a day. Even at the Academy, he was called "Baby Face" until Hell Week when his Tai Kwon Do classes as a kid kicked in and he applied the wrist turnout, gooseneck lock, and straight arm bar lock with such agility his partners smarted for days. No one teased him then about still liking to play Fortnite.

He keyed in the password and up came the feed. As expected, many people used the line to anonymously complain about stray dogs, a noisy neighbor's crying newborn, or a teenager's garage band. At least the operators at Crimestoppers got to talk to people and take down names for the offered reward. He settled into the unglamorous job of sifting through the insults and suggestive comments.

> It was Sasquatch. He been out because of the rains and he mad.
> It's the Chinee. There trying a poison they wanted to put in the meat
> Why do you all want to find out, anyway? Mister Diedrich had it coming.
> It's because of him that we're all flooded in poo. Good riddance.

I would of done it myself but someone beat me
to it!
Don't waste my tax dollars on this dam wild
goose chase.
I seen Mexican workers spit on the company
sign with his name on it. Shouldn't have these
illegals here in the first place.
Glad he's dead. Now go back on patroll
Nothing like a man in uniform. For a good time,
click reply.
Everyone knows Richie done it.

That was the most interesting one.

They hadn't released that name to anyone yet.

Still, it wasn't as if they hadn't considered it.

The identity of the sender might be more relevant than the sender identifying Richie as the perp.

Too bad the comment was truly anonymous and untraceable through the third party that scrubbed all the identifiers.

McWhorter, the desk sergeant, called him on Line One. "Hey, Paulie. Visitor up front for you."

"Oh, great. Is it who I think it is?"

"Yup. Cute little tank top, cut off dungaree britches tighter than my compression socks, and a plate of peanut butter cookies."

CHAPTER 20

STEPHANIE RETURNED TO THE HOUSE, assured after a drive-by that Frank wasn't still there. She felt too upset for lunch. Maybe just a beer. No, too early. Even for a light? Yes, even for a light. She poured "fuzzy water" instead and remembered to turn her phone back on. She'd silenced it at Caitlin's, in no mood to talk to Frank.

Of course, she'd missed an important message. Happens every time. Mark Warren, the go-get-em thumbs-in-the-lapels Chicago lawyer advising the No CAFO group, left a voicemail:

Hey, Stephie. It's Mark. By now you heard that Mr. Diedrich met his unhappy end. With that, it's a good idea we discuss the next move, don't you think? How about we meet at the same restaurant as last time? It's just convenient to the interstate. I won't be staying overnight this time. Call me.

She floated a finger over *reply* before deciding to text him instead. The less talk, the better. That captive hug at the restaurant, the time he seized her hand before raising a glass in a toast, the walk into the hotel lobby and the crooning invitation upstairs for a nightcap ("There are ready-made Bloody Marys in the room fridge") gave her pause. Still, with the Diedrich death, the game had changed.

She had to see him again and give him what he wanted.

CHAPTER 21

"SORRY, FRANCIS, I already sent that bolt gun to the state lab."

Anderson's smirk through the opposite open car window disquieted Gordon. "But you said—"

"Here are the photos I thought you should see."

Anderson, wearing a blue nitrile glove, held up the first eight-by-ten in a clear three-ring-binder folder.

It wasn't the truck.

There was Stephanie in a head-to-shoulder embrace of a man in a pricey sports jacket. She was on tiptoe with one foot and the other kicked up behind her.

Anderson flipped it over. The two at a window booth, the man's left hand resting atop Stephanie's as they raised glasses of wine.

Withdrew it. Produced a third. The man holding open the front glass door of the TripleTree Gardens Hotel as Stephanie passed through with a tilted glance at him.

Gordon's heart leaped to his throat. "What—what is this?"

"Well, I can tell you what it *looks* like," Anderson said, withdrawing the photo into his cab. "And it's not good."

"Who is that?"

"It's a slick lawyer from Chicago. Schaumberg, to be exact, named Mark Warren. Divorced, two kids, working with your wife. I mean to say, working with your wife's activist group."

"Why are you doing surveillance on Stephie?"

"Well, first off, *he's* trouble. It's good to keep an eye on him. He gets people riled up. Like at the town hall. And second, after what your wife said at the town hall, she was a person of interest."

"Maybe they're just—just discussing legal business."

"Til two in the morning? I wonder."

"You've got no right—"

"I got every right to check a suspect's alibi, *Detective*," Anderson said. "The good news is that the photos establish an alibi for her whereabouts on the night of the murder."

Gordon felt the top of his head might blow off. "Why didn't you bring this up in the war room?"

"So as not to embarrass you, Francis. But you know, if these photos got out, people may get the wrong ideas."

"You wouldn't," Gordon said, indignant. "They're—they're evidence."

"If that's what you want to call it," Anderson said. "But evidence of what? What's a normal person gonna think? The worst."

"Who else has seen these?"

"Just us. As a favor to you," Anderson said. "I'll keep them in a separate file and be rid of them when I get proper consideration at the solve."

"You want to receive all the credit when there's a solve announced?"

"Oh, now, now, Francis. Why should I take *all* the credit?"

To boost your election campaign. "This is blackmail."

"This is teamwork," Anderson said. "It must feel good to know your wife isn't— suspected—anymore. And I'll be in touch about the truck."

Anderson *whirred* up the window and sped off.

Gordon sat quietly. His eyes ached. His belly ached. His chest was pressed in a vise of uncertainty. This wasn't just Anderson's way of getting even about releasing Tyler. This was more serious. A heat rose slowly in his head, a demon of suspicion wanting him to believe what was worst. There were the photos. Could they lie? But what truth did they reveal? He resolved to go on loving Stephie, even if the not-knowing felt unbearable. Just business. Til 2:00a.m.? Why had she hesitated when asked *"Is there someone else?"*

"*It's you*," she had said. What was that called? Projection? Deflection? Or did it mean yes, there is, and yes, it's *because* of you.

CHAPTER 22

ON TV, COP WORK IS FULL OF ACTION. High-speed chases. Shoot outs. Roughing up a gang banger on the street. Bar fights. Building searches. *Clear!* Surveillance that sees something suspicious right away. Running through back yards and ducking clotheslines, gun drawn. Dramatic table-pounding interviews in the block. And sure, you see cops on the phones. But no one tells you that working the phone is most of the job.

Oh, and typing. Lots of typing.

It's not sexy.

Gordon sipped his decaffeinated mud before picking up the corded landline blinking at him. He tucked the receiver into his neck to keep his hands free. Who had these phones anymore except cops and old ladies? The caller ID told him it was Anderson.

Gordon's stomach cramped. He still had to work with the man. He flipped open his phone log to jot notes of his calls with a mechanical pencil. He could always check the transcripts later. 911 calls were recorded and kept as public records, and in a small-town station like this, two lines: line one at the front desk and the detective desk. There was no customer-service robotic voice declaring *Your call will be recorded or monitored for quality assurance,* but a beep sounded every twenty seconds to indicate it. If Illinois ever became a single consent state, that would be helpfully unnecessary.

He punched the button.

"Gordon here. Go ahead, Deputy."

"Hey, Francis. How the heck are you?"

"How do you think?" Gordon snapped.

"Good, good. Say, we're returning the truck to Krystyl Spinney. I'll email you the report."

"Spinney? Okay, that's her real name, huh? She reminded me that Valera wasn't her name."

"So, you saw her today?"

"Yeah. I went to the trailer first, but it looked abandoned. All boarded up. Her sister told me she was at Buck Carter's fishing shack."

"One loser for another. But look, I'm legally bound to return it where I picked it up. Maybe Buck can drive her back there. If he doesn't get busted on the way for DUI."

"Yeah, he was already drinking when I was there."

"Say, just curious—why'd you ask about a baby seat?"

"The baby wasn't with Krystyl. She said it was with her mom in Joslin Corners."

"Madeleine Spinney. Sure. I arrested her once for speeding. She was late for her shift at the chicken plant there. Still works there, far as I know. How would she have time to look after a kid?"

"Vacation time? Medical leave?" Gordon liked this less and less.

"Not likely. I dunno. Funny how it runs in the family."

"What? Speeding?"

"Nah. I mean, Krystyl works at the Diedrich shop."

"No kidding? Doing what?"

"Maintenance. Janitor stuff. Oh, man. Can you imagine the mess in there? At least that's what she said for the intake. So, about the truck—" Anderson was ready to move on.

"Whoa, whoa. Maintenance? What shift?"

"Didn't say. Didn't ask. Why would I at the time? Diedrich

was found later in the day, after the intake. She wasn't in custody for questioning regarding that."

"Maybe we need to pick her up again."

"You'll need probable cause. You think she saw something?"

"Maybe. Janitors have keys. She'd have access to the building even between shifts."

"Really? If she saw something, don't you think she would have told you before?"

Gordon shook his head, even though Anderson couldn't see him. "Not if she had something to hide."

"C'mon, Frank. Are you saying that puny thing dragged Diedrich's dead weight into the kill room, shackled and hung him up, and then stuck him? And no one saw it?

"She's not puny. She's got muscles, from lifting buckets and hoses, I guess."

"She's still short."

"Maybe she just unlocked the door so the killer or killers could do it."

"She hated Richie. She wouldn't have helped him." Anderson seemed set in this decision.

"I'm just saying that since we canvassed all the shift workers, we need to question her about it, too."

"Have at it. Go talk to her again. And tell her the truck is waiting for her at the trailer."

Gordon hung up. There was no use in trying to get Anderson to keep helping him right now when he wanted to be doing anything else. When he was done playing call center, he'd swing by and let Krystyl and Buck know. And ask her about her shift at the plant. But he still had a few more calls to make.

He called Jerry Davis for the slaughterhouse canvas report.

"Hey, Jerry. Any news from your canvasing?"

"Sorry, Frank. The second shift workers didn't see anything unusual. They left at the usual time to clear for the cleaning crew."

"The cleaning crew?" Gordon wanted to make sure he'd heard that right.

"Yeah, there's a power-washing and sanitizing crew that comes in when they leave. They call it the third shift, but isn't really. I'd call it the graveyard shift."

"Cute. Okay, so that would be around—hmmm—"

"Second shift is out by 1:00 a.m., so I'd say one-thirty in the morning, thereabouts. They're gone by the first shift, which starts at 4:30 a.m."

"Who's on that crew?"

"I'll find out and call you back. Say, Frank, you ever been in that place?"

"Nope."

"Good grief, the smell. Somehow, I didn't blow my lunch. They warned me before I went in, twice, but nothin' prepares you for the blood. Worse than that semi-accident on Route 251 two years ago, remember, when the roof was sheared off of that compact with the four teenagers—"

"I remember. Get the names of the cleaning crew, okay?"

"Roger."

Gordon hung up.

Was Krystyl on that crew? Or was she a day-janitor in the offices, emptying waste baskets, cleaning sinks and toilets, wiping lunchroom counters, and swabbing floors? How many on that crew?

McWhorter, working the front desk, poked his head in. "Lou Willis called, asked for a callback."

The coroner answered on the first ring.

"Hey, Frank. I'm done with the prelim report on the driver."

"Lo Phat."

"Right. The Chinese came to ID him. Even though he had half a face, they knew it was Xi Lo Phan. I think I pronounced that right. *Shee Low Fan.* He was an intern with them, a grad student at the U of I in swine genetics and insemination."

Gordon almost laughed. "Pigs in love, huh?"

"No, it's quite fascinating, really. With shoulder-length gloves and a spiral tip catheter—"

"Spare me, Lou. Anything I need to know?"

"Point blank range. I'm betting ballistics will match the pellets to Richie's favorite brand. If we had bullets, we could match to the gun more easily. But—"

"No such luck."

"The Chinese claimed the remains; they'll cremate and ship them back to Shanghai. They were pretty adamant about solving the case before they put Lo Phat—I mean, Lo Phan—in the mail. Oh, Chelsea Diedrich was with them."

"Funny how she came for the driver but not her dad. Bet she translates for them."

"Yeah, she did. It seems she was the backup to Lo Phan, who was an excellent English speaker."

Gordon thought for a moment. "Did she ask to see her dad?"

"Nope. I asked. She declined. Her lawyer had already finalized details on a private interment next week. It all had been pre-arranged and paid for in advance."

"Speaking of payment, it makes me think. Maybe she paid Richie to do it, or the Chinese did, or both, because the talks were stalled or difficult—Diedrich could be a bully about such things—and they believed they'd get better terms with the kids in charge. I'll check his accounts."

"You probably need to call the DA to set it up. I'd call the local banks and credit unions first, though. I'm guessing that folks like Richie don't even *have* bank accounts."

CHAPTER 23

XI LO PHAN'S DORMITORY ROOM in the Bao Shan District of Shanghai, just blocks from the Bioinformatics and Immunophysiology Lab, had felt just as confined as the university's hog facility pens where a virulent flu had decimated the herd and thousands of carcasses were thrown into the Huangpu River by night. That's when the doctoral candidate was chosen for a research fellowship in the University of Illinois' Applied Swine Science Program.

A lifelong urbanite—although both grandfathers had been swineherds in the Guangdong Province countryside— Lo Phan had never seen wide open spaces except for the endless Pacific. He missed most of the expanse of the U.S. at thirty-five-thousand feet, and there was little to see in the sleepy hop from O'Hare to Willard near Champaign-Urbana.

It was only when the International Student Friends Committee offered campus and country tours that beyond I-74 and a few minutes' drive down West Cardinal Road he saw the full arc of the planet's horizon, alive with wave upon ocean wave of emerald corn and the silver glint of grain elevators. The host driver, an MBA student taking a Chinese language class, was politely asking him about his family in passable Mandarin, but his minders had ordered him to say little so that no one could trace him to the People's Security Bureau which was counting on his patriotism and filial piety to transmit his adviser's data on the Swine Genome Project.

Instead, he stared at kilometer after kilometer of fruitful stalks, field after fertile field, rolling, rolling, and he covered his face with both palms to conceal the tears.

"Lo Phan," the driver said, alarmed, "are you feeling well? Are you ill?"

"No—no," he stammered, and then gathered himself.

"What is wrong?"

"No—no one will ever starve here."

Chelsea Diedrich decided not to tell him that most of the corn was earmarked for livestock feed and ethanol.

CHAPTER 24

DORIS WEAVER AT SINNISSIPPI BANK AND TRUST came on the phone line to answer Gordon's question about Richie's accounts.

"We can't give that information. Don't bother calling anyone else, Flash. They'll tell you the same thing. You'll have to call the DA. Based on an affidavit of probable cause, his office would issue a subpoena. But a search warrant for bank statements, or any other financial records, I should add, is subject to many additional requirements because bank and financial records are protected by federal law, namely, The Right to Financial Privacy Act of 1978. Under that law, federal prosecutors have to notify the person affected by the search warrant that their records were obtained."

Gordon sat through the legal speech and took a deep breath before saying, "The person affected is dead."

"Oh." Weaver recovered. "That's different. So that would probably be an inactive account."

"You're telling me."

"If there's no POD, a 'payable on death' beneficiary named, and no debts to be paid, then the bank turns the account over to the state. It's called 'escheating' an account, where a bank will turn over the funds from that inactive account to the state treasury. Once the account is sent to the state, the funds are held as unclaimed property. So, you could call the state treasury and ask if they have received it."

"Okay, but what if there is a POD beneficiary? Or if it was a joint account?"

"Well, you're back to what I said before. Call the DA—"

"I got it. If it's at the state treasury, could they tell me if there was recent activity in the account? Like a large deposit?"

Weaver sounded bored. "No, just the final amount."

"An exact round figure, say, ten grand or twenty-five grand, would imply a payment. Don't you think?"

Weaver considered this. "Not really. Could be a lottery payout. But it wouldn't be an even number after taxes, come to think of it. Can I be honest with you, Flash? People who are—let's say, economically challenged—don't have savings accounts and investments. Like I just said, they roll up cash in plastic bags and stuff them into the cinderblocks or play the lottery. Haven't you noticed at QuikStop or Value Mart? They'll buy smokes or tins of Skoal, in cash, on payday, and if anything is left over, they'll get a Powerball ticket or a scratch-off like Pick Three. I call it a tax on the poor. They don't use banks and credit unions; they use title loan companies and pawn shops. It's a different economy. A lot of it's a barter economy. Services are paid in sides of ham or bales of hay. Or weed. I get that you're trying to follow a money trail, but— you follow what I'm trying to say?"

"There might be money involved but no trail."

And their concept of a safety deposit box would be a shoebox under the bed.

"Thanks Doris." He hung up.

He turned to the computer and checked the DMV and arrest records for Madeline Spinney's violations in order to get a last-known address. There it was. He'd visit there, too, to verify she had the kid.

The email notification pinged. It was from Davis, sending the HR/receptionist visitor list and the CAFO Shipping and Receiving vehicle log Gordon had asked for. He replied *THX* and printed the visitor list to review later. Then he scrolled down the vehicle list, right hand on the mouse, left hand index finger tracing the list down on the screen as though it made the lettering clearer. Livestock transports, more livestock transports, still more, a vet, feed delivery, and last on the list, at 4:00 a.m., was the Sanitation Unit.

Driver: K.S.

Krystyl Spinney.

CHAPTER 25

BAM BAM. GORDON SLAMMED HIS FIST against the door.

"Krystyl Spinney? Open up. River Falls Police."

Odds were, Gordon deduced, she wasn't in the cabin. The truck was gone. The radio was off. Buck didn't answer the door or call out *buzz off* or something worse. No, they must have been notified about the truck and gone to the trailer park to retrieve it. Or grandma time was over, and she'd gone to fetch the kid. Or both. Either way, she'd end up at Grandma's. So, he would go directly there.

Joplin's Corners was exactly that, an asphalted four-corners intersection in the middle of Flatland with Teddy's Discount Tires, a Casey's General Store (hawking a Hawaiian pizza special), an undulating corn field with a ruffled collar of St. Anne's Lace, and a chain-link-fenced Memorial Garden where a granite obelisk and a twelve-pounder "Napoleon" Civil War cannon marked the resting place of Robert Daniel Joplin himself, a twenty-three-year-old married farmer who joined the 37th Illinois Infantry Regiment in August 1862, according to the wind-worn inscription on the marker. The 37th spent so much time pursuing and fighting guerilla forces in Missouri that its soldiers were dubbed the Illinois Greyhounds. Eventually, the 37th was sent to the Siege of Vicksburg, a critical campaign that decided whether the North or the South controlled the Mississippi River. Pvt. Joplin died there in September 1863—not of battle wounds but of scarlet fever. After the war, his widow had him exhumed and shipped home for reburial here, across the road from the family farm, and the town was renamed in his honor. Smaller stones nearby remembered other men who served in Mercer, Rock Island, and Sinnissippi County units but were buried in the battlefields of Murfreesboro and Chattanooga. Their descendants still lived in these farmhouses, clapboard ranches, and tin-roofed trailers, tilling the same land, raising the same breed of chickens, and fixing cars instead of carriages.

Madeleine Spinney likely descended from such a line. Her brown brick hovel cringed in the shadows of three cobalt blue Harvestore silos; a gravel driveway spit from a tumble-down porch strung with Christmas lights and decorated in junk: stacked flowerpots, rusted folding chairs, old tires, and trash bags. A barbed-wire fence separated it from the pasture next door; the heat advisory from earlier in the day had probably compelled the farmer to move his cattle inside the barn.

No sign of Richie's truck.

But a Chevy beater suggested Madeleine was in.

The door knock was answered by a staccato barking of an ankle biter and the cries of "Chester! Be quiet! Chester! Come here!"

The Venetian blinds in the front window split open a moment, then closed. The front door clicked and a sixty-ish woman in a sleeveless floral print blouse and turquoise shorts peered through the opening. A miniature fox terrier with bandit mask coloring wriggled in the crook of her arm. The woman's heavily mascaraed eyes squinted from below a bottle blonde fringe, and the heavily rouged cheeks made her look like a cadaver in search of a wake.

"Help you?" she said.

"Madeleine Spinney?"

"What do you want?"

"Ma'am, I'm looking for your daughter, Krystyl. Is she here?"

"No." The dog growled and yipped once. "That's enough out of you," Spinney scolded with a little shake.

"Has she been here recently?" Gordon pressed.

"Why would she be?"

"For the baby."

"The baby?"

"Her baby."

"Krystyl had a baby?"

"You didn't know?"

Spinney laughed hoarsely. It was the rasp of someone who snored all night from drinking too much. "A baby. That's too much."

"She never called you, or ..."

"We haven't talked in years. She run off when her daddy did. She don't tell me nuthin."

"So, you didn't babysit the child recently."

"Oh, heck, no. This here is the only baby in the house," she said, rubbing her pinked nose in the terrier's ear. "Aren't you, angel?"

"How about Lucy? Do you hear from her?"

"Lucy who?"

"Her sister. Your other daughter?"

"Krystyl's my only. Well, I got me two in heaven, as I like to say."

"Krystyl calls Lucy her sister. She lives in the place next door to her."

"Don't know no Lucy. No probability, she means her sister-in-crime." A wheezy laugh. "If you catch my drift."

Gordon produced his card. "If you hear from Krystyl, please call me."

She one-eyed it like it was a three-dollar bill. "So, what is it? Boy or girl?"

"A boy, ma'am."

"Name?"

He had to think a second. "Cody, ma'am."

"Who's the daddy?"

"Fellow she was living with named Richie Valera."

"Never heard of him. You sure it was him?"

"I'm not *exactly* sure—"

"I bet she ain't sure, either."

CHAPTER 26

"I'm really sorry, Frank, but if no one has reported a child missing, there's no justification for a court-ordered deadline to produce the child." Lieutenant Simms waved his eyeglass frames as though trying to hit no-see-ums.

"I'm reporting it."

"You don't count. It must be a person with standing. And I don't see what this has to do with the Diedrich case, either," he added. "We're forty-eight hours out already, and I don't want us wasting time on a minor distraction."

"A distraction?" Gordon gruffed. "Suspicion of child endangerment is no distraction if there's a—"

"You're right, Frank, that's exactly what it is, suspicion. That's all it is. A hunch. A funny feeling. There's been no complaint. And gee—who would have thought—a single mom with a drug history in a trailer. Get DCFS on it, if you want to. Look, I need a solve on the Diedrich case. Representative Harmon is coming here tomorrow morning with his pal Commissioner Sellers in tow for an update— after church, of course—and I'm not telling them my lead investigator is spending time and tax dollars chasing a deadbeat mom instead of evidence for a capital murder case."

"All we have is circumstantial evidence that Richie—"

Simms slammed his palm on the desk. "Maybe they didn't teach you about *circumstantial evidence* at the community college, Frank. It's typically enough to convict a defendant if the evidence and the inferences drawn from the evidence can be used to establish that the defendant is guilty beyond a reasonable doubt."

"Sounds the same as a hunch and a funny feeling to me, huh?" Gordon said.

Simms reddened. "Is this a funny feeling?" he asked. He splayed his left-hand fingers and counted off each one with his right. "There's evidence of an opportunity to commit the offense, of the accused's state of mind when the offense was committed, of the accused preparing for the crime, of the accused having items that could be used to commit the offense, namely the knife, gun, and shells and a stun pistol he was known to have used in his job, the stolen tie clip, the fact that the accused behaved in a bizarre and suspicious way before and after the offense, at the diner, then in his trailer, the fact that the accused was in the area when the offense was committed, namely, the truck. Not to mention the tattoo carved in the vic that matches his. What more do you want?"

Gordon drilled his eyes into Fisk. "A motive."

"Do we really need one?" Simms asked. "Look at his record: domestic violence by strangulation, aggravated battery, burglary, aggravated assault with a deadly weapon. It's like, what he does."

"That's not enough."

Simms leaned back in his chair and twirled his eyeglasses. Okay, you want a motive? The union just voted to authorize a strike. Didn't you hear? How's that for a motive?"

"How is that a motive?"

"The contract talks were stalled," Simms reminded him. "Diedrich was stalling them. Hoping to wear the union down. With the whole town mad at him, and the workers feeling hopeless and powerless, Richie saw an opportunity to be their hero. So, he took him out. It worked. Things moved forward."

"We don't know that," Gordon objected.

"Well, then you could ask him. But he's dead. Do you have any other suspects? Didn't think so. Sounds like closure to me."

"Someone paid him."

"We don't know that," Simms echoed him.

"Someone helped him."

"We don't know that, either."

"I'll find out."

Simms glanced at the clock. "You've got until ten in the morning, Frank. Then you can come back and tell me, Representative Harmon, and Commissioner Sellers what you found."

Back at his desk, Gordon tapped a pencil and then snapped it in two. His boss wanted this over with, lickety-split. Good for a promotion. His boss's political pals wanted this over with. Good for profits. Were they protecting somebody? Were they deliberately trying to frame Richie with planted evidence? Anderson had done it with Tyler Williams using that old trick associated more often with urban drug stings: *find* some dope on the guy in a pat-down and pin him for it. Of course, he'd loudly insist it wasn't his and he didn't know how it got there; they always did, even if it was theirs. It wasn't in Tyler's case. But this multiple planting of circumstantial clues to pin Richie was more complicated. Maybe coordinated. Simms had finger-counted the long list of *evidence*. It was quite a list.

A list. He'd almost forgotten. The receptionist's log of visitors to the Diedrich facility that he'd printed. He crossed the room to the common printer. It wasn't in the tray. But it wasn't likely someone would remove it to hide the names. He still had the email, after all.

There it was, in the *Jobs Completed* basket. He snatched both pages and returned to his disheveled desk. The first thing he noticed was that Jacob Diedrich had worked in the CAFO office on Tuesday, the day before the town hall meeting. He did not have appointments with the sales reps for metal roofing, industrial fans, sanitation supplies and such; they dealt with mid-managers. But he met Owen Charles, the public health inspector from the state department of agriculture, who defended Diedrich's operations by attacking the credibility of the other experts. They'd probably conferred about their strategy for the next day's town hall meeting. And look who followed: State Representative Jeb Harmon with County Commissioner Terence B. Sellers, fellow swine operation owners who were, at this moment, pressuring his boss to close the matter immediately, if not sooner.

Were they now afraid of something coming to light? Would they try to take him out—have him end up as dead meat?

Focus, he commanded himself. *Don't get paranoid.*

Farther down the list, he noted a pair of attorneys with *Bentley, Dean, and Morin Law Associates* whose names Gordon didn't recognize. Nothing unusual about lawyers meeting with a man who thrived on legal intimidation, buyouts, and lawsuits.

But the next appointment was unusual. Shawn Elliot, Caitlin's real estate husband.

What was *he* doing there? He hopped in his cruiser and headed over. He'd need to talk with Shawn.

—⚒—

The outer office of *Prairie Property Partners* cheerfully announced Broker Manager Shawn's recent sales with blown-up color photos and bold diagonal SOLD stickers.

The eighty-acre Robbins' farm for $759,900, Mrs. Pitt's thirty-eight-acre farmette for $375,000, The Bakers' twenty-seven-acre creekfront ranch at $339,000, along with Mrs. Fairmont's three bed, two bath retirement-home-of-her-dreams with ten acres of horse pasture for $210,000. The Everetts' cattle operation that had been in their family for generations: 1.2 million. A few others. All of them bordering the Diedrich properties. In his patrolling, Gordon hadn't seen *For Sale* signs.

Not hard to figure out, then, who was buying them. And who was making a healthy commission.

"Help you, Officer?" A twenty-something in a loosened tie leaned out a cubicle, every hair of his pompadour moussed in place. The nameplate said CHAD PEDERSON. Gordon didn't recognize him. New in town.

"I was hoping to find Shawn in the office," Gordon said. "Is he here?"

"He's with a client," Chad said.

"It's official business," Gordon said. "Please tell him Detective Sergeant Gordon of the River Falls police is here, and I need to speak with him right away."

"Real estate business?"

"None of your business, junior. Now get him."

Chad's snake-oil smile drooped. "He doesn't like to be disturbed."

"He'll be more disturbed if I kick in his door."

"You wouldn't."

"Watch me." Gordon snap-kicked a table beside a waiting room chair. It flew against the wall and shattered into flying pieces. Splintered wood clattered to the floor and spun.

"Hey, hey, you can't do that!" the kid objected.

"I just did. Now tell him I'm here."

The kid swung out of his chair. "I'll get him."

The door at the end of the hall popped open. "What the fat was that?" Shawn demanded.

Chad stopped dead in his tracks and pointed over his shoulder. "There's a cop here—"

"Frank?" Shawn called, looking past Chad. "Frank, what's

this all about?"

"What do you think it's about?" Gordon growled.

"If this is about Stephie coming to our house, you've got no right to come in here—"

"It's about Diedrich."

Shawn clapped his mouth shut. He turned aside. "I'll be right back," he said to the client in the office. "Chad, could you wait in here with Mr. and Mrs. Crawford while I help Officer Gordon?"

Chad slipped into the office and secured the door.

"For heaven's sake, Frank," Shawn said, pointing to the mess on the floor, "you didn't have to bust up my place to see me."

"What were you doing at Diedrich's office the day before the murder?"

"What am I, a suspect? Are you trying to smear me because Caitlin and I tried to help Stephie?"

"This has nothing to do with Stephanie and me," Gordon rumbled.

"Well, if you think I got mad at Old Man Diedrich over a big deal gone bad and had a tiff about it and a reason to hurt him, you're dead wrong. It's the opposite. He's been good for business. Very good. I wish he was still alive."

Gordon nodded at the SOLD posters. "You brokered all the sales of adjoining properties, didn't you?"

"Nothing illegal about that. Who wanted to be next to a stinkin' pig factory and an open manure lake? No one. I helped them to sell fast and get out."

"I never saw any For Sale signs."

"That's common practice, Frank. Deals are often made privately in advance, and by law, a listing must be made with Multiple Listing Service even though it's already sold, and a sign is optional. I'm doing it right now with the Crawfords."

"They're about a mile from those barns."

"Yup. And flooded with manure. A lotta people want out,
Frank. I have days full of appointments with people whose
home values have plunged because of that lagoon flood."

"Diedrich buys them."

"Nothing wrong with that. The sellers get something
rather than nothing. He gets room to expand."

"He lowballs them."

"He's a businessman, Frank. You buy low. Especially if you
know no one else will buy."

"And you get a commission."

"I'm a salesman. Of course I get a commission. And a
finder's fee."

"Pretty good fee. That's your Mercedes outside, isn't it? I
thought you had a Buick."

"I can't deny it. You probably ran the plates. And why
would I? My buyer has been generous, and the sellers have
been grateful. Like the Wyatts."

"Stephanie's folks? You sold their farm?"

"Who else? Stephie is friends with Caitlin, so I got asked
first."

"They sold the herd so they could *keep* the farm."

"It didn't work out. I guess Stephie didn't tell you. But
you've been away and kinda out of touch because—"

"You sold the Wyatt Farm to the snake who forced them
out of business?"

"Look, Frank, a buyer is a buyer."

Gordon bunched his fist and drove a right cross to
Shawn's nose. It sent him sprawling to the floor. He struggled
up to one elbow and wiped his nose. His sleeve streaked with
blood.

"Are you—are you crazy, Frank? Geez."

"A snake is a snake," he said.

"I'm going to report this," Shawn squealed. "I'll file a
complaint."

"It won't be the first one," Gordon countered sharply, and left.

Back in the cruiser, Gordon turned off the *do not disturb* feature on his phone. The voicemail had a message. It was State Homicide Detective "Jerry" Davis. "Hey, Frank. I've got an update on getting the names of the cleaning crew. Call me back."

He did.

"Sorry it took a little while, Detective, but the sanitation unit, the so-called Third Shift, is managed by a third party," Davis reported. "Their workers are non-union, and HR has no records of them."

"So, did you call the third-party employer? Who is it?"

"Sinnissippi Staffing Services, or *Servisios de Personal*. What a racket. It's minimum wage, non-contract temp work for a piece of the paycheck, but it works for undocumented workers, hires with drug histories, and ex-cons. The Diedrich plant doesn't mind using them; they don't have to report injuries to OSHA, and there's a lot of them. Last month a guy's sleeve got caught in a conveyor belt and he lost—"

"Do you mind?"

"Sorry. As you can imagine, they weren't open to sharing their files. Protecting their clients, they said."

"Sure they are. Call again. Ask if they'd rather give us a few names or have ICE give them a visit and shut down the whole operation for good. If they still stiff-arm you, tell them we're getting a court order on Monday and bringing the IRS Fraud Investigation Unit in with us. Hey, maybe we won't wait 'til Monday and call in a DEA SWAT team to raid the place based on a tip. Or tell them if—"

"I get it, Frank. Put the screws on. I'll get back to you."

Gordon hung up.

I can't wait until Monday, he groused. *Simms is ready to clear the case and get captain's bars for a speedy closure.*

Anderson is ready to close the case and run for sheriff, claiming he solved it. The Chinese are ready to bury the case and close on a multimillion-dollar deal with Chelsea Diedrich who wants to deflect any investigation into her complicity. The politicians are ready to close the case to placate the Chinese, keep the stock value high and grease their own palms while promising legal protections. Heck, even Stephanie will want to close the case so her organization is off the hook, and I can maybe find the time to get back to her and make things right so that we can—

The phone trilled. Davis.

"It worked. Ready to write down the names?"

"Hang on." Gordon pulled over to a full stop and opened the laptop. "Okay, shoot."

"Here goes: Lucinda Maldonado, Buck Carter, Krystyl Spinney. It's spelled funny."

"I know how it's spelled," Gordon said, his pulse quickening.

"And Buck, I mean do you think that's his real name—'Buck'?"

"It is," Gordon said. "You know what this means?"

"That you know him?"

"More than that," Gordon said, nearly breathless. "It means this crew was in both places the night Jacob Diedrich was killed."

"Is that normal?"

"I plan to find out," Gordon said. "I'll have to go talk to them tonight when their shift starts. They won't be there tomorrow night with the strike starting."

"I'd go with you, but I can't put in for more overtime, you understand, since—"

"I got it," Gordon said.

He hung up.

His heart hammered to the beat of the clock ticking.

CHAPTER 27

HER CLOCK WAS TICKING.

Her own mother reminded her of this each year on her birthday. *Happy birthday to me.* Stephie popped the beer can and sucked in the foam. She never told her mom that they were *trying* because the next embarrassing question would be *how often? Because you know, dear, you have to be together, if you know what I mean, every other day for the fourteen days after you ovulate,* even if Frank's twelve-hour shifts and frequent impromptu overtime had complicated things, and then Daddy would say *honey, leave the poor girl alone,* and Mom would go on *why don't you try standing on your head, why don't you try some raspberry tea, why don't you why don't you* when in fact they had tried all the serious medical options, shy of spending fifteen thousand dollars or more for an egg extraction and freezing because she wanted no part of *Brave New World's* factory farrowing of humans. No CAFO. No Concentrated Alternative Fertility Operation.

Of course, Mother's Day was the worst. Strangely, the second-worst day was Christmas, with all those toy ads for kids, baby-in-a-manger displays and carolers hymning Handel's "For Unto Us A Child Is Born".

Then there was the first day of preschool. Day after tomorrow. She had never expected she would not be dropping off her own at a place like this, and the anxiety of separation other moms felt was replaced by the anxiety of never being separated at all. It's why she spent the weekend before the first day of school scrolling through infertility blogs, for support, for comfort, for understanding, for some explanation, for some affirmation that she was not abnormal, even though *My Eggsperience, The Hannah Project, Sarai Laughed, Baby Bumped, Baby One More Time, Back in The Stirrups Again,* and most others ended up with a resigned resolve to move on, maybe adopt. Would it help to start her own blog or podcast? To share her thoughts beyond a personal journal?

But it was hard to do so when she spent her workday with other women's children, wiping four-year-old noses and playing dominoes, connecting dots with letters, drying tears and kicking balls of different colors, hiding stuffed animals for hide-and-seek, construction paper weaving and storytelling and jigsaw puzzling and making clocks with paper plates, and—

She braced herself for her coworker's probing inquiry and polite elbowing: *Sooo—how's it going?* actually meaning *Sooo—did you and Frank—you know—get any results yet?*

She tilted her head back for a big swig and then planted the beer can on a coaster. Well, she was a couple days late. It hadn't meant anything before. The hormones had played with her schedule. But Winifred would poke and persist, and Stephie needed more than a glib answer. She'd take the strip test in the morning just to shut her up.

She exited her screens, folded the laptop, and carried the beer can to the kitchen. She poured the remaining portion fizzing down the drain. She arced the can into the trash. *Padink.* Two points. She brushed, dressed for bed in gym shorts and a tank top, clicked on the fan and set the alarm.

Like Mom said: the clock was ticking.

CHAPTER 28

WITH THE CAR CLOCK WINKING 1:30:00 a.m., Gordon parked outside the chain-link fence of the processing plant. There was no military-style guard house here, no razor wire, and no panning cameras as at the CAFO, just corner floodlights and the lidless fisheyes of security cameras. The vacant employee lot, black asphalt with yellow parking grids, looked like an enormous grill.

When he stepped outside, the humidity swallowed him, and the iron in the air, the smell of warm blood, pawed at him. No amount of bleach could overcome it.

A chalk-white box van squatted inside the fencing, rear-ended to one of the two receiving ramps. The steel-and-chrome framing and absence of markings made him wonder if the white-out of the CAFO security footage was actually this truck blocking the camera. In any event, the sanitation crew had already arrived. Someone noisily unloaded a chemical drum with a hose attachment on a dolly truck. If there had been evidence that Diedrich was bled out here, it was all sanitized away.

He tapped his watch. 1:34:31. 32. 33. If only Paul could have come for backup. No money in the budget for overtime, he was told. Frank never did it for the money, and it annoyed Stephie to no end that he neglected the paperwork. He just kept putting it off and off and before you knew it, you—

Get going, he rebuked himself. No one else on regular patrol was likely to show up. He shifted his duty belt and tugged his vest. "Hot even at night," he grumbled.

Sheet lightning replied from behind the brooding clouds, like struck matches that didn't catch.

He leaped up to the steel ramp with a thud. Not as supple as in his track days. The frosted glare of the suspended LED lights inside cast ghostly shadows through the maw of the garage door.

"Hey! You! You can't come in here!"

A gangly male in safety glasses, high boots, and an overall apron smeared in blood pointed a yellow-gloved finger at him.

"Shut up, Buck," said a woman nearby, releasing the trigger on a hand-held high pressure washer hose. Streamlets of steam rose from the conveyor belt rollers and stainless steel tables beyond her and the grated floor beneath her like exorcised spirits. "It's just our friend, Officer Gordon. Ya come to see how the sausage is made?"

"I came to ask a few questions," he said.

"That prob'ly wasn't one of them," Krystyl said, lifting the visor on her polycarbonate face shield.

Another woman emerged from a utility closet pulling a wheeled bucket with mops and squeegees attached. She cussed. "What's this? A raid?"

"It's no raid, Lucy," Krystyl said. "It's someone who done come for a personal tour and has a question for the guide."

"You're not really her sister, are you?" Gordon nodded at Lucy.

"Not by blood," Lucy said. "But who else would do this work?"

"And Buck—I thought you said you were a stunner."

"I *was*," he stressed. "Til a month ago. The other guy got caught in the scalder—"

"Buck," Krystyl cut him off, "there's no need."

"Yeah, so, I had enough of the kill floor and took this. It's just part time but I don't mind because—"

"Officer Gordon ain't interested," Krystyl said. "Are you?"

"Were the three of you working the night Jacob Diedrich was killed?" Gordon said.

Buck shrugged. Krystyl made a face at him. "'Course we were," she said, matter-of-factly. "It's our job. You can check the time sheets."

"Anyone else with you?"

"Why would there be?"

"To bring Mr. Diedrich for a visit."

"Visit my britches," Krystyl said. "You think maybe someone done kilt him here or tried to grind him up or sumpin'."

"Was Richie here?"

"Why would Richie come here at night? He hates this place."

"So, did you see anyone else? Anything out of the ordinary?"

"Cain't say I did," Krystyl hiked up a shoulder. "You, Buck? Didn't think so. Lucy? You? Nope. Kin we get back to work, now?"

"Where's the baby?"

"You're awful concerned 'bout my baby, ain't you?"

"You lied when you said it was with your mother. I checked. She doesn't even know you had a kid."

"We don't talk," Krystyl said. "She wouldn't know."

"You said she was babysitting for you."

"I meant I wish she could. It'd be convenient. I give him to the wife of one of the workers here."

"Who would that be?"

"I don't even know her name. The undocumenteds, you know, don't want to be known. She picks him up, brings him back. I pay cash. It's all good. What's it to you, anyway?"

"What's the worker's name?"

"I dunno. Juan or sumpin'. They're all named Juan or Pedro."

"You really don't even know the name of the worker whose wife takes your child?"

"I don't know, and it's prob'ly a fake name, anyway. You don't get us, do you? The ones who gotta live with the blood and guts and the shinola, we gotta take from the law and from people with money. Now stop harrassin' us so we kin get back to work."

"Where does this woman take your baby?" Gordon pressured. "It isn't your trailer; that's boarded up. It isn't Buck's; there are no baby things in the place. No highchair, no teething rings, no toys, no nothing that says that a baby lives here."

"What if I told you everything's in the back?"

"What if I got a search warrant? Would I find baby things in the back rooms? Would I find a baby at all?"

"Go ahead and get your blinkin' warrant, cowboy. You'll be wastin' your time, like you are now."

"One more thing: Do you work at the CAFO when you're done here?"

"It's part of the contract," Krystyl admitted. "We got the power washers to do a good job to flush everything into the lake. Why? You want us to come do the police station and jail, too?"

Gordon suppressed a cough. The pungent mist of disinfectant was burning his lungs. "I'm not done with this," he said.

"I am," Krystyl said. "Now show yourself out."

She placed her finger on the trigger of the pressure washer, the rifle-like barrel pointed at the floor.

Gordon backtracked to the steps, not willing to turn his back. A blast from the washer could knock him off his feet, incapacitate him. Once at the stairway, he spun and exited, feeling Krystyl's sharp stare daggering him in the back.

CHAPTER 29

THE TWO MINUTES WERE UP. Two colored lines appeared, the testing line and the control line, pale, shadowed, struggling to show. Unsure. Afraid. Hoping.

Pregnant.

Pregnant?

Stephie clutched and then checked the expiration date on the box. Nowhere near. Still good. What did Dr. Feldman say about false positives? *It can happen if you take a pregnancy test too soon after taking a fertility drug that contains HCG. That's because after a fertilized egg attaches to the uterine lining, the placenta forms and produces a hormone called Human Chorionic Gondotropin, and so the test might be detecting the drug, not an actual implantation.*

So, which was it? When was the last shot? And when had she and Frank—yes, that night—*oh, no, that night*—she'd been drinking, *again*. No, she didn't dare to hope. It's not even like they were trying that time. It just happened. Should she tell him? Not yet. She couldn't bear to be disappointed.

Should she take another reading? The test claimed ninety-nine percent accuracy if done a day after a missed period. But those shots had skewed the rhythm. What was the point? She would need to call Dr. Feldman for confirmation.

Naturally, she reached the clinic's answering service. She tapped her nails while listening through the recorded office location and hours and *if this is an emergency, dial 911* and *leave your message after the tone.* She did.

In the shower, she rubbed her belly—no, caressed it, two-handed, still unwilling to believe that a new life was conceived there, feeling for a tenderness, a swelling, something, for assurance. Morning sickness wouldn't begin for another four to six weeks, and she didn't feel queasy in the least, except for the thought that she'd have to apologize to Frankie for all the grief she had caused by her self-absorption and frustration and inconveniences and crying and lack of faith and—

The phone trilled. *Dr. Feldman. Now?* She wouldn't let it go to voicemail. She flung aside the curtain, swung the robe around her shoulders like a cape and stretched for the cell on the vanity. The call ID wasn't Feldman's; she knew it by heart. A crank call? Another death threat? She hovered a finger over the phone. She answered.

"Stephanie, it's Mark, how are you doing today?"

The lawyer.

"Mark. Yes, hello. I'm fine. Yes, fine," she lied.

"Maybe you heard the union at the Diedrich plant voted to approve a strike action," he said. "It's effective as of the first shift early tomorrow morning."

"I did. I guess the union saw Mr. Diedrich's death as an opportunity for leverage."

"So do I," said the attorney. "Remember how I explained to you at the hotel that filing a nuisance suit was probably the best way to fight?"

"Under certain conditions, I think you said," she began, securing the robe's belt. Soon there would be a bump there and the belt wouldn't fit.

"The conditions are right," Warren said, "all four of them: physical damage to the plaintiff's property, economic harm to the property's market value, harm to the plaintiff's health, psychological harm to the plaintiff's peace of mind. These were all evident at the town hall meeting, wouldn't you agree?"

"Of course."

"So, it's not just the smell and the truck traffic, it's the flooding. There is now substantial evidence—about ten million gallons worth—to prove legal injury and to get legal relief in the form of monetary damages and an injunction. And with the added pressure of the strike, they'll be eager to settle."

"What makes you think they won't dig in their heels?"

"Diedrich's dead," Warren said. "I'm betting the kids want to cut their losses and keep most of their inheritance. But we have to do it now while the pressure is on and before a year is up since the CAFO opened. That's the only catch."

"Why is that?"

"The so-called 'Illinois Right to Farm Act' that Diedrich pushed with his pals in the legislature, like Jeb Harmon, who sponsored it," Warren explained. "It was passed to protect ag operations by curtailing an individual's right to sue for nuisance. They saw how nuisance actions were winning big-time against hog CAFOs in North Carolina."

"Where Diedrich also owns hog farms."

"Yup. Darned if he'd let it happen in Illinois. It cost him just over two-hundred million. But like I said, the suit must be filed within a year of opening. The sooner, the better. If we wait, we need to prove the nuisance conditions existed substantially for the whole period, and if the court says they did not, the plaintiff pays for the ag operation's costs in its defense. That's a lot of money. And an individual must bring the action, not a group. Your house wasn't directly affected, I'll bet."

"Are you kidding? Everyone in town can smell it."

"Not enough. We need to meet with some of those folks who stood up at the town meeting to complain about illnesses and sewage on their property and convince them to sign on immediately. Are you game?"

Stephie rested her palm on her abdomen.

"Stephanie? You still there?"

"I'm in."

"Super. I'll get up a list of people you and I need to approach. I'll get back to you on that. Meanwhile, we need to make a public announcement that we plan to move forward with this, while the news of the strike is fresh," he said, the adrenalined words rapid-firing. "I've already got news crews arriving at noon. They'll cut the story in time for the evening news and the morning papers. I need to confirm the location; I want the CAFO in the shot. Say, we could do an early lunch at the hotel and go from there. What do you say?"

"That's not going to work today," she equivocated.

"That's too bad. We could discuss plans and have a few laughs. C'mon."

"I—I have plans. Just call or text me, okay?"

"All right. Another time, then. I'll get back to you. *Ciao.*"

They rang off.

Stephie clasped her hands around her belly. She suppressed a queasiness that wasn't morning sickness, for sure. It wasn't even excitement about possibly killing the CAFO. It was—what was it? That odd feeling whenever she was with Mark, the need to brush her teeth afterward.

CHAPTER 30

When he'd returned to the apartment around 2:00 a.m., Gordon smelled something worse than himself. Batman had left another present on the stoop, but it wasn't half a chipmunk. It was a digested one. The pieces—half a skull with teeth, boney claws, a matted tail, and the rest—sat in a foamy yellow-brown puddle. Batman mewed pitifully in the bushes and gagged, gagged, heaved again.

"I don't like the look of this," Gordon muttered. He checked the water bowl he left outside. Empty. "I'll get you some more," he said. "And I'll call the vet first thing in the morning. Maybe she'll see you before my meeting."

He fetched an evidence bag from the car and, hearing no more heaving, whistled the cat inside. He collected the sample and lumbered to the bathroom where he stripped off his clothes and stuffed them into a sealable trash bag to wash later. After a quick, hot, lemony shower he plopped bleary-eyed into bed where Batman had propped up, washing himself.

—⁂—

"Dr. Judy will see you now."

Gordon thanked the veterinarian's receptionist for scheduling him so early, lifted the cat carrier, and gripped the sack holding the evidence bag full of chipmunk parts. Batman hunkered down in his portable jail, ears flat.

Gordon took a seat in the tiny examining room once the receptionist closed the door. He studied the posters warning about the dangers of fleas, ticks, and worms. So many ways to die in the wild. A series of photos depicting the bleeding gum stages of periodontitis in dogs reminded him of morgue shots and how Diedrich's mouth gaped open in disbelief that everything could end so suddenly.

Dr. Judith Meyers stepped in, holding a clipboard. "Flash," she said merrily, "how are we doing?"

"I'm fine," he said. "The cat, not so much."

"Stomach trouble, you say?"

"He just ate something he shouldn't. He heaved it up. I didn't like the look of it. I brought it."

He fished the sealed sample out of the plastic bag. Out of habit, he'd noted the location, date, and time with a marker.

"Batman, Batman, what did you do?" The vet held the ziplocked baggie up in the light, turned it this way and that. "Chipmunk alfredo. Not part of his regular diet, I presume."

"It might be. He's outside a lot."

She handed back the evidence pouch and flipped a page on her clipboard. "His last wellness checkup was all normal," she noted. "Up to date on shots. Okay. Let's have a look."

Gordon knew well enough to be quiet while she assessed her patient's alertness, appearance, gait, skin, coat, and weight. She fingered his paws, used an otoscope for the ears, passed a finger by his eyes, thumbed up his lips, pressed his gums, and listened to the heart and lungs with the stethoscope. She felt his abdomen and glands and took his temperature in the rear.

Now was the time to talk. She asked questions about the cat's diet: Any changes? Treats? Any other vomiting? Any other symptoms: diarrhea, weight loss, discolored stools, unusual fatigue? Like a good detective, she was looking for clues.

"Well, Batman," she said while stroking his pointy ears, "it looks like you have a case of dietary indiscretion."

"That's it?" Gordon asked. "What about the yellow stuff?"

"It's probably bile," she said. "Cats will vomit bile when they have an empty stomach. It can happen if you're only feeding your cat in the morning and they go twenty-four hours without food. Does he get fed once or twice a day?"

Gordon felt his cheeks pinking. "Just the morning," he said. "I've got twelve-hour shifts, and I've been working pretty much non-stop since Mr. Diedrich passed so—"

"Stephie doesn't feed him?"

"She left—uh—I mean, she leaves it to me."

"Well, it's probably why he decided to supplement his diet on his own."

"Plus he's a natural killer."

"True. There *is* that," she said. "But probably not whoever did in Boss Hogg Diedrich."

"We don't know that yet."

"You know, they asked me to come out once when one of their regular inspectors couldn't make it. I refused. They threatened to challenge my license. Can you believe it?"

"You don't do large animals anyway, right?"

"Even if I did, I wouldn't. You know they bribe these so-called inspectors to clear their hogs. I wasn't going to be counted among them."

"Of course not. Good for you."

She scratched Batman's chin. "Okay, buddy, that's all. Lay off the rodent buffet. And meow a little louder for dinner. Food stimulates the gall bladder to contract, and when that happens, bile won't back up into your belly."

"Got it," Gordon said.

"You're good to go." The vet breathed a tired sigh. "You know, that was the point of vet inspections at the plant. To verify that the swine were healthy enough to be slaughtered. Ironic, isn't it?"

"Yeah."

"Here, the euthanasias at the end of the day are only for animals that are sick beyond helping. I can't imagine what it's like for Autumn Hale at the shelter. She has to put down healthy ones. You got Batman there, right? You saved his life, Flash."

CHAPTER 31

GORDON CRUISED BY the Sinnissippi Humane Society Animal Shelter for the third time, deciding whether to go in. The director, Autumn Hale, attended the town hall meeting and had shouted an incendiary opinion. She surely despised the cruelty of the CAFO and the brutish indifference of the man in charge, but she wouldn't kill him—even if she was accustomed to killing. She used needles, not knives. Not a suspect. But maybe she'd seen something after the meeting. Heard something. He had to ask. Even if she was a high school chum of Stephanie's. And she was a fellow board member of NO CAFO. They spoke frequently, so awkward questions were sure to come his way.

He pulled into the parking lot after a fourth pass-by.

A bell chimed when he stepped inside. The service desk was unstaffed, but the hissing of water and the clank of a bucket told him someone was cleaning the kennels.

"Be right with you!" Autumn called, her voice muffled by the closed door. Dogs replied with barks.

He tried the handle. Locked. Through the wire mesh glass window, he saw Autumn approach, tugging off her blue rubber gloves. Still no wedding ring.

"Hey, Flash," she said with a toothy smile and a raised shoulder. The yips and woofs amplified until she clicked the door behind her. "You here for another cat? I've got just the one."

"I've got questions about pigs."

"Sorry. We don't have any here to adopt."

"I meant the CAFO, of course."

"Yeah, he was a pig, wasn't he?"

"So, you know."

"C'mon, Flash. Small town. Everyone knows. By the way, thanks for not arresting me at the town hall for my little outburst." She looked him up and down. "Though I wouldn't mind being put in cuffs by you."

She punctuated the line by brushing back a tendril of hair behind her ear.

"Don't worry. You're not a suspect."

"Too bad."

"I'm just wondering if, in mingling with the crowd afterward, you heard anything unusual? Any threats? Any mention of harming Mr. Diedrich?"

"Sheesh, people were mad, that's for sure. But no—the only threat I heard was from Stephie. *Everyone* heard *that*."

"Right." He shuffled his feet. "Did you see anything unusual? Someone going up to Mr. Diedrich and shaking a fist, or getting in his face, anything, you know, belligerent?"

"He left in a hurry. Made a beeline for the exit. I think he had a car waiting."

"You *think* he did, or he *did*?"

"There was an Asian guy standing at the exit," she said, tapping her lower lip, remembering. "Young guy. Twenties, I'd say. Short hair. Shaven. Black slacks, white shirt. Like a waiter, y'know? But I heard someone say it was his driver. When the mayor ended the meeting, the guy left and Diedrich followed, so I think he had a car waiting, based on that."

"Anyone else close behind Diedrich?"

"Nope. He hustled out by himself."

"Okay. Good to know."

"Anything else?"

"No, thanks, Autumn, that's helpful."

"Can't interest you in another cat?"

"Not now. Batman's great."

"Have a heart, Flash. I've got this cute little guy who's been here a week. You could call him Robin."

"Save him for someone else."

"I can't. After a week, an animal here is—well, you know."

"Just a week?"

"Standard practice," she said. "Some places only allow 72 hours. They're overwhelmed. It comes to just over two million per year. Six per minute."

"What happens to them all?"

"You don't wanna know."

"Cremation, right?"

"I said you don't wanna know."

"Landfill?"

"Flash, don't go there."

"What if it changes my mind?"

She pinched her lips. "Please don't hate me," she said. "They're processed into livestock feed."

"No."

"Guess who does it?"

"Don't tell me."

"Too late. Diedrich Agri-Products." Her eyes welled up. Her lower lip trembled. "I'm—I'm sorry, Flash. I hate them. I really do. But it's good money."

CHAPTER 32

"IF YOUR SUSPECT IS DEAD, is there still a trial to make sure he was the real killer?"

State Representative Jeb Harmon, accustomed to making deals in smoke-filled back rooms like The Right to Farm Act, twiddled his unlit cigar as he shifted squeakily in the vinyl chair.

"No, Jeb, there's no point to a trial," Lieutenant Simms answered from behind his desk, fingers laced behind his neck, elbows high. "Any defense lawyer would file—oh, Detective Gordon. G'mornin. Come on in."

"Am I late?"

"No, no, right on time, as always. Close the door."

Gordon nudged the door closed and stood at parade rest. "Sirs," he acknowledged.

County Commissioner Terence B. Sellers, in a wide-collared shirt he'd saved from the 1970s and dungarees for his farm chores, lifted his double chin. Sheriff's Deputy Anderson wedged in a folding chair below the lieutenant's overstuffed file cabinets.

"So, Jeb, like I was saying," continued Simms, "the defense lawyer would file what they call a 'Motion In Suggestion Of Death' and attach the defendant's death certificate. The prosecutor verifies it and at that point the judge would dismiss the charges. But I don't know of any jurisdiction in America that would waste the court's time and tax dollars trying a dead man."

Sellers stabbed a finger sharply at Simms. "So, we're sure it was this Richie Valera fellow."

"'Sure as shootin', as the saying goes," Anderson quipped.

Simms swung in Gordon's direction. Arched an eyebrow. "Detective, you agree?" It sounded more like a command than a question.

"We're still not sure if there was an accessory, sir," Gordon said.

"So, you found nothing since we last spoke?" Simms pressed.

"I know Mr. Harmon and Mr. Sellers here visited Mr. Diedrich the day before the murder."

Harmon glared at him. "What's that supposed to mean? Are you insinuatin' somethin'?"

"I'd just be curious why," Gordon said. "Did you argue about anything? Have a bone to pick?"

"None of your tootin' business," Harmon spat.

"It's just business, is all," Sellers snapped.

"I'm just wondering—" Gordon continued.

"We're not up for 'wondering,' Detective Sergeant Gordon," Simms said severely. "Do we have evidence?"

"No, but—"

"No 'buts'," Simms said. "That does it, then. We'll pass it on to the state's attorney's office and let them decide if they want to keep a cold case file on it to look for an accessory. We'll transfer the case file and evidence in hand to them for storage. The DNA evidence has already been submitted to the FBI's Combined DNA Index System for later probative profiles. One thing left to do, Detective."

"What's that, sir?"

"Inform the family that, while there isn't the 'closure' they may have wanted, there is resolution, and the case is officially cleared."

Harmon leaned forward. The vinyl squeaked. "Don't you mean *solved* or *closed*?"

"No, Jeb; the FBI allows for clearances by what they call 'exceptional means' when charges aren't filed. It's usually because a suspect has died."

"Like our Richie," Anderson chimed in.

Simms crossed his arms in finality. "Detective, notify the family in person right away. Take Officer Balfour along if you like. They need to hear it from us before the chief and I hold our press conference this afternoon."

"Shouldn't I be there?" Gordon asked, a slow burn in his gut.

Simms shrugged. "What's the point? The investigation is over. I'll add your final report to the case file. Hand it in tomorrow. That's all, everyone. It's a win. Thanks for coming."

Chairs slid and creaked, handshakes were exchanged all around. Gordon slipped out, tugged a handkerchief from a hip pocket and mopped his brow. *Everything but champagne.* He felt his cheeks burning, his nostrils flaring. He thumbed a Rolaids from the foil, popped it in and gritted his teeth so hard he thought a tooth might crack. *This can't be over,* he growled.

Something smells.

CHAPTER 33

"I CAN'T DO IT, CHRIS," Gordon said, palming the steering wheel left into the driveway. "I'd be lying to say the case is closed."

"It's not closed, Flash, it's cleared, right?" Chaplain Christine Balfour said. "Isn't there a difference?"

"Not to me," Gordon huffed. "And not to relatives, regular citizens. It's all the same to them."

"It brings closure," Balfour said. "Consolation. Families need that."

"Not in this case." Gordon shifted into park behind Chelsea Diedrich's Audi. He sighed. "Look, everyone hated this guy. Even his kids. I'm the victim's only advocate for justice; it's my job. And I want to do it right. Look, Christine, if the kids had anything to do with this, I don't want them *consoled*. I want them a little worried that I'm on to them, and that this isn't over. Not by a long shot."

"You still think Richie was paid?"

Gordon shook his head like a pitcher shaking off a catcher's sign. "I'm still not sure Richie did it alone. And if he was paid, it was by somebody with access to enough cash, and wanting something worth the cost."

"How about the union?" Balfour said. "They have money. They had a motive."

"No, it's too public. Unions have finance officers and state reps that oversee accounts. Someone would blow the whistle." He released the steering wheel; his iron grip hurt his fingers. "But Diedrich's kids had such money. And the Chinese. Either way, with Daddy out of the way, Chelsea would get the deal with the Chinese that her father resisted and earn millions. And Logan? I'm wondering where he got his drugs from. I wouldn't be surprised if it turned out to be Richie, and that's how Chelsea connected with him to do away with Daddykins. Dumb Richie wouldn't do it to gain leverage in the strike. He'd do it for money. A lot of it."

"Calm down, Frank. You're getting yourself worked up. Breathe."

"I know, I know. I just don't like it." He sucked in a lungful of cooled air. "Okay. Let's rock'n'roll."

He stepped out into the glue soup that was August. The humidity clung to him like film on a pond. The polyester uniform didn't breathe well and neither did Gordon. Balfour swung out, stood, and exhaled sharply as though gut-punched.

"Oh, this is bad," she said with a squint at the turbulent sky. Olive-green clouds were already bunching into fists. Cicadas mourned in the honey locusts.

Chelsea answered after the second knock.

"This can't be good," she said, eyeing one, then the other.

"That depends," Gordon said. "We're here to inform you that the department is officially clearing the case of your father's death. That means we're announcing the end of our investigation this afternoon, since the only suspect is dead. We believe a packing plant worker high on drugs, Richard Valera, ambushed your dad's car after the town hall meeting, shot him and his driver and, after pushing the car and driver into the Sinnissippi River, decided to hide the other body in the CAFO lake. Soon after, Mr. Valera was killed by a coworker in a dispute. We wanted the family to know before it became public knowledge later today."

"So that's it?"

"For the time being, yes," Gordon said matter-of-factly. "The district attorney's office will hold onto the case files in the event new evidence emerges about accomplices or accessories. So, if someone else had a part in this, we'll find him." He lowered his chin a moment, then lifted his stern gaze. "Or *her*."

Her brows knitted. "Are you implying something?"

"Am I?"

"We're awfully sorry for your loss," Balfour cut in, "and we hope this resolution brings you some relief."

Chelsea puffed air from the side of her mouth. Big eyeroll. "Relief? I was relieved when he died," she said.

Gordon stitched his lips to avoid saying *See? Told you so.*

"Please let us know if there's any way we can be of help," Balfour said.

"I doubt if there is," Chelsea said. "I'll tell Logan. He can be hard to find."

"We'd much rather do it in person," Gordon said. *He might say something useful.* "Is he still at Beverly's apartment?"

"I don't know. You can try there. He didn't move back here, if that's what you mean."

"Do you have his phone number?"

"Sure, but he won't answer, believe me."

"Try it."

She reached into her back pocket, extracted the phone, and called.

Your call is being redirected to an automated voicemail messaging system. [tone] The voicemail box for this number is full. Goodbye.

Chelsea swiped it off. "Like I said."

They dismissed themselves and seat-belted in. Halfway to the apartment building, Gordon bit his lip.

"I should have asked her to call Beverly," he reproached

himself. "She'll call Beverly instead, you know, and tell them both to make themselves scarce."

"You could stake out the place."

"That could take hours, Chris. I won't put you through that. I have to submit a final report, and the chief will probably want you at the press conference like last time."

"Oh, no, not me," she said, crisscrossing her hands. "Those reporters will be on them like turkey vultures on roadkill."

CHAPTER 34

CHELSEA SHOULDERED THE DOOR SHUT and slid the bolt home.

"Are they gone?"

"They're gone, Logan," she answered. "You can come out now."

He slinked from the hall, combing his fingers through his hair, straight back, like his father did.

"So, you heard?" she asked.

"It sounds like they won't be asking us any more questions," he said.

"Don't be so sure, you idiot. That flat top seemed to be saying he thought we had a part in this. He looks like the kind of dog that won't let go of a bone easily. I'll bet he still has questions for you."

Logan splayed his fingers. "Me? About what?"

"You know about what. I'll take you to the lake house where you can lay low. Don't you dare tell anyone I promised the Chinese a good deal with or without Dad. If word gets out, the Chinese will be *yǎo yá qiè chǐ*, super mad, because they'll be suspected of plotting his death and lose face. You hear me?"

"Can I bring Bunny?"

Chelsea slapped him hard. Logan spun half-way around and brought a palm to his cheek.

"No wonder Dad threw you out," Chelsea reprimanded.

"You're an idiot and a loser, just like Dad said. Bunny got you in this trouble by introducing you to that dealer in the plant—"

"Richie wasn't a dealer, he was—"

"He was a loser like you, and if you're not careful, they'll connect you to him, and then try to connect me to him, and it'll ruin everything, and you'll probably end up like him. And I won't be sorry. Just like I'm not sorry Dad is out of the way. Are you listening?"

Logan straightened and rubbed his jaw. "Can I have my phone back?"

"No way."

Logan chuffed. "Then how will I stay in touch?"

"You won't. You'll be as good as dead."

CHAPTER 35

"STEPHIE, HURRY UP, the news is on. It's starting."

Live! Local! Late breaking! It's NewsNow 4! With Brad Nickelson! And Donegal O'Neill! With meteorologist—

"You want ice in your water, Caitlin?"

"Never mind that!" Caitlin called out. "Come on! You're probably the lead story."

Stephanie emerged from the kitchen and set down the glasses, ice rattling, just as the urgent intro music hit the stinger.

The search for the killer of agriculture giant Jacob Diedrich is over. Hi, I'm Brad Nickelson.

And I'm Donegal O'Neill. In a joint press briefing of the River Falls Police Department and Sinnissippi County Sheriff's Office, Chief Raymond Fisk declared the case officially "cleared" now that the only suspect is dead. Our Rachel Miller was on the scene. Rachel?

"I should have figured," Caitlin said with a sigh. "If it bleeds, it leads, right?"

Stephanie studied the screen where the blow-dried reporter summed up the case's official outcome: a drugged-up Richie ambushed and killed Diedrich and his driver and then dumped the bodies in the lagoon and the river, acting out of spite for the stalled union talks. It probably wasn't the full story, but that was the point. Make it a good story.

"I don't see Frank," Caitlin said, leaning forward.

"Wouldn't he be there? Wouldn't he be working that case? Why isn't he at the mic?"

"Only the brass talks," Stephie answered absently, figuring Frank was in the field on another call.

Rachel the Talking Head chattered on. *The Chief reminded everyone that the Diedrich company and the packers' union had deadlocked in contract talks and anger had been building for some time. The union has voted to strike beginning with tomorrow's first shift at 4:30 a.m. union president Jayden Lieber issued a statement denouncing the violence—*

"That's new. But who couldn't see that coming?" Caitlin said cynically. "It's just what we needed, right?"

That's exactly what Mark Warren had whispered in her ear as he steered her into position for her statement, the CAFO barns artfully framed in the background. His palm in the small of her back pushed more than it guided. Warren carefully scripted her statement as an irresistible, no-need-to-edit soundbite. His barrel-curled Gal Friday struggled with the cue cards in the wind, and Stephie had to repeat five takes before she got the timing right.

Back to the anchors.

That union strike has prompted two local animal rights and environmental groups, NO CAFO and S.O.S., Save Our Soil, to file a nuisance suit against the Diedrich operations. Citing the Wednesday night breach of the swine manure lagoon that released millions of gallons of sewage into—

"Okay, okay, this is you," Caitlin exulted with a clap of her hands.

I probably look nervous, Stephie worried. *My hair must be a mess.*

—waterways, fields, and roads. NO CAFO's spokesperson Stephanie Wyatt Gordon had this to say:

She had practically memorized it. She lip-synched to the screen. "The catastrophic pollution of our rivers, streams, and wells by millions of gallons of untreated hog waste, the poisonous release of tons of ammonia and hydrogen sulfide into the air, and the ruinous harm to crops and soil is more than a nuisance or an inconvenience. It is a toxic danger for the incalculable damage done to the health of our environment, our economy, our homes, our families, and especially to our, to, to our children."

"Oh, I love the lip trembling at the end," Caitlin applauded. "Nice touch."

It wasn't faked. Stephie had felt a deep cramp in her belly. The environmental cause was suddenly much more personal. She couldn't tell Caitlin yet why. "We can turn that off now," she said.

"Don't you want to see the reactions?"

"There won't be any," Stephie replied, picking up the remote. "Their PR guy will send out a statement praising the business for uplifting the rural economy, and politicians will conveniently neglect to return calls." She clicked off the TV.

"One thing is for sure," Caitlin said. "After seeing this, people will start calling *you*. They have a way of finding the number even if it's not listed. Most of them will be mean. You'd better turn off your phone or let me answer it."

As if on cue, Stephie's phone trilled.

Again, and again, and again.

CHAPTER 36

AFTER SCREENING A DOZEN CALLS and hanging up each time, Caitlin cupped her palm over the cell phone's mouthpiece. "Stephie, I think you should answer this one."

"Credible death threat this time?" she said, flippant. "Not like the others?"

"It's someone on your side," Caitlin said, "or so she says. A woman who works at the plant."

"No kidding?" She reached for the phone. "I guess it's a good thing after all that I didn't just turn this thing off." She took it and tapped the speakerphone. "This is Stephanie."

"Hi? Stephanie Gordon?"

"Who is this?"

"Hey. I work at the packing plant and at the CAFO on the cleanup detail, like, overnight? When no one else is there? Well, except my team. There's a coupla others. Okay, so, I saw you on TV and I thought we can really help each other."

"How?"

"Like I said, no one else is here and hardly not no one at the barns after second shift, when we come in to wash everything down, and with the strike beginning in the morning, this will be my last night here for a while."

"What is your point?"

"It's like this: we're all really mad about the company dissing us and no one wants to strike and lose wages, know what I mean? So, you can help us make the strike short, and

I can help you with that suit you was talkin' about on the news."

"I don't know how." Stephanie shrugged at Caitlin. *What's this?* She mouthed.

Caitlin twirled her finger to indicate *keep her talking.*

"I was thinkin' that if you was to come tonight with some home security cameras— they're cheap now, and real small, and they send pictures to your phone, you know. You'd get some pictures of what goes on here and at the barns and use them to back up your case, you know, and that kind of pressure helps us, too."

"It's—it's really the CAFO barns we're interested in," Stephie said, tentative.

"Yeah, but you can't go there direct because of the guards," the caller said. "I gotta sneak you in, with you in the back of my truck. They don't check it. So, you gotta come to the plant first. They just got a gate, is all."

"This is something I'll have to discuss with others, especially our lawyer—"

"You got no time," the caller said. "Our shift starts at one in the morning and we're out of both places by four. After tomorrow, we won't be here, and there'll be picket lines and police besides, even if we was here."

Caitlin pinched her fingers on her right hand and twisted, like a screwdriver. *We'll stick it to them*, she was saying. *Tighten the screws.*

"One o'clock, you said?" Stephanie said.

"You had better come by yourself," the woman said. "There's no room in the truck for anyone else, with the cleaning supplies and all. And I wouldn't tell no one, neither. That goes for you, too, lady, you, the one screening the calls. Word gets around. It'll spoil it."

Caitlin made shoving motions with her palms forward. *Go, go.*

"One o'clock, then," Stephanie confirmed.

"Don't be late. We lock the gate behind us, and we won't hear ya with the power washers runnin'."

"What was your name again?"

"It's better if you don't know."

The call went dead.

CHAPTER 37

OF COURSE, LOGAN WAS NOWHERE TO BE SEEN. Gordon dropped off Balfour at the United Methodist Church's manse and then threaded his way through town streets to the QuikStop for an iced coffee.

Donny Delmonico, squatting to restock the Skoal tins behind the counter, stood with a grunt. "Frankie, how ya doin'? See the news today? On the TV?"

"Yeah, I know, the department closed the Diedrich case," he said, thumbing open his wallet. "Sorry, *cleared. Cleared* is the word we use—"

"No, no, I mean your wife, Stephie. She was on."

Gordon's gut twisted. "For what?"

"You don't know?"

"We don't talk about everything," Gordon sidestepped.

"It was about the CAFO barns and the manure leak and all that. She and her group are suing their pants off."

Gordon handed over a couple of bills. "Well, if you ask me, it's a little late for that."

"They figure it's the right time, you know, with the strike on, and all the stink from the spill and all. As it were." He tapped at the register. "I been selling more air fresheners than usual, that's for sure. I got a few left. Need one?"

"Why? Do I smell again?"

"Not as bad as before," Donny teased.

Once back in his car, Gordon grimly hammered out

his report on the cruiser's Toughbook, pounding the keys two-fingered. It was perfunctory now, a dutiful wipe of the mess that had been this case. Others were pending, and he'd get back to Paul Pembroke about his progress on them tomorrow. Given his percussive typing and pulsing forehead, he knew his mood might turn sharp and say something he'd regret. For now, the best thing to do was to cruise a bit before the weather turned nasty.

Dips in the toll road shimmered like mirrors, and more than once he was fooled into thinking he was driving toward standing water. The watery mirages glimmered in the gathering humidity, and the cumulonimbus clouds began to boil into high cauliflower heads. By early evening, the systems would cluster along a cold squall line and curl into thunderheads. The leafy cornstalks, marching implacably in parade greens across Flatland, whispered to each other across their endless rows, *a storm is coming, a storm.*

URGENT – IMMEDIATE BROADCAST REQUESTED
Tornado Watch Number 8
NWS Storm Prediction Center Springfield IL
6:00 pm CST Sun Aug 18
The NWS Storm Prediction Center has issued a
* Tornado Watch for portions of Western and
Central Illinois Southwest Wisconsin Eastern Iowa
* Effective this Sunday afternoon from 600 PM
until Monday morning 200 AM CST.
* Primary threats include...
A few tornadoes likely with a couple intense
tornadoes possible
Widespread damaging winds and isolated
significant gusts to 80 mph likely
Isolated large hail events to 1.5 inches in
diameter possible

SUMMARY...Elongated squall line will progress
east/northeast across the Mississippi and
Sinnissippi Valleys through eastern Iowa into
Western and central Illinois early this morning
with a couple supercells possible ahead of the
line. Damaging winds and embedded tornadoes
are anticipated.
The tornado watch area is approximately along
65 statute miles east and west of a line from 60
miles northwest of Davenport IA to 50 miles
south southeast of Moline IL. For a complete
depiction of the watch see the associated watch
outline update (NWS64 NOAA/IL NOAA/IA).
PRECAUTIONARY/PREPAREDNESS ACTIONS...
REMEMBER...A Tornado Watch means
conditions are favorable for tornadoes and
severe thunderstorms in and close to the watch
area. Persons in these areas should be on the
lookout for threatening weather conditions
and listen for later statements and possible
warnings.

Gordon minimized the alert on his laptop screen. Natives
didn't pay particular attention to watches. *Conditions are
favorable for the development of ...* C'mon. Conditions were
favorable *every* day in a sweaty central Illinois August.
Couldn't help it with thousands of acres of corn and
soybeans breathing into the air. A *watch* was the same as
saying *it's another August afternoon in Illinois.* A *warning* was
different; the sirens howled, and the Weather Service robot
droned *Doppler radar indicates a strongly rotating column of
air ... weather spotters report seeing a funnel cloud one mile
southwest of Mendota ... take cover immediately.* But *watch*
announcements like this were as commonplace as TV jewelry

ads in December, weight loss ads in January, and chocolate ads in February. Everyone knew that.

Just like everyone knew that tornadoes hated trailer parks.

He thought of swinging by the Prairie View park to see if Krystyl or Lucy were there. But with the case cleared, what was the point? The lieutenant would not be pleased with a rogue cop pursuing a case he'd publicly and dramatically ended. Best to stay away.

And what about Stephie? She also made a dramatic announcement that surely would anger a lot of folks. Did they know where she lived? It wasn't hard to find out on the Internet. If she felt unsafe, would she call him? Probably not. Best to stay away?

Probably not. Definitely not.

He'd drive by after dark. Just in case. Late. When she was in bed for sure. Wouldn't see him. Wouldn't get mad. By now she knew he had popped Shawn and wouldn't be keen on seeing him.

Circling back, he patrolled past the drive-thrus, detail shops, dollar stores, and car washes staffed by the town's high school grads not smart enough or rich enough or fast enough for college. Well into the night, they'd spin their jacked-up pickups around the downtown Civil War monument, the one flanked by two black cannons aimed at the Sinnissippi River in case Jeff Davis' fleet of Merrimacs showed up. Harmless, really, until Salvatore and Rose D'Amato called to complain they were keeping their pizza customers away. Mrs. Hirsch had phoned in a nuisance call once. He might check on her, with the storm coming and all.

It made him think of the wellness call he made two years ago in a week of hundred-degree temperatures. *My father lives alone in the country, and I don't think he has air conditioning,* the woman had said on the phone. *He's forgetful and might not even have a fan going. He's not answering my calls.* She lived in Baton Rouge and couldn't make the trip.

The smell was strong, even with the windows shut. He called for backup, tied a kerchief around his lower face, and crowbarred the door open. Mr. Langley in his boxer shorts was stuck to his faux leather chair—well, his skin. The rest of him had slid out to the floor, a putrid mess covered by flies and fleas. He had hated wellness calls since.

A hot wind stirred the skies into a cauldron, a slowly rotating mix of steely rain heads and cerulean swirls. The already-crisping leaves on the red maples that lined Mrs. Hirsch's street chattered.

Keeping a close eye on the show was Mrs. Hirsch, rocking on the porch, stem wineglass in hand.

Gordon unfolded out of the patrol car and locked it behind him.

"I knew you'd be back, Frankie," she called.

"You did?"

"Sure. To fix that sticky screen door you had trouble closing last time."

"I'll need some tools I don't have in the squad car."

"Take your time. If it flies off in the storm, there's the inside door."

"So, you know that there's a tornado watch."

She lifted her glass to the sky. "I'm watching."

"You may want to be inside."

"Inside, it's so hot, even with the windows open, I'm schvitzing."

"I meant be ready to go to a safe interior space."

"Man makes his plans, and God laughs," she said. "Like your case with Mr. Diedrich. I saw on the TV that you got it all figured out."

"Not everything."

"In due time. And that little Stephie, all grown up, was

there, too. She must be proud of you. When are you having babies?"

Gordon felt his cheeks grow hot. "We're, we're talking about it."

"Talking won't work. It takes a little pushing." She winked.

"10-53, fallen tree, Route 251, mile marker fifteen," the dispatcher crackled. "Code 32, need one unit, over."

Gordon reached across his badge to the shoulder mic. "Bravo-twelve, copy. En route."

"Bravo-twelve, copy," Dispatch confirmed.

"Duty calls, Mrs. Hirsch."

The woman shrugged and smiled. "If you don't learn to endure the bad, you won't live to enjoy the good."

By eleven o'clock, the wind picked up; it amplified the haunting keen of the Union Pacific train and its distant *kerclack kerclack kerclack.* Gordon hoped no one was stupid enough to try to outrun the roaring locomotive at the ungated crossing. Gusts came in unsettled spurts now, spinning up little dust devils; tattered County Fair signs shivered on telephone poles, and a tilted mailbox shaped like an old Allis Chalmers tractor rocked back and forth as though trying to climb a grade.

By the time he swung onto his street at midnight with the headlamps off, the honey locusts were waving and the utility lines harping. By habit, he parked a block away. He checked overhead to make sure he wasn't going to be an easy target for a falling limb. He snorted at the memory of a heavy branch crunching the corner of his roof and twisting the gutter last August, and his insurance agent, Chip Swindell, denying the claim because his adjustor said his estimate for repairs didn't exceed the deductible. *You know the game, Flash,* he said. *Higher deductible, lower premiums. Lower deductible, higher premiums. Would you like to adjust the deductible?* What a gotcha gamble. All legal. Swindell cheated in high school wrestling, too. With those so-called supplements.

The streetlamps blinked. If the power went out, he'd need to move to a traffic-lighted intersection until Commonwealth Edison put things to rights. He kept the engine purring. The car rocked once in a windblast. The radio squawked. "Bravo-twelve, code 101, please copy."

He answered, "10-106, over." He was secure. Routine. He twisted down the volume.

He surveyed the house, dark as expected. The Venetian blinds were closed, the curtains drawn, largely to keep heat out and cooled air in during the sweltering day. The street looked empty as he had hoped. If anyone scoped out the place, hoping to harass Stephie or prank the house, they'd see the squad car and move on. He'd sit here a while. He shuffled lower in the seat and crossed his arms. He pictured Stephie asleep on her side with her knee drawn up, her freckled shoulder poking from the sheet, her strawberry hair fanned across the pillow, her lips pursed in a wistful dream.

CHAPTER 38

STEPHANIE TILTED THE REAR-VIEW MIRROR down so she could pull her hair back into a tight ponytail and slip a band over it; the blustery wind was sure to blow her mop awry. She wished Caitlin could have come along to calm her jitters, but the woman on the phone had been adamant, hadn't she? *You better come by yourself.* Steph asked Caitlin if she might just stay in the car while Stephie went inside to set up the cameras. But there was no way to know how long she'd have to sit there, anxious about being discovered and questioned. Besides, what would she do when the woman took Stephie to the CAFO? Accompanying her to buy the cameras and then setting them up on her phone was enough. *Just call me when it's over.*

That's when Caitlin spilled the beans about Frank busting into the real estate office to clobber Shawn. *And he did you such a favor, helping your folks out.*

Maybe he was feeling...protective. It's in his blood.

He's just mad, Stephie. Mad about everything. Watch out.

Stephie grasped the vinyl backpack with the cameras, zip ties, and tape. The mounts that came with the gear might not be right; better to have some options. The cameras would not be hard to secure, hardly bigger than her thumbs.

She levered out of the car with a solid grip on the door, lest a gust blow it wide open. The sky flickered and a grumble followed with a spit of rain. The weather report had been threatening but she couldn't pass up this chance to close down the CAFO. She swung the backpack over her shoulder, shut the car door, and headed for the loading docks bathed in a couple of floodlamps.

The white truck at one of them, she surmised, was the cleanup crew's vehicle that would slip her into the CAFO. The garage door yawned open, a square mouth howling light. Her legs suddenly felt rubbery, and a chill snaked up her spine. Was this a good idea? What if the cameras were detected? And if not, how would they be later removed? By that woman on the phone, supposedly. Maybe she hadn't thought this through.

Would any *evidence* gathered outweigh the corporation's expensive lawyers accusing her of trespassing? What if the whole thing was a setup? A trap? *Let's nip the lawsuit in the bud by catching that big-mouth activist trespassing with a load of cameras. Late Breaking! Here's the surveillance footage, and here are the photos the security team took.* What would a jury say? Never mind—what would Frank say?

She could turn around now and forget it. Get back in the car and drive away. The suit was going forward without this. Wasn't it? Wouldn't it?

The clouds lit up here, there, over there, and an angry *ba-boom* rattled the building's sheet metal siding. The spatter of rain turned steady, needling her face.

"I am really glad ya come, Mrs. Gordon." A stout woman in coveralls, her thumbs tucked into a tool belt, spoke from the landing. "Better get in before the sky opens up."

Stephie hurried up the concrete steps beside the ramp and squinted at the top, adjusting to the blaring fluorescent light. She ducked inside and shook off rain.

"You're the one I spoke to on the phone?" Stephie asked.

"The same," the woman answered. "Them the cameras?"

Stephie slipped the backpack from her shoulder. "I

brought three. They're for home security, actually."

"They'll do. Let's have a look. Bring 'em on in here." She gestured to an inner room with a table, chairs, and lockers. "After you."

"Where is the rest of your crew?" Stephie asked over her shoulder.

The blow from behind sent a shock through her skull and a flash of pure white before there was nothing.

CHAPTER 39

RAIN CASCADED OVER THE CRUISER'S WINDSHIELD, making it harder to keep watch on the house. The shower swept the neighborhood in curtains; the wipers did *no-good, no-good, no-good*. A crack of thunder shook the cruiser, and the throaty after-rumble reverberated in Gordon's chest. Might Stephie be awakened by the storm and spot him? The radio squealed a code 47, but someone else was closer to the emergency road repair call. He may as well stay put; patrolling in the downpour didn't make much sense, though he might check on the QuikStop once it let up since—

His phone trilled. Local number. He lifted it to his ear. "Gordon."

"Hello? Can you hear me?" Female.

"Yes, who is this?"

"Hey, it's Krystyl. So, you told me to call this number if I remembered something. You know, something about Richie?"

"Right."

"So, like, I remembered something."

"Go ahead."

"Well, it's something I gotta show you."

"Can't you just tell me on the phone?"

"Come see me at the plant when I start my shift, at one-thirty."

"Just tell me what it is."

"It's about Richie and the baby you're so concerned about."

"I'm listening."

"One-thirty."

Click.

CHAPTER 40

SEVERE THUNDERSTORM WARNING
IAC155-ILC045-095-131-121715-
/O.NEW.WMEG.SV.W.0057.200312T1641Z-
200312T1715Z/
BULLETIN - IMMEDIATE BROADCAST
REQUESTED
Severe Thunderstorm Warning
National Weather Service Moline IL
100 AM CDT Sun Aug 18
The National Weather Service in Moline has
issued a
* Severe Thunderstorm Warning for...
East central Scott County in eastern Iowa...
Rock Island County in western Illinois...
North central Mercer County in western
Illinois...
Western Sinnissippi County in western Illinois...
Southern Whiteside County in western Illinois...
* Until 300 AM CDT.
* At 100 AM CDT, a severe thunderstorm was
located over Clinton Iowa, moving northeast at
40 mph.
HAZARD...60 mph wind gusts and quarter size
hail.
SOURCE...Radar indicated.
IMPACT...Hail damage to vehicles is expected.

Expect wind damage
to roofs, siding, and trees, and scattered power
outages.
* Locations impacted include...
Clinton and Comanche Iowa, Rock Island,
Moline, Port Byron, Erie, Prophetstown, Joslin
Corners, Sinnissippi State Park, River Falls, and
Sterling, Illinois.
PRECAUTIONARY/PREPAREDNESS
ACTIONS...
For your protection move to an interior room on
the lowest floor of a building.
HAIL...1.00IN
WIND...60MPH
XXX

—ᴍ—

In the deluge of rain, Gordon nearly smashed into a
coiling pile of sheet metal, the blown-off top of a concrete
silo. Corn leaves skittered across the road. Roof shingles spun
over the pavement. His tires hissed through puddles, leaving
a high spray behind him, and the buffeting wind seemed to
wrestle for the steering wheel.

Should have just said no, he groused. The case is cleared,
and the Lieutenant won't be happy to know I went on this
chase. Can't call in Paulie for backup. Lord knows that if
more fallen trees block roads or if there are accidents, I'll
need to call this whole thing off and—

"5-85, toll road exit 5, car in the ditch, possible injuries,
copy."

Gordon reached for the handset. Raised it to his face as
he heard:

"Bravo-15, copy, I'm not far. 76."

It was Pembroke replying, enroute to the accident.

Gordon hesitated, and then replaced the handset. He could go on. But for sure, Paul would now be occupied and not available at all. Gordon didn't trust anyone else. Surely not Anderson and his men.

"Bravo-15, sending a 10-51 out, with—before—and the EMT Unit—*spaaatzz ...*"

The radio static cued the sky to blaze white, like a giant flash bulb, and a peal of thunder split the clouds.

CHAPTER 41

THE SHARP CRACK SNAPPED Stephie to awareness, and the pebbled pelting of the roof shook her awake. Her arms ached horribly, the elbows high and on her ears and she grasped with a start that she was suspended over the floor by her wrists bound above. She gasped, but her lungs hurt, and her breathing came in panting puffs.

"Don't try to talk too much, and it'll feel better," said the woman, rising from a folding chair in front of her.

Stephie's head throbbed where she'd been struck. She wriggled and the chains around her wrists bit into her skin. She hitched her breath sharply in pain.

"Yeah, and don't move too much, neither," the woman said.

Stephie sucked in a gulp of air. "Help!" she shrieked. "Help me! Someone!"

The thunder answered with a timpani roll.

The woman stuck her thumbs in her tool belt. "Scream all ya want," she said. "There's no one around. Just like I tol' you. There won't be nobody around til mornin' when the first picketers show up with their tent and signs and big blow-up rat."

Stephie gulped air and then dropped her chin to see the metal grate beneath her, a kind of ditch that extended to the right where a fenced area narrowed. The pipe above extended from this spot around a corner. The floor on either side was grated, too, and she realized with a gasp and a skip in her heartbeat that it was for blood to drain.

"What—What do you want? Why are you doing this?" Stephie squeezed a tear from her eye. "I haven't hurt you!"

"No, ma'am, but your busy-body snoop of a husband might."

"What does—what does Frank have to do with you?" Her shoulders creaked. Could they be dislocated if she hung there?

"He's been asking me too many questions. I don't 'ppreciate it. I want to tell him so. You're my insurance that he'll show up. I called him. I think he's on the way. But he don't know you're here. If he don't come, I'll call again and put you on the line. Then he's sure to show up."

Stephie blinked away a stinging tear, caused by the agony in her arms and chest as much as from the terror that gnawed her belly. She squeezed her eyes shut. *Frank will come. He'll come for sure. He doesn't give up easy.*

"He'll come with backup, you know," Stephie said. "A tactical team. They'll surround the place. They'll take you down. You—you won't get away."

A spatter of hail struck the roof, a thousand little tack hammers, and stopped.

The woman glanced up to the ceiling. "What a night," she laughed. She returned a cold stare to Stephie. "He'll come alone. You'll see."

"What do you want from him?"

"Honey, I just want him to leave me alone. He promises that to my face, everyone can go home. If not, well, there'll be a different outcome."

"Please don't hurt me."

The woman checked a wall clock. 1:26 a.m. "Ain't it ironic," she said. She crimped her mouth. "Is that the word? Ironic? You bein' on the kill floor. Hung up on the line we hang the hogs on after they get stunned. Just before they get stuck."

She pulled a knife from the tool belt.

"Please," Stephanie begged. "Please don't."

"This is what they use to stick 'em. Richie showed me how."

"Please! Don't hurt me! I'm pregnant!"

The woman turned the blade so that it glinted. "Ain't that a shame?"

CHAPTER 42

GORDON SPUN INTO THE SLICK PARKING LOT, hydroplaning to a stop. Rain beat the roof and looked like a million little eruptions on the pavement. In the hazy cast of the dock's floodlight, he spotted the familiar truck. But unlike before, he spied a car parked along the fence. In the next flash of lightning, he saw it more clearly. Stephanie's Jeep.

No, no, oh no, he breathed, heart accelerating to a gallop. He fumbled for the radio handset. Dropped it. Picked it up. "Bravo-12, copy."

Dispatch responded. "Bravo-12, go ahead."

"Code 35, emergency, possible hostage situation in progress, need backup, right now. Diedrich packing plant."

Breathe. Breathe. Don't hyperventilate.

A gust quaked the cruiser.

"12, say again, the signal is *zkarrzzat ssppich* to hear you *zzisskrrak.*"

"Code 35, 35, emergency. Hostage situation in progress, notify all units, Diedrich plant on North River Road, need back—"

The sky boomed. Gordon's seat shook.

"Flash, we have a 10-1, can you hear me? The signal is cutting out—can't—if—"

Gordon raised his voice. "Paulie, you there? Any unit? Come back."

That's when he heard the scream.

CHAPTER 43

"THAT'S JUST TO SHOW I'M SERIOUS," the woman said. She wiped the blade on her coveralls.

Stephanie sobbed and her breath came in short gasps. The slash across her abdomen was made jagged by her twisting away in vain. The wound bloomed red, and rivulets of blood ran into her slacks.

"That oughta get him inside," the woman said. "I thought I heard him pull up."

The dock entrance suddenly lit up like fireworks, strobing blue and red.

"Yup," the woman said. "He's here."

Stephie drew a lungful of air, winced, and belted, "Frankie! Frankie!"

CHAPTER 44

GORDON HIT THE LIGHT BAR to make it seem like he wasn't alone. The side of the building erupted into Fourth of July colors. If any backup arrived, they'd see where he was located immediately. He'd lose any element of surprise, but she was expecting him anyway. He switched off the shoulder mic. No need to agitate her further. He leaped out into the storm.

"Frankie! Frankie!"

The cry ripped his heart. She was here and in bad trouble. How bad? No time to think about that.

He drew his service weapon. Sprinted to the dock steps. Bounded up by twos. He couldn't go in blazing. For a hostage situation, he needed calm. Find out what Krystyl wanted. Was she high? Drunk? Armed? Alone?

He crouched and made his way along the wall, aware of any ambush. This had to be the staging trough where the swine were unloaded and forced forward through a narrowing path. The railings tapered and the floor changed from sealed concrete to a metal grid in the shallow ditch and waffle-looking resin sidewalks alongside. The track curved around a bend, emptying into the beginning of the kill floor. The insulated railings sat low enough for the stunners to reach over with the twin-forked stun wands, hung in a row on wall brackets, recharging, their green lights staring like snake eyes. A rack for rubber boots and rubber aprons was mounted on the side.

And just ahead, strung from the overhead slaughter rail, the blood-drains below, Stephanie dangled by her chained wrists.

"Don't come no farther," Krystyl barked. "Hold it right there."

She planted herself behind Stephie, her human shield, a fearsome pig sticker blade in her fist.

Gordon lowered his gun and took another step.

"I said hold it," Krystyl warned, pressing the tip of the blade to Stephie's bare midriff where she'd rolled up the t-shirt.

Gordon's gut twisted at the sight of the jagged line there, oozing crimson.

"What I started, I can finish, you know," Krystyl hissed.

Stephie whimpered. "Don't. Don't let her kill me, Frank. Don't let her! I'm pregnant!"

Gordon's heart nearly punched its way out of his chest. Was it his? Or that sleazy lawyer's? *Stop it, stop it.* He forced his shaking gun arm to stay down. He might have emptied the magazine all at once in rage if he didn't risk hitting Stephanie.

"Stephie, sweetie, we're gonna, we're gonna, get. Through. This," he said. He tried not to grit his teeth. "Krystyl, listen to me, now. Are you listening? Huh? You don't need to do this. We can all still walk out of here."

She chortled. "That's just what you tol' Richie. Look what happened to him. Course, he deserved it."

"No one deserves that, even if he killed Diedrich."

"You all still think that?" She laughed hoarsely. "Imagine that."

The sandpapery snicker might have been a sign she'd been drinking or she had snorted something.

"It really worked," she went on, amused. "We made you think it was that poor dopehead."

"It was you, wasn't it?"

"Me and the other dopehead, Billy. He come along for the ride, so to speak. But I wasn't gonna let Richie the Raper take that baby from me."

"He raped you?"

"I didn't want the baby. But this couple in Wisconsin, couldn't have a baby theirselves, denied adoption over and over, they advertised and I said, dang, twenty-five thousand buckaroos for a baby I don't want. I'm in."

"Richie was trying to *save* the baby."

"Like he knew what to do with one. Pathetic." She shook her head. "But I was trying to save *myself*. Maybe you don't get how much twenty-five grand means to someone like me. It means a new start. A new life. Away from Richie."

"You didn't need to kill Diedrich for that. Just Richie. And you did."

"After the fact," she retorted with a sniff. "You cops ain't got no imagination. I figured if'n I could get him arrested for a big-publicity hit on that arrogant cuss no one liked, using Richie's truck, his gun, some knife he stole for his collection, and his bad record, me an' Buck could take the money and run. It worked out even better, cuz Richie got kilt. Then your big nose done come along."

"Where's Buck now?"

"He's waiting at a un-dis-closed lo-ca-tion, let's say. He don't have the stomach for this. He's just a stunner, remember?"

"He used the stun gun on Diedrich, didn't he?"

"And put it in Richie's truck. After I wiped it."

"Did he shoot the driver?"

"Ain't you listenin'? He don't got the stomach for it. After he rammed the car over and pulled the old man out and the Chinee done rolled down his window to yell at me, I popped him."

"And Lucy helped you, too."

"Nah, she looked the other way. She didn't want her whacko religious pals to be blamed."

"You've been careful, huh? You both went through a lot of trouble." His training kicked in, high gear. *Keep her talking. Flatter a little. They love to brag. Buy time. Backup might show up.*

"Had to make it really look like that loser Richie done it," Krystyl said, almost nostalgically. "Beyond a reasonable doubt—is that what you all say? So, I made that tattoo in Boss Hogg, too. It ain't pretty, but it was the best I could remember Richie's. But then I thought, I can't leave him hangin' in here, to hang it on Richie, so to speak. Cuz they'll know I had a key for this time of day, not Richie. So we washed the place down, put him in the back of our truck, parked in front of the cameras, and put him in the lake. It looked like we was workin' a normal shift. Say, that lake was just the right place for that pig, dontcha think?"

Stephanie whimpered. Gordon planted his feet. He couldn't make a move. Not yet.

"You're a good planner," Gordon said. "A logical person, huh? The smart one on the team, huh? Practical. I get that. I appreciate that."

"Do you, now? Well, the plan screwed up. I had to stick Richie before you guys could put him away. Either way woulda worked. I still get away with it."

"So, what's your plan now? What do you want? How does this end well for you? I can help you, Krystyl. My backup is surrounding the place and unless I tell them not to, they'll bust in and take you out the first chance they get—"

"Oh, puh-lease," she pshawed. "You tol' *that* to Richie, too. No one's comin'. I saw the TV. The case is closed. That light show? It's just your car. You're on your own."

The wind howled and the building shuddered. The lights

overhead swayed, winked, and flickered.

"Frankie," Stephanie cried weakly, "do—do something."

"Here's what ya do," Krystyl said. "I want you to toss me that gun of yours, or I'll finish her off. You can see how I started it. I'll stick her just like I did Richie."

Stephie shook her head vigorously. "Frankie, don't, don't do it, she'll—"

Krystyl touched the tip of the knife to Stephie's side. Stephie sucked in her breath.

"You can't get away with this," Gordon said.

Krystyl knit her brow. "Watch me." She pushed on the hilt a bit. Blood spurt from the puncture.

Stephie pinched her lips hard and groaned.

"Okay, okay," Gordon said. He crouched. He wished the Glock had a regular safety he could engage; it might be that Krystyl didn't know how one worked, and he could wrestle her down as she fumbled with the gun. But the passive safety on a Glock only prevented it from discharging from a drop. The trigger had to be pulled. That's all she had to do.

"Here it comes," he said.

He slid it across the grated floor. It clattered to a pinging stop between them.

"That was stupid," Krystyl growled. "Halfway? Halfway?"

As he hoped. "Want me to come over and kick it closer?" Gordon said.

Then she might be in taser range. Could he draw fast enough—

"You'll be too close to me, then," Krystyl protested. "You did that on purpose!"

"It just didn't slide like I thought. I'll kick it—"

"Stay there!"

The clouds cannoned an ear-splitting rip, rain daggered the roof, and the light fixtures swayed, flickered. Flickered once more.

"So now what?" Gordon shouted over the clamor of the rain.

"Back up! Get up against the wall!"

Gordon reversed a few steps.

"I said, against the wall!"

Keeping his focus on Krystyl, Gordon backtracked to the green cinderblocks by the boot rack and apron hooks. The recharging stun wands, with their twin antennae, blinked at him like cicadas. His crepe-bottom shoes squeaked on the concrete.

"And stay put!" Krystyl said. "You move this way, and you know I'll reach her quicker'n you reach me!"

She held the knife to her chest, regarded Gordon with a cocked head, and feinted a lurch forward.

Gordon stayed glued to the wall.

"Good move!" Krystyl said. "That's the right thing! Stay right there!"

She took two steps before the thunder artillaried again and the lights went out. The emergency LEDS snapped on, blinding white stars. The overheads clicked back on. Sputtered, hesitant.

Krystyl looked this way and that, for a moment losing the gun. Spotted it.

Gordon twisted around, seized a stunner. Rushed to the railing edge. Aimed the prongs at Krystyl.

Krystyl sneered, the Glock already in her hand. Pointed at him. "That's no ray gun, Flash Gordon. Ya gotta touch me behind both ears with that thing."

Gordon thumbed it on. It hummed to life. "No, I don't."

He leaned forward, tilted the prongs down, and touched the metal grate.

The electric shock jerked Krystyl back in a wide-eyed shudder, and she crashed to the lattice with a ringing of steel on steel. Her body spasmed until Gordon lifted the prongs.

Switched off the current. Her jerking body lay still.

Stephie swung above the floor, untouched by the paralyzing voltage, her breath short. She strained to look over her aching shoulder. "Is she—is she—dead?"

"Just shocked. Like a taser. Hold on," Gordon said as he tossed the stun wand aside, vaulted the rail, and sprinted to Krystyl's side. He pried the Glock from her grip, holstered it, and cast the knife out of reach. He flipped her over and snapped on the cuffs—one to her wrist, one to the railing. She might return to consciousness more quickly than he knew. He stood and reached for his wife.

Stephie breathed in labored puffs, tears brimming her eyes. "Frankie, I—I was so s-scared, I'm so, so sorry—"

He shushed her gently. Embraced her and lifted her to relieve the pressure on her arms and wrists. "I'm gonna let you down now, sweetie, slow, and just for a sec, so I can unhook that chain."

He released her gently, stretched up, and said, "You're going to drop a few feet. Ready?"

She nodded.

He thumbed open the spring that clipped the shackles. She fell to the grating, weak-kneed, crumpled forward, but Gordon caught her up. In a moment, she was upright and enveloped in his arms on the floor. Her chest heaved in sobs. He tightened his hold.

"You're okay now. You're okay," he soothed. "You're safe."

"Why?" she sniveled. "Why would she, I mean, who—who could ever—"

"I could still pin it on her," he said. "So, she was going to shoot us both and make it look like I did it. The good cop shooting a trespasser, who turned out to be his own wife, and he killed himself in regret. She was pretty good about making up stories."

"How—How would she explain this—this cut?"

"Who knows? You ran away. You fell. My fault. On second thought, she wouldn't have to explain anything. She'd be long gone with Buck somewhere off the grid."

A police siren wailed in the distance. And another. Getting closer.

Gordon placed his palm over her blood-streaked belly. "Did you say pregnant?"

She planted her palm over his. "We did it, Frankie, we did it. That night you came home. Remember? That was the charm."

He wrapped his big arms around her. How could he have suspected her? It wasn't that lizard of a lawyer. It was his, it was theirs, it was—

"Such a purty scene," gruffed a man's voice from the entry.

"Otis," Gordon acknowledged, a stone dropping in his belly.

Otis Anderson oiled his way across the floor, oozing charm. "Your boss won't like it much that you acted on your own here, Flash, but I'll vouch for you, don't you worry. Care to explain? I just wanna get our stories straight."

"Krystyl and Buck ambushed Diedrich and his driver and worked hard to frame Richie for it. She wanted him out of the way so she could sell her baby. I was on to her, and she used Stephie to make me promise not to squeal."

"What brought you here, Mrs. G?" Otis asked, one eye squinting.

"I was going to—meet her. To talk about the strike. Work together. Then she attacked me and—well, what Frank said."

"Sure, sure," Otis said out of the corner of his mouth, disbelievingly. "You okay now, Mrs. G?"

Stephie nodded, her eyes narrowed in caution.

"That's mighty fine, mighty fine," Otis said, feigning care. He glanced around, quickly assessing the scene. "Not the taser," he concluded. "That stunner over there." He smiled broadly, not to congratulate Gordon, but to celebrate his opportunity. "As soon as Sleeping Beauty here wakes up, I'll make the arrest and take her in. Where's Buck? He run off?"

"He was never here," Gordon said through clenched teeth.

Stephie felt him tighten his grip. "It's all right, Frankie. Let him have this one."

A second cruiser pulled up outside, lights strobing.

Anderson produced his cell phone. "That's Creasy out there. I'll send him to go find Buck. At the office, we'll make one of them squeal, as you put it. Meanwhile, I'll just take a few photos. Routine, as you know. Having photos is *so* important. Don't you agree, Francis?"

Stephie tugged at Frank's sleeve. "What's he mean?"

"It's routine," Gordon replied. But it wasn't. Anderson was making sure he kept Gordon quiet. Even if the baby was his, the hotel photos would be bad publicity and cast doubt. Anderson would receive credit for the solve, and Gordon wouldn't be surprised if Anderson now took a selfie with the unconscious Krystyl in the background to use in his sheriff's election campaign.

"We'll finish up here, Francis," Anderson said. "We'll get your statement tomorrow. You better get yourselves to the clinic and have that cut looked at."

CHAPTER 45

CHARGE NURSE SUZIE PENDERGRASS tore off the BP strap from Stephanie's arm with a loud Velcro rip.

"One-forty over eighty, somewhat elevated, but looking much better after last night," she said with a dimpled smile. "Dr. Feldman is on the way up."

"What do you think she'll say?" Stephanie asked.

Pendergrass checked the IV drip and the EKG monitor's jagged line. "Well, for the grade three concussion that knocked you out, Dr. Feldman might order a CT scan or an MRI to rule out bleeding or any brain injury. I think you'll be all right, though. You're coordinated, your reflexes are fine, and you're answering questions without a problem. She'll tell you to take it easy and to take acetaminophen for any headache and the ache in your wrists, neck, and shoulders, and for that stomach scar, if it throbs."

Stephanie folded her hands over her lower belly. "That's not what we really want to know about," she said with a tremor.

"Or is it too early?" Gordon asked. He shifted uneasily in his patrol blues; he was perspiring under the vest from the anxiety. "Won't Dr. Feldman need to do an ultrasound to check if it was a false positive?"

Pendergrass double-dimpled. "Not at all," she said. "The urine and blood tests were all. You've got a measurable level of HCG. Congratulations."

Stephie reached up to Gordon. "Frankie, did you hear? We're going to have a—we're going to be—"

"Busy," he said.

They laced fingers.

"When Dr. Feldman comes in," Pendergrass said, beaming, "she'll discuss prenatal care with you. I'll leave you two alone." She winked at Gordon. "You're a lucky gal, Stephie," she swooned and padded out.

Stephie squeezed Gordon's hand. Brought it to her cheek. "Come home, Frankie," she said with a kiss on his knuckles. "Come home. I mean it."

His radio shoulder mic squawked. "Downtown units, 10-56 at Main and Walnut. Bravo-twelve, do you copy?"

Duty called. Gordon pulled his hand away from Stephie's, detached the hand mic, and brought it to his mouth.

And switched it off.

THE END

EPILOGUE

{OPENER THEME MUSIC}
{VOICEOVER}
ANNOUNCER: Live! Local! Late breaking!
It's NewsNow 4! With Brad Nickelson! And
Donegal O'Neil! Meteorologist Courtney
Willow, and sports director Gary Kowalski!
{WIPE: SHERIFF'S DEPUTY OTIS ANDERSON
MUG}
BRAD: The sheriff's deputy running for his
boss's job makes a dramatic arrest in the
Diedrich murder case.
{WIPE: STRIKER TENT WITH BLOW-UP RAT}
DONEGAL: The Diedrich packing plant strike is
suspended as the new Chinese owners promise
a deal.
{WIPE: CHELSEA DIEDRICH IN BLACK VEIL
STANDUP}
BRAD: Meanwhile, former CEO Jacob Diedrich
is laid to rest in an unmarked site in an
undisclosed location, says the family.
{WIPE: STOCK FOOTAGE: COP FLASH BARS}
DONEGAL: And an Illinois mother and
Wisconsin couple are arrested in an alleged
baby selling scheme.
{ISO COURTNEY ON LOCATION, WRECKED
BARN}

COURNEY: Also, I'll have a full report on last
night's damaging storm: Is another on the way?
BRAD: NewsNow 4 starts right now!

"Turn that off, Flash," Paul Pembroke urged. "You know they get it all wrong."

Gordon seized the remote, switched the wall-mounted TV to a weather service, and muted it.

"They don't always get it all *wrong*, Paulie," Gordon groused. "Usually they just don't get it *all*, period."

"How's that?"

"They've only got twenty-two minutes, and most of it is melodrama or fluff. They're not going to bore an audience that likes shiny things with long explanations. That Donegal O'Neill woman interviewed me for an hour, and she won't use one line, guaranteed."

"That's because you're boring."

"No, it's because Otis Anderson gave her a good soundbite story of him arresting a child trafficker and a killer who works in a slaughterhouse. It was, as news people say, sexy."

"Speaking of sexy, how about that Chelsea Diedrich? She's not so innocent."

"She's only guilty of being greedy like her dad. She struck a sweet deal with the Chinese real fast once Daddy was gone, that's all. She didn't arrange or pay for his demise like I thought she might have. She just profited by it, big time. And so did all the political snakes invested in the business: Sellers, Harmon, and the rest. It's why they wanted this over fast."

"You putting that in your report?"

Gordon guffawed. "Are you kidding? And lose my job?"

"I'm surprised you won't lose it over this little episode, going rogue with a phone tip—"

"I was responding to a hostage situation," Gordon snapped. "It was my *wife*, for godsakes. I didn't go rogue on the Diedrich case. That was cleared. Closed. Remember?"

"Okay, okay, no need to bite off my head."

"This was *different. Get* it, huh?"

"I get it. I'm sorry Stephie was hurt. I really am."

And another thing, Rookie. Anderson didn't arrive first and taze Krystyl Spinney just as I got there; he tazed her after I left to make it look like he—

McWhorter, the desk sergeant, poked into the squad room. "Paulie, there's a visitor for you up front."

Pembroke sighed, a release of the tension in the room. "Don't tell me. Is it who I think it is?"

"Yup. In Daisy Dukes and a halter top small as my bandana. Oh, and chocolate chip cookies this time. They're good."

Pembroke arched a questioning eyebrow at Gordon.

"Go ahead," Gordon said. "Send her in."

ACKNOWLEDGEMENTS

I WANT TO THANK the officers and instructors of the Rockford, Illinois, Citizens' Police Academy for their professional advice and my fellow writers of the Saluda, North Carolina, Story Circle for their encouragement.

ABOUT THE AUTHOR

A FORMER PRODUCER for Wisconsin Public Radio, John Desjarlais taught English for 25 years at Kishwaukee College (IL). His novels include *The Throne of Tara* (Crossway 1990), *The Light of Tara* (KDP 2020), *Relics* (Thomas Nelson 1993), *Bleeder, Viper, Specter* (Chesterton Press, 2008, 2011,  2015), and *The Kill Floor* (Torchflame Books 2022). His short stories and poems have appeared in literary journals such as *The Critic, Conclave, Lit Noir,* and *Dappled Things.*

A member of *Mystery Writers of America* and *The North Carolina Writers Network,* John is listed in *Who's Who in Entertainment* and *Who's Who Among America's Teachers.* He is a graduate of the writing program at Illinois State University and the Writers Police Academy. He resides in Hendersonville, NC.

Follow John Desjarlais:

johndesjarlais.com
facebook.com/jdesjarlais1
twitter.com/johndesjarlais; @johndesjarlais
linkedin.com/in/johnjdesjarlais
goodreads.com/johndesjarlais
crimespace.ning.com/profile/JohnDesjarlais
amazon.com/author/jdesjarlais